"Jessie, we

Cadde's deep voice demanded Jessie's attention.

She looked up, trying to appear as innocent as possible. "About what?"

"You know damn well about what. We spoke last night and you seemed in agreement about the next steps for Shilah Oil."

"I didn't promise you my vote."

"Oh, no, you're way too smart for that." Anger now edged his voice. "Do you get some kind of perverse pleasure out of blocking my every move?"

"Actually, no."

"Then what the hell is it?" He waved a hand around the green-and-white room. "If the oil company goes under, so will all of this. Why are you keeping Shilah stagnant? It's me, isn't it? You're not comfortable with me taking over Roscoe's position so you're trying to stick it to me every way you can."

She shook her head. "No. I think you're more than qualified to fill Daddy's shoes."

"Then what the hell is it, Jessie? What do I have to do to get your support? What do you want?"

"It's quite simple. I want a baby."

Dear Reader,

I'm happy to present you with the second book in The Hardin Boys series. Cadde Hardin and Jessie Murdock are two strong-willed people who know exactly what they want. Cadde has worked years toward one goal: owning an oil company. Jessie wants a family. She has the power to make his dream come true and vice versa. But as we all know, life doesn't come with a blueprint.

As far back as I can remember I wanted to be a nurse. I took all the right courses and worked as a nurse's aide. My dream was set, but like I said, life's blueprint is different from our own. In college I was diagnosed with rheumatoid arthritis and I had to adjust, regroup and create new goals. Today I write happy-ever-after books for Harlequin. Not too bad of an adjustment.

Cadde and Jessie think their goals are set, but they get derailed for a lot of reasons. Through some heartache the two of them learn a hard lesson—love is not a business arrangement. I have to admit I shed a few tears while writing this book. I have a box of tissues on my desk that is now almost empty.

You know this story has a happy ending, so hang in there. I hope you enjoy *The Texan's Bride*. It took a piece of my heart. Please look for the third book in the series, *The Texan's Christmas*, Cisco's (Kid's) story, in December.

With love and thanks,

Linda Warren

P.S.—It's always a pleasure to hear from readers. You can email me at Lw1508@aol.com or write me at P.O. Box 5182, Bryan, TX 77805. Visit my website at www.lindawarren.net or www.facebook.com/authorlindawarren. I will answer your letters as soon as I can.

The Texan's Bride
Linda Warren

Harlequin®

TORONTO NEW YORK LONDON
AMSTERDAM PARIS SYDNEY HAMBURG
STOCKHOLM ATHENS TOKYO MILAN MADRID
PRAGUE WARSAW BUDAPEST AUCKLAND

Recycling programs
for this product may
not exist in your area.

ISBN-13: 978-0-373-71735-4

THE TEXAN'S BRIDE

Copyright © 2011 by Linda Warren

ABOUT THE AUTHOR

RITA® Award-nominated and award-winning author Linda Warren has written twenty-nine books for Harlequin, including Superromance, American Romance and Everlasting Love. Drawing upon her years of growing up on a farm/ranch in Texas, she writes about sexy heroes, feisty heroines and broken families with an emotional punch, all set against the backdrop of Texas. When she's not writing or at the mall, she's sitting on her patio with her husband watching the wildlife and plotting her next book. Visit her website at www.LindaWarren.net.

Books by Linda Warren

HARLEQUIN SUPERROMANCE

HARLEQUIN AMERICAN ROMANCE

*The Belles Of Texas
**The Hardin Boys

To Jennifer...may all your dreams come true.

Acknowledgments

I would like to thank the following people
who answered my many questions and
made this book possible:
Vicki, Jennifer, James O., Phyllis, Lauren, Mark,
Laura and Scott.
All errors are strictly mine.

CHAPTER ONE

CADDE HARDIN ALWAYS THOUGHT he'd eventually get married. He just never dreamed it would be a marriage of convenience.

And a pain in the ass.

"One of these days I'm going to wring her damn pretty neck."

He threw his briefcase onto the desk, scattering piles of folders, and slam-dunked his body into a leather chair, which protested with loud, annoying squeaks. He was so angry he could barely breathe.

How many more times was Jessie, his wife, going to stab him in the back?

His brothers, Cisco—known as Kid—and Chance stood in the doorway. "Is it safe to come in?" Kid asked.

Cadde nodded.

"What the hell happened?" Kid wanted to know. "You said you had it handled, but once again Jessie shot down your proposal."

Cadde yanked off his tie. "I'm well aware of that." For a whole week he'd been telling Jessie how much he needed her vote at Shilah Oil's next board meeting. The company had to move forward. She had agreed, but evidently she'd changed her mind, voting against expanding drilling outside of Texas. He could feel his blood pressure rising by the minute.

"What did she say when you told her about the proposal?" Chance asked, taking a seat.

Cadde threw the tie onto the desk. "She said it sounded like something her father, Roscoe, would do. He was always a wildcatter, a risk-taker."

"Did she agree to vote your way?" Kid plopped into a chair and rested his boots on the desk. Usually, Cadde would knock them off, but today he wasn't in a mood to fight with Kid. Jessie and her about-face was all he had on his mind.

"No," he muttered.

"Sounds as if she's still pissed about the marriage," Kid commented.

"I didn't force her into this arrangement. Roscoe was dying and he wanted me to protect her, to take care of her, and I agreed."

"For a piece of the pie," Kid murmured under his breath.

He glared at Kid. "Don't start with me today."

Chance spoke up. "Face it, Cadde, she has to be upset at having her husband chosen for her."

"She was there when Roscoe made his wishes known. She didn't object or get angry. She accepted her father's decision."

"Still…"

"Dammit, Chance." Cadde swung out of his chair and stood to gaze at the view of Houston, but all he saw were Jessie's dark eyes. Swinging back, he said, "Don't you think I'm aware of that? I'm at my wit's end on how to handle Jessie."

"Since I'm an expert on women—" Kid formed a steeple with his fingers and looked at Cadde over the top "—I'd say Jessie wants something…and she wants it from you."

"What would that be, Kid?" Cadde asked in a sarcastic tone.

"I don't know, but whatever she's angry about is aimed at you."

"That's for damn sure."

"Shilah Oil is going nowhere without her support on the board," Chance said. "So your best bet is to have an honest-to-God talk with her."

"It might be as simple as a divorce," Kid added.

Cadde frowned. "You think she wants a divorce?"

Kid shrugged. "What else could it be? I mean, Roscoe sheltered her all her life. She's probably looking for some sort of freedom. And fun—preferably not with a man handpicked by her father."

Chance turned on Kid. "You don't know that. He needs to talk—"

"I'll see y'all later," Cadde said, grabbing his briefcase and heading for the door.

"What? No orders?" Kid's pesky voice followed him.

"Get your damn feet off my desk! Chance, I want the drilling log on the Carver well when I return." Why had he brought his brothers in on this oil venture? They had a way of getting under his skin. But the truth was he needed their expertise to make Shilah Oil a successful company. Besides, they were brothers who stood together in rough times and in good times.

Right now Cadde didn't want to think about his siblings. Jessie occupied every corner of his mind.

In record time he was in his truck and driving north out of Houston toward Brenham. Maybe he and Jessie could talk and work things out. The knot in his gut eased a little.

Lord knew he didn't enjoy the marriage any more than she did. The first time he had dinner at the Murdock estate Roscoe had made it very clear that his daughter was off-limits, so he was shocked when Roscoe had brought up the suggestion of them marrying. He'd told the man he would look out for Jessie, but he didn't see any reason for a legal ceremony. They didn't love each other. They were barely more than acquaintances.

He'd never paid much attention to Roscoe's daughter, and he'd thought she'd grown to be an unattractive old maid without much appeal, except her father's wealth. As for Roscoe—it had been said that he resembled the back end of a horse going the wrong way. The man wasn't handsome by any means and Cadde had assumed his daughter favored him. He'd been mistaken.

Roscoe was big and barrel-chested with a booming voice that could make babies cry. Jessie was just the opposite; slim, feminine and beautiful with long dark hair and the blackest eyes he'd ever seen. She obviously took after her mother. Roscoe never spoke about his wife and there were no photos of her in the house.

That first night Cadde had dined with the two of

them, he looked everywhere but at the gorgeous woman sitting across from him. No way did he want Roscoe to catch him eyeing his daughter. That would put an end to his oil career. He played the part of cool indifference well, and the status quo remained the same every time he visited the Murdock estate.

He'd spent a lot of years working toward one goal—owning his own company. He, Kid and Chance had roughnecked all over Texas. They knew the oil business. He wasn't jeopardizing that goal by acting stupid. Jessie was his boss's daughter and in his eyes that meant she was off-limits.

Then, Roscoe being the gambling wildcatter that he was, sweetened the pot.

"How long have I known you, boy?" Roscoe had asked that day in his hospital room.

"A little over ten years."

Roscoe nodded. "You roughnecked on a wildcatter well. I saw you had potential and I brought you into the office. You've been my right hand since then."

"Yes, sir. I've learned from you and I'll always appreciate the opportunity you gave me."

"It's payback time, boy. Don't you know that?"

"What?" Cadde wasn't sure where the old man was headed with the conversation.

"I'm not asking you to marry Jessie. I'm telling you."

That took a moment for Cadde to digest.

"I've always been a gambler. You know that. Tomorrow I'm taking the biggest gamble of all…they'll remove the tumor from my brain. The doctors say I have a fifty-fifty chance of surviving the surgery and I'm willing to take that risk. I'm damn tired of the headaches and losing my eyesight, but I can't go under the knife until I know Jessie's future is secure."

"Sir..."

"Okay, boy," Roscoe interrupted, not willing to listen to anything he had to say. "I'm gonna make this easy for you. Marry Jessie and I'll give you half of my shares in Shilah Oil. Jessie gets the other half."

That sent Cadde's heart galloping like a wild steed.

"The papers are there on the nightstand. They require your signature to become the CEO of Shilah Oil." Roscoe took a labored breath. "Sign it, boy, because I'm not giving you any other choice. You've got integrity. I've known that from the start, and you'll keep Jessie safe."

Fear choked the man's voice. Roscoe's paranoia was never more evident than it was that day, but Cadde had to ask, "How does your daughter feel about this?"

Jessie walked into the room in a brown pantsuit and heels. Her dark hair was coiled into a knot at her nape. She looked elegant, sophisticated and uptight as any woman could be. The only sign she was nervous was the false smile on her face.

"Here's my baby," Roscoe said, and held out his hand.

She grasped it. "Daddy, I'm hardly a baby. What are you doing talking business with Mr. Hardin? You should be resting."

"I can't rest until I know your life is secure."

"Oh, Daddy."

"I'm serious, Jessie. Marry Cadde." Roscoe took another tortured breath. "We've talked about this and it's the right thing to do. Cadde knows the oil business and he'll keep Shilah profitable so you'll never want for anything. Please, baby."

Jessie met Cadde's eyes for the first time and their depths bore right through him. "Has Mr. Hardin agreed to this?"

"Yes," Roscoe said before Cadde could answer.

She turned back to Roscoe. "Daddy, you do realize I can take care of myself? I'm twenty-nine years old."

"Don't argue with me, Jessie. Please let me die in peace. I have to know you're safe."

Tears welled up in her eyes and Cadde felt a sucker punch to his chest. She hugged her father tightly and then straightened. "Okay. I guess I'm getting married."

They had the ceremony that afternoon by Roscoe's bedside and Cadde signed the papers that gave him a large interest in Shilah Oil. The next few hours were tense as they waited for news that Roscoe had survived the surgery. He hadn't. He'd died on the operating table.

Losing Roscoe had been a big blow. He thought the old man could win at anything, but the stakes were too high this time. Pushing aside his grief, he tried to comfort Jessie by offering to take her home. That was a huge mistake. She lit into him like a dog in a chicken coop.

"Contrary to what my father believes, Mr. Hardin, I can take care of myself and deal with Daddy's death... on my own."

That's when the iceberg set in—big-time.

She was stoic at the services. At the grave site, she stumbled and he caught her. She leaned on him for a second before she'd pushed away, thus setting the tone for their eighteen months of marriage.

The reading of the will was an eye-opener. Everything Roscoe owned was equally divided between him and Jessie, except Shilah and the Murdock estate. The house belonged to Jessie, and Roscoe's shares in the oil company were split twenty-five percent to Cadde and twenty-six percent to Jessie.

Roscoe omitted mentioning that little tidbit, which gave Jessie the upper hand. She used it every time she could—like today. Roscoe's cronies, who owned the remaining percentage of shares and sat on the board, always voted her way.

He never understood why Roscoe had done that. Jessie didn't know anything about the oil business, yet she was the one calling the shots—not him. That irritated the hell out of him on a good day. On a bad day he cursed a lot. If Shilah Oil was going to succeed, he had to find a way to reach Jessie.

Cadde sped down the paved road leading to the Murdock estate. Climbing Mount Olympus might be easier than reaching Jessie. And definitely less painful. But today he was angry and he was having his say. She wasn't giving him the cold shoulder and walking out of the room as she usually did. If he had to tie her to a chair, they were discussing their farce of a marriage, and most definitely her sabotage of Shilah Oil.

He drove up to the double wrought-iron gates leading to the house. As he touched a button on his windshield visor, the gates swung open. An eight-foot steel fence surrounded the entire property and was held in place with brick cornerstones every twelve feet. Razor wire curled across the top. The entire structure was linked to a state-of-the-art security system. To say Roscoe was paranoid about Jessie's safety was putting it mildly. But Cadde knew he had good reasons.

Roscoe's brother, Al, who had started Shilah Oil with Roscoe back in the forties, had a six-year-old daughter who'd been kidnapped. The child had fought so vigorously that the kidnapper had broken her neck. The man had been a roustabout who Al had fired.

Al's wife couldn't handle the grief and died six months later. Al followed her the next year. After the tragedy, Roscoe made sure nothing would happen to Jessie. He had her guarded twenty-four hours a day, even when she went away to college. That couldn't have been easy for her.

Usually, a guard was at the gate, but today no one was there. Jessie had dismissed them a week after the funeral. It was their first marital argument, if you could call it that. He told her he didn't think it was wise and she told him to mind his own business. They went back and forth until she stormed out of the room, leaving him in no doubt what she thought of his opinions.

She never rehired the guards and neither did he. Somehow he felt he had failed Roscoe, but he knew if he hired new security, she'd fire them. So maybe for once in Kid's life he was right. Jessie wanted her freedom.

The house loomed in front of him, and he had the same thought he did every time he visited—the structure resembled a fortress or a castle in England with its turrets, tower and mullioned windows with bars. It was impressive, but seemed out of place in Texas.

That was Roscoe, though. He never did anything the normal way.

Cadde parked at the garages and got out. Two Dobermans ran to greet him, sniffed at his boots and trotted back to their spot at the door. At his first visit he almost had a heart attack when the dogs lunged at him, intending to take him down as if he was no more than a poodle. Roscoe had shouted, "Stay," and they'd immediately backed off. He had the dogs sniff him so they'd know his scent. From then on the Dobermans never gave him a problem.

For the first time Cadde realized that Jessie virtually lived in a prison of Roscoe's making. Why wouldn't she want to spread her wings?

The stifling August breeze almost took his Stetson. Anchoring it with his hand, he headed for the house. The heat was almost suffocating, but soon the temperatures would drop as fall arrived.

It certainly was a time for a new direction.

JESSIE WENT THROUGH THE document once again. Hal, her lawyer, had drawn it up just like she'd asked. She paused for a moment, thinking over what she was about to do. A small shiver ran through her.

The small mixed Jack Russell terrier at her feet whined for attention. "What's the matter, Mirry?" she cooed. She'd named her Miracle but she always called her Mirry. The dog sat on her foot as if all she needed was to know that someone cared. The poor thing looked pathetic with no tail or ears.

Jessie had found her on the side of the road and had

taken her home and nourished her back to health. She couldn't believe that some people could be so cruel, but no one was going to hurt Mirry again. She'd make sure of that.

The grandfather clock chimed in the hallway. *It was time.* Cadde would be here any minute. She'd bet money on it.

She straightened the dark suit and white silk blouse she'd worn to the board meeting this morning. Her hands went to her hair to check for loose strands that had worked their way out of her knot. She didn't want to appear vulnerable.

Rosa, the housekeeper, walked in. "Can I get you anything, Miss Jessie?"

"No, thank you. If I need anything I'll get it myself," she chided softly. "Besides, I have iced tea." She held up the glass. "That's all I need." A shot of vodka wouldn't hurt, she mused to herself. Rosa would faint at the mention of such a thing. But if courage came in a bottle, she could definitely use it.

Round and barely five feet tall, Rosa was like her mother. She'd raised Jessie since she was seven years old. Sometimes she felt suffocated by all the sheltering. Her father never saw her as anyone but his baby girl who needed protection, as did Rosa. Jessie was thirty now and she was determined to have the life and freedom that she wanted.

"You've been so sad since Mr. Roscoe's passing."

"I'm okay," she said, and smiled at the woman who would do anything for her. "Thank you for your concern, but I'm really fine. When Cadde arrives, tell him I'm in the sunroom."

Rosa frowned. "What's Mr. Cadde doing here this time of day?"

"Now, Rosa, don't pry," she teased.

Rosa shook a finger at her. "You're up to something, Miss Jessie, I know that look." Rosa had called her "Miss Jessie" ever since she could remember. She'd often asked Rosa to just call her Jessie, but Rosa never heeded her wishes.

They heard the back door open and close.

Rosa clicked her tongue as she went to confront their visitor. Jessie held her breath as she listened to the stomp-stomp of his boots against the hardwood floor. In a few seconds he was standing in the doorway, fury etched across his strong features. His jacket and tie from the morning were gone, but the jeans, white shirt, Stetson and boots were the same. The shirt was opened at the neck, revealing tiny swirls of dark chest hair. Her stomach tightened.

The first time she'd met him she'd thought how handsome he was: strong, powerful and everything a woman could want. There was just one problem. He treated her like a piece of the furniture. Today she was going to change that. She was going to rock Cadde Hardin's world.

Without speaking to her, he walked into the room and carefully placed his hat on the table, as if he was gauging his next words.

"Okay, Jessie, we need to talk." His deep voice demanded her attention.

She looked up, trying to appear as innocent as possible. "About what?"

"You know damn well about what. We talked last night and you seemed in agreement that Shilah should explore drilling outside of Texas, especially the Louisiana leases that Roscoe kept up-to-date. But once again you did a flip-flop. Why?"

"I didn't promise you my vote."

"Oh, no, you're way too smart for that." Anger now edged his voice and she could see that he was keeping a tight rein on his temper. His muscles were taut and his brown eyes intense. She refused to squirm. "Do you get some kind of perverse pleasure out of blocking my every move?"

"Actually, no."

"Then what the hell is it?" He waved a hand around the green-and-white room. "This is paid for by Shilah. If the oil company goes under, so will all of this. Do you understand that?"

"I'm not stupid." She could feel her anger bubbling to the surface and that's the last thing she wanted. She had to remain calm, but that was hard to do with a six-foot-plus all-male glaring at her and demanding answers.

"Then why are you keeping Shilah stagnant? It has to grow to succeed." He didn't give her time to respond. "It's me, isn't it? You're not comfortable with me taking over Roscoe's position so you're trying to stick it to me every way you can."

She shook her head. "No. I think you're more than qualified to fill Daddy's shoes."

"Then what the hell is it, Jessie? What do I have to do to get your support? What do you want?"

She played with the pen lying on top of the document for a second and then raised her eyes to his. "It's quite simple. I want a baby."

CHAPTER TWO

A BABY!

Had he heard her correctly?

Cadde swallowed. "What did you say?"

"A baby. I want a family." She stated each word clearly.

His brow knotted together so tightly it made his brain hurt. Was she out of her mind?

"You mean you want to adopt?" That was the only explanation he could think of. "You don't need my permission for that." Or maybe she did. He didn't know.

Her dark eyes flared like charcoal being lit by a match. "It may surprise you, but I don't need *your* permission for anything."

"Whoa." He held up a hand. "I can see that pushes a button, but I'm out here in left field. What the hell are you talking about."

"I'll say it one more time, slowly, so you'll understand."

He gritted his teeth at her condescending tone and kept a leash on the curse words burning his throat.

"I want a baby. I want to conceive, feel the life grow inside me and give birth to my son or daughter."

"Oh." That pretty much obliterated every response from his mind.

"Since Daddy died I'm all alone in the world. I have no relatives that I know of. I want someone to call my own...someone to love."

He heard the sadness in her voice and he felt himself weakening toward something he didn't even understand. "If you're talking about being artificially inseminated, as you pointed out, you don't need my permission."

She slapped the folder in front of her, drawing his attention to the file. On it, he saw the words *Jessie Hardin*. He wasn't aware she went by her married name.

"Good grief, are you dense or what?" The first sign of emotion flashed across her pretty face. "Why would I need to go to a sperm bank? I have a husband."

The creases on his forehead became tighter. "You mean you're asking me to donate...?"

"No," she interrupted him. "I want to have my husband's child the old-fashioned way."

What! It took a moment for him to catch his breath.

"You want *us* to make a baby?" he asked, motioning from her to him.

"Yes. You asked what I wanted and that's it."

His brow was so furrowed now he could barely think. "You do realize we'd have to have sex to accomplish that?"

"Yes."

"Have you ever had sex?"

Resentment flashed across her face. "Of course. I'm thirty years old."

"When, Jessie?" he probed. "When have you had sex? Your father had you guarded twenty-four hours a day even in college."

"There are ways to escape the guards," she said with a lift of a dark eyebrow. "I've learned every trick in the book."

"Did Roscoe know?"

"Of course not. The guards didn't want to lose their jobs."

He placed his hands on his hips. "Who did you sleep with?" He had no idea why he was asking her this. It was none of his business, but for some unknown reason it seemed important.

"I resent that question." Like a shade being drawn to block the light, her eyes shut out any emotion other than anger. How he wished he could see beyond that veil of darkness.

"I am your husband," he reminded, just to needle her.

She glanced at him. "Who I've slept with in the past is no concern of yours."

He nodded, conceding her that point.

"We're getting sidetracked," she said. "Let's get back to my request."

Cadde rubbed his jaw. "Frankly, Jessie, I'm surprised. You've never shown one sign of making this marriage legit in every way."

"Neither have you." Her eyes held his like a trap held an animal.

The thought made his tone sharper than usual. "It's damn difficult to get close to an iceberg."

She bristled just as he knew she would. "And it's even more difficult to attract a machine whose only focus is the oil business."

"Damn, Jessie, this is the longest conversation we've ever had."

She twisted the iced tea glass on her right. "I'd like an answer to my request."

The word *request* irritated him. "I'm not Roscoe and I don't automatically grant your every wish."

"Fine," she answered without pausing, "I'll continue to block your proposals at Shilah."

"That's not fair, Jessie."

"Whoever said life was fair?"

He swiped his hand through his hair. "Honestly, Jessie, I'm not ready to be a father. I spend every waking minute I can trying to get Shilah back on its feet. Roscoe wasn't feeling well his last year and made some bad decisions."

She stood in a quick movement. "My father never made a bad decision."

"Okay," he replied to pacify her.

"Don't patronize me," she snapped.

He took a long breath, giving them both some time to cool off. "As I said, I'm not ready to be a father."

"You're almost forty," she shot back. "When will you be ready?"

"When Shilah is making a steady profit."

"Oh, please, you had time to go out to dinner with Karen Harvey—twice."

He did a double take. How did she know that? "It was a business dinner—a reward for a job well done on a lawsuit pending against Shilah."

One dark eyebrow lifted again. "You rewarded her twice?"

He tried not to appear guilty but he feared he failed. "There's nothing between Karen and me. It was only business. I didn't cheat on our sham of a marriage."

"I'll have to take your word for that."

At that moment the crazy dog of hers sniffed at his boots. The mutt was small with a ring of brown around her left eye and another brown spot on her white body. "If she pees on my jeans one more time…"

Jessie bent and patted her leg. "Come, Mirry."

The dog immediately trotted to her and Jessie stroked Mirry's head. The little thing looked weird without any ears or tail, but that didn't matter to Jessie. Her classical features softened as she cooed to the animal. He remembered Roscoe talking about her love of animals and it showed in her expression. None of that emotion had ever been bestowed upon him. He thought it best to get back to the matter at hand.

"A baby should be conceived between two people who are in love and building a life together," he told her.

She straightened from petting the dog. "In most cases that's true. It's quite different for us, though. We were forced into this marriage and I've decided to make the best of it. I do not intend to remain childless."

"But—"

"I thought sex to a man was like turning on a faucet…anywhere, anytime type of thing."

He studied her face. "You're so unemotional about this."

"You want emotion, Cadde?" She reached down and opened the file. Pulling out a document, she slid it on the glass table in front of him. "Here's the kind you will understand. The day I give birth I will sign over one share of my stock to you. I'll then have twenty-five percent and you'll have twenty-six, giving you control of Shilah. Isn't that what you want more than anything in the world? Well, there it is in black and white."

For the first time in his life words failed him. He couldn't push a single syllable through his throat. *Was she serious?*

"I want full custody. You will give up your parental rights." She tapped the paper. "It's in the document. You can see the baby whenever you want, but I will raise the child, leaving you free to run Shilah. You have twenty-four hours to think it over and then the deal's off the table."

She brushed past him and he came to his senses, grabbing her arm. "Oh, no, you don't get to walk away after delivering a bombshell like that."

Her skin felt as soft and inviting as anything he'd ever touched, reminding him of a magnolia blossom from the tree his mother had planted in their yard in High Cotton, Texas. Jessie's chest rose and fell with each labored breath. His eyes were glued to her breasts pressing against the white silk. A delicate, tantalizing scent reached him.

She was petite, barely five foot four, and all woman. Suddenly he could feel the heat building between them and he wondered why she didn't pull away or why he didn't let go.

"There's nothing left to say," she said in a hoarse voice he'd never heard before. "The next move is up to you."

Reluctantly, he released her. "I thought you wanted a divorce or an annulment."

"Quite the contrary."

"So this is a business deal?"

"If you want to call it that."

He shook his head. "You really are Roscoe's daughter."

"I learned from the best." She left the room with that weird dog following her.

He jammed both hands through his hair. All it took was for him to get Jessie pregnant and he'd be in control of Shilah. He almost laughed out loud. What man wouldn't want to go to bed with her? Why was he hesitating? He didn't understand it. He didn't understand the whole damn conversation he'd just had with her. But once again he knew Jessie was in control.

JESSIE QUICKLY CHANGED OUT of her suit and into jeans and a T-shirt. She had animals to feed. She paused for a moment to let her heart rate subside. Her hand went to the spot where Cadde had held her. His fingers were firm, powerful, but the touch of his skin against hers was warm, tempting, and she wanted him to wrap her in his arms and say…what? He didn't love her. She knew that. Cadde loved the oil business. Her father had said that Cadde had oil in his blood and she now believed that was true.

She had practically offered herself to him and he had to think it over. He wasn't ready to be a father. That was crap. He just didn't want her. He preferred the blond willowy type—like Karen Harvey.

Her pulse quickened at the sheer jealousy running through her. And then she laughed. What did she have to be jealous about? She and Cadde were married, yet they went their own ways. She certainly never asked him to be faithful to her. Dealing with her only parent's death was hard enough without contending with a new husband.

Walking over to the window, she gazed outside in time to see Cadde's truck drive away. Her father had once told her that if she wanted something to go after it no matter the consequences. She wanted Cadde Hardin and she went after him in the only way she knew. Time would tell if he would take the bait. Daddy was a gambler to his soul but she'd never thought of herself that way.

Until today.

Once you make a decision, stick to your guns, Jessie. His words came back to her. It wasn't that simple, though. She was gambling with her heart—so dangerous. The consequence of getting hurt didn't deter her and, like her father, she was willing to take the risk.

Her eyes went to the bars on the window. The prison especially built for her. She never had a normal childhood, a normal life, and that was her dream—to have a real family living without fear. She wanted to fill this big house with kids, laughter and love. And she wanted to do that with Cadde.

He'd called her an iceberg. *Ouch.* Well, she had to admit that in part it was true. She had thought her father would survive the surgery, but he hadn't. In shock, she'd pushed everyone away, even her new husband.

She hated that Cadde had to be forced to marry her. She hated that he treated her like a piece of furniture. She hated that life had been so cruel.

After her grief had subsided somewhat she decided to try and make her marriage work. But first she had to get Cadde's attention and doing that proved more difficult than she'd ever imagined. Therefore she aimed for his heart.

Now she waited.

CADDE SAT AT HIS DESK going over the document Jessie had drawn up. She was willing to give him control of Shilah for a baby. That should be easy—for any man. Why wasn't it easy for him?

The door opened and his brothers burst in. They had extrasensory perception where he was concerned because they always seemed to know when he was in the building.

"Hey, any news?" Not being afraid of the devil, Kid dove right in.

"From the look on your face I'd say the talk with Jessie didn't go well," Chance said.

"Depends on how you label *well*." His hand rested on the document. He was still wrestling with its content.

"What the hell does that mean?" Kid asked with his usual tact.

"Jessie didn't want a divorce. You need to brush up on your women skills, Kid, because that was the last thing she wanted."

"Damn." Kid snapped his fingers. "I'm hardly ever wrong when it comes to the fairer sex."

"I won't take that to the bank."

"What did Jessie want?" Chance asked in his calm way. Of the three brothers Chance was the youngest and the one with a heart of gold. The night their parents had died, Chance had been sleeping in the backseat of the car. He was the only one who'd survived the crash. To protect his brothers he'd kept a secret for over twenty years. Their parents screaming at each other had awakened him. Seemed the man they adored was leaving their mom for someone else.

Chance had struggled with his demons for a lot of years, only telling them recently the real story behind the accident. But then fate dealt him another severe blow. He fell in love with the daughter of the woman who had destroyed their family. Chance, with his heart of gold, had worked through all the pain. He and Shay were happy and they had a nine-year-old adopted daughter, Darcy, who was the light of Chance's life. His brother had found true happiness, but Cadde had to wonder if that was in the cards for him.

"Cadde?" Chance prompted him and he realized his thoughts had drifted.

He cleared his throat. "Jessie wants a baby."

"What!" echoed through the large office.

Kid frowned. "You mean those little creatures who crawl around and slobber all over themselves?"

"If Shay and I have a child you're never holding it," Chance told him.

"I didn't ask to," Kid fired back.

Cadde got up and walked to the floor-to-ceiling windows that looked out over Houston. It was a magnificent view and he swore he could see Galveston in the distance. But it was only an illusion. He was having a hard time with fact and reality today.

His thoughts turned once again to his father. Cadde was in the oil business because of him. Chuck Hardin roughnecked his entire life, but he'd said his sons would do better. They'd get an education and work their way up the ladder into a position of power.

Cadde had worked toward that one goal and now it was within his grasp. Somehow, though, it was tainted by the betrayal of his father. The man who'd taught him about family values and honor was a phony. Cadde didn't want any son or daughter of his to think that of him. He wanted to be in his child's life one hundred percent of every day. And he didn't want a baby conceived as part of a business deal.

Damn Jessie!

"Cadde," Chance prompted again.

Cadde swung from the window and walked back to his desk. "Are you two through arguing?"

"Yeah," Chance replied. "We decided Kid's an ass and left it at that."

"We did not!" Kid protested.

Cadde held up his hand. "Enough. I have some important things to discuss with you." He glanced at the document. "The day that Jessie gives birth she'll sign over a share of her stock to me…giving me control of Shilah."

"Hot damn, now we're talking." Kid jumped to his

feet in excitement and then stilled. "What's wrong? I can see something is by the look on your face."

Cadde remained silent, having a hard time explaining the situation to his brothers. But they had a stake in Shilah, as well.

Chance leaned forward. "What you're saying is that you and Jessie haven't had a real marriage and she wants to make it real in every way possible."

"That's about it," Cadde had to admit.

"So what's the problem?" Kid wanted to know. "You've worked your ass off for Roscoe for years and now it's time for the big reward you've been waiting for. Jessie's handing it to you on a platter. All you have to do is get her pregnant. Easy as pie." Kid's eyes narrowed on him. "You're hesitating. Why?" Before he could form a reply Kid added, "You're not impotent, are you?"

Chance slapped Kid's shoulder. "Shut up, you idiot."

"I'm not shutting up!" Kid yelled. "I have a stake in this business, and if you hit me one more time I'm gonna knock you on your ass."

"Just try." Chance faced him—two brothers, same height, same build, both angry and neither afraid to fight.

"Cut it out, dammit. I don't need you two at each other's throats."

"Hell, Cadde, that's what we do best—fight with one another." Kid was back to his usual cheerful self. "Just tell us why you're finding it hard to accept Jessie's offer."

"Because it's a business deal. I never planned on my firstborn being part of a negotiated legal document."

"So?" Kid pressed. "It gives you control of Shilah. That's what you've wanted."

Cadde eased into his leather chair. "I keep thinking about Dad."

"Oh, God." Kid closed his eyes. "Let's not go down that road."

"When we were boys," Cadde went on, as if Kid hadn't spoken, "he was a good father. I thought there wasn't anything he couldn't do. I hung on his every word, but in the end he tarnished all of those childhood memories with his betrayal. I don't want a child of mine to have bad memories of me."

"Why would he or she have anything but love for you?" Chance asked.

"Because Jessie wants full custody."

"Oh, my God." Clearly, Chance was shocked. "She's asking you to give up your flesh and blood?"

"She says I can see the child whenever I want, but basically I'd be trading the baby for Shilah." His eyes swung to Kid. "Now do you understand my hesitation? Imagine how that child is going to feel about me later in life. I don't want any kid of mine to have bad feelings about his father."

Kid looked straight at him. "Then do something. You're a wheeling-dealing gambler just like Roscoe. You can do anything if you put your mind to it. Remember that little old lady in Midland who said she'd die before she'd lease her land? Even I couldn't sweet-talk her, but you mentioned her kids and how the money would benefit them. You had her eating out of the palm of your hand. You have to do that now. Find a way around this business deal. Make it work for you and Shilah."

"For once I agree with Kid," Chance said. "Whatever you do, though, do not give up your rights as a father."

"I've got a handle on it now, guys. Thanks."

"That's what brothers are for," Kid replied as he and Chance headed for the door.

Cadde drew the document forward. Jessie wasn't going to have it all her way. He picked up a pen and began to scratch out lines he didn't like and then he added his demands. At the bottom he scribbled his name.

Jessie was in for a shock.

CHAPTER THREE

CADDE MARCHED THROUGH the back door of the Murdock house. "Jessie," he called.

No one answered, but he found Rosa in the kitchen. "Where's Jessie?"

"Mr. Cadde," Rosa acknowledged in surprise. "I wasn't expecting you again."

"Where's Jessie?"

Rosa wiped her hands on her apron. "Probably at the barn. She went to feed her animals."

Animals? What the hell was Rosa talking about? It suddenly hit him that he knew absolutely nothing about his wife other than she was Roscoe's daughter and a pain to deal with at board meetings. He had no idea how she filled her days. He just had this vision of her lying across the bed in that big master bedroom eating bonbons. Obviously, she had more animals than that silly dog.

Before he could question Rosa, Jessie came through the door looking flushed. He did a double take and wasn't really sure it was her at first. She wore jeans, a blue T-shirt and work boots. Dark stains smeared her T-shirt and strands of dark brown hair had worked loose from her knot, curling around her face. She looked like a teenager bent on a day of mischief.

"Cadde," she said, breathing heavily. Evidently she'd run to the house. "I saw your truck…"

He held up the document in his hand. "We need to talk."

"Oh. Okay. Let me wash my hands first." She hurried into the bathroom off the kitchen.

"You don't really know Miss Jessie, do you?" Rosa asked in a disapproving voice.

"No, ma'am. I don't," Cadde answered truthfully.

Rosa shook her head. "Mr. Roscoe was a good man but paranoid about his daughter. He never allowed her any freedom and…"

Jessie came back, interrupting Rosa. "I'll check on Mirry and I'll meet you in the sunroom," she said to him.

"The dog can wait. We need to talk."

"I'm checking on Mirry." Her dark eyes narrowed and she brushed past him.

He charged into the sunroom, anger eating at his insides. Was she always going to have the upper hand? Whipping off his hat, he slammed it onto the glass table along with the damn document. He eased into a rattan chair, feeling out of place in the green-and-white room that overlooked the closed-in pool. Plants seemed to be everywhere, even hanging from the ceiling.

He took a long breath, trying to relax. He'd been negotiating business deals for years and he never felt as nervous as he did today. Jessie had a way of making him crazy, but this time he was going to be in control.

From the sunroof of the pool, sunlight danced off the water. He watched as if mesmerized…and waited.

AFTER CHECKING ON MIRRY, Jessie paused at the bottom of the stairs and drew a calming breath. She wanted to change her clothes, but that was pointless since Cadde had already seen her looking like one of the hired hands.

Why had he returned so soon? Could this unexpected visit mean he was accepting the offer? Or throwing it back in her face? Could this be the one thing Cadde Hardin wouldn't do to gain control of Shilah—have a baby with her?

It was an insane idea in the first place. Yet they were married and she wanted a child. This old house was so lonely. Next time she would rethink her father's advice.

She walked into the kitchen and got two glasses from the cabinet.

"What are you doing?" Rosa asked.

"Getting iced tea for Cadde and me."

"That's my job." Rosa took the glasses from her.

"Rosa."

Rosa paid her no attention, as always. In a matter of seconds she had them filled with ice and tea. She reached for two napkins off the granite kitchen island and handed them to Jessie.

Jessie kissed her cheek as she took them. "I love you."

"You need someone else to love," Rosa told her. "And I don't mean all those animals out there." She thumbed over her shoulder.

Jessie winked. "I'm working on it."

"Miss Jessie, what are you up to?"

"I'll tell you later."

She breezed out of the kitchen and braced herself for

the scene with Cadde. Her courage intact, she walked into the sunroom and placed a glass of tea and a napkin in front of him.

"Thank you," he muttered, taking a swallow.

Jessie sipped hers before taking the seat across from him.

He pushed the document lying on the table toward her. "I signed it."

"Oh." Relief rushed through her. She hadn't expected him to concede so quickly.

"But I made some changes."

"Oh." His abrupt attitude was making her edgy.

"Read it, sign on the dotted line and we have a deal."

She flipped through the document and stopped when she saw his bold handwriting. She reread the page, not quite believing her eyes. "You…you…want a real marriage?"

"That's what it says. When the deal is official, I'll be moving into that big master bedroom."

Her eyes caught his. "I sleep alone. I always have."

"Not if you sign that document."

"Why can't you sleep in your own room?" She didn't want him to know her secret. She slept with the bathroom light on. All those fears from her childhood were still there. She was seven when her cousin, Crissy, had been kidnapped and killed, but she remembered it. They'd lived in Houston then and after the murder her father had slept on a cot in her room with a gun across his chest. That frightened her even more.

"Because married couples sleep together."

"But we don't have to."

He poked the document with a long finger, his brown eyes determined. "That's the deal, Jessie."

She clenched her hands in her lap until they were numb and then she forced herself to continue reading his other demands. "You claim all your rights as a father, which are granted in our marriage vows."

"Yes."

"And you insist on my full support at future board meetings after the marriage is consummated."

"Yes."

She raised her head and looked into his steady, unwavering gaze. "You're asking an awful lot."

"How bad do you want a baby?" he asked, and her insides quivered at the magnitude of her actions.

He reached for his hat and stood. "You have twenty-four hours to think it over." With an in-your-face nod, he strolled from the room.

"Wait just a minute," she called, infuriated that he was turning her tactics around on her.

He paused at the door and faced her. "What?"

"We need to talk."

"Jessie, we've talked this to death. Bottom line I refuse to walk away from a kid of mine. I will be there from day one. Sign it or not. It's up to you. If you don't, we're getting an annulment because I'm not living in this sham of a marriage any longer."

"I see." She should have known it wouldn't be simple. Cadde was a skillful businessman and he had upped the stakes. She had to accept them or live the rest of her life alone. And if Cadde left she would truly be alone.

She gulped a breath. What were her options—loneliness or a real sleep-in-her-bed-every-night marriage? She'd started this out of desperation and she had to have the courage to finish it.

Her hand shook as she picked up the pen that was still lying there from the morning. She took another breath and wrote her name beneath Cadde's. The action caused her to feel limp, weak and defeated somehow.

Cadde strolled back into the room and placed both hands on the table. Leaning in close to her, he asked, "Wanna go upstairs?"

She drew away. "I'm not a hooker, Cadde."

"That's how you make a baby, Jessie." His eyes sparkled with glee at his victory, and she wanted to smack him.

"I want to get to know you better first."

He straightened. "Now there are rules?"

"Yes," she told him, taking the wind out of his sails. "We're going out to dinner tonight."

"Tonight! I've been fooling with this insanity most of the day. I have work piled up. I don't have time to go out."

She stood and picked up the document. "I'll get this to my lawyer." Her eyes locked with his. "Be here at eight or the deal is off." After delivering that blow, she brushed past him. He didn't grab her arm this time but she heard him curse. She smiled all the way up the stairs. At least she had the last word. Now she had to fulfill his demands.

CADDE TRIED TO CONCENTRATE on the Louisiana leases. With Jessie's approval, he planned to move on them quickly. First they had to consummate the marriage.

He tapped his pen on the papers in front of him. That would be a big step. It would make their relationship real, but he had to wonder how a marriage could survive without love.

He ran both hands over his face. How much did love matter? His parents had been in love until... Would he be like his father and cheat on Jessie? He didn't know, but he hadn't cheated on her in eighteen months and it had been a strain. He could have with Karen. Something held him back, though. It had to be that integrity thing Roscoe had talked about. He didn't want to be like Chuck Hardin even if the marriage wasn't real.

Sleeping with Jessie could turn out to be rather pleasant. If only he could get those off-limits notices out of his head. Who knew she wanted to change their relationship? She showed no signs of doing so...until today.

Fatherhood. He hadn't thought much about it. He'd been too busy building a career. How was he going to balance his job and Jessie and a baby?

A baby! He couldn't quite wrap his mind around that just yet. But as Jessie had mentioned, he was almost forty. It was time to think about a family.

With Jessie.

Shaking his head, he brought his concentration back to the leases. After they consummated the marriage, the first thing on his schedule was to call an emergency board meeting. He had to have their approval to move on anything.

He'd already talked to his geologist and engineers. They felt if they could drill deep enough they'd hit a big well. As soon as he decided which lease had the most potential, he'd get Kid out there to inform the lease hold-ers. In this economy he was hoping they'd be grateful for some extra income. Roscoe had sat on those leases for a reason and now Cadde had to make it work.

Reading through the engineers' notes, he glanced at his watch. Dammit! He didn't have time to go out to dinner. Irritated, he found himself looking at the time every few minutes. At first, Jessie'd balked at the real marriage thing, but then she'd caved. His moment of victory was short-lived, though. Living up to his own demands wasn't going to be easy.

The luxury of having an apartment down the hall from his office was something he was used to. Now he had to make the drive in every day. What was he think-ing? At the time he was angry and wanted to get back at her. After cooling off, he realized some things were not going to work in his favor.

He slept about three nights a week at the house to keep an eye on Jessie, as he'd promised Roscoe. But he rarely saw her. He worked long hours and she was usu-ally in bed when he came home and still asleep when he left. Through Rosa he knew she was okay and ev-erything was running smoothly. If he needed to talk to her about business, he'd call and come home early.

"Damn you, Jessie, for screwing up my life," he said under his breath. Her biological clock was ticking and she'd zeroed in on him, her husband, like a buzzard on a carcass. But he was the logical candidate. They couldn't continue to live in their farce of a marriage. It would have been so much simpler if she had wanted a divorce or an annulment. Then they could have gone their separate ways. Still, he wouldn't have felt good about that. He'd made a promise to Roscoe and, unlike his father, his word meant something to him.

Closing the files he got to his feet and headed to the apartment to get ready for a date with his wife. And God help him, it was the last thing he wanted to do.

JESSIE WENT THROUGH ALMOST every dress in her closet and finally shimmied into a black slim-fitting one with a V-neck. Looking in the mirror, she frowned. The V showed too much cleavage and she actually had some to show off. For so long she'd been flat-chested.

Taking another glance, she decided to wear the dress. After all, tonight she was starting a new role—being a wife and hopefully a mother. She sighed. Why did it have to take a business deal to bring them together? Why couldn't they have magically fallen in love? Because Cadde never saw her as anyone other than Roscoe Murdock's daughter.

Pushing the depressing thought aside, she sat at her dressing table. With her olive complexion, dark hair and eyes she needed very little makeup. She applied liner to her eyes and brows and then added some lip gloss. That would do. She brushed her long tresses until the static electricity almost ate her brush. Rarely did she wear her hair loose, but tonight she let it flow down her back.

She glanced at herself in the mirror and wondered like she had so many times in her life—who did she favor? Her father had blue eyes and blond hair. Without a doubt she took after her mother. When she'd asked

about her, he'd say, "Jessie, baby, your mother left us
a long time ago. You've got me, so put a smile on that
pretty face." Then she'd feel guilty for asking about a
woman who would leave her child. It didn't keep her
from wondering, though.

She'd even asked Rosa, but Rosa had come to work
for them after the tragedy. She'd never met Jessie's
mother.

As a child she'd dream about the mysterious woman
coming back, but she didn't. In her teens Jessie had finally accepted that. Her mother had made her choices
for whatever reasons and Jessie seldom thought about
her these days.

Glancing at the crystal clock on her vanity she saw it
was after eight. Damn! Where was Cadde? If he bailed
on her, she'd make his life a living hell. She laughed
out loud. She really was her father's daughter. But she
wasn't making anyone's life a living hell. If he didn't
come, they'd go back to the status quo of ignoring each
other. That would be her living hell.

"Get a grip, Jessie," she said to herself as she reached
for a long strand of pearls her father had bought her in
New York. Slipping into high heels, she hurried downstairs to wait.

CADDE WAS RUNNING LATE, but he couldn't help it. He'd
had a call from one of his engineers and they talked
about the Louisiana leases.

He rushed through the back door and found Jessie pacing in the living room, her dog trailing her
every step.

"I'm sorry I'm late." The rest of his excuse evaporated as he stared at his wife. He knew the poised Jessie in business suits and the casual Jessie in jeans, but the sexy siren in front of him was someone else entirely. He could feel his blood pressure taking a hit.

She looked at the gold watch on her arm. "Fifteen minutes, to be precise."

"I told you I had a lot of work to do and I got away as quickly as I could."

"And so gallant about it, too."

"Let's go then." He struggled to look anywhere but at her cleavage. He felt like a teenager seeing breasts for the first time.

Jessie bent to pat the dog. "Go upstairs to your bed, Mirry. I'll be back later." The little thing trotted away as if she understood every word.

"Where did you get her?" he asked to focus his attention on something beside her. If it was up to him, they'd just go upstairs but he knew that wasn't what she wanted—just yet. Damn! Why did women have to be so picky?

"I found her on the side of the road," Jessie was saying. "Someone abused her severely and left her for dead."

He experienced a moment of guilt for not liking the little dog. The cruelty of people floored him, but Mirry seemed to have found a savior in Jessie.

"You're staring," she said.

He blinked. "I've never seen you with your hair down."

She called his bluff immediately. "My hair is here." She touched her head.

"Okay, I was staring at your breasts," he admitted like the honest Christian boy that he was. "I never realized you had…"

"Breasts," she finished for him.

He nodded, wishing they'd never started this conversion.

"They're pretty much standard equipment, Cadde."

He sighed. "Could we go?"

"Sure." She picked up a small purse from the coffee table.

"Do you want to go in my truck or your Suburban?"

"Your truck," she replied. "My vehicle has feed in it and it's smelly."

"What do you feed?"

"Animals that would starve if I didn't."

They talked as they walked through the dining room to the kitchen. Rosa had said something about animals and now he was curious.

"What kind of animals?"

"I have five horses from the Houston SPCA. Their owner left them to starve to death in a pasture. I know someone there and she calls me when they have an animal that's been mistreated or abused and needs a home. I also have a donkey that had an infected eye and a ram with one horn. Gavin cut off the other one and operated on the donkey's eye. They're doing very well. The horses were skittish at first, but between Gavin, Felix and me we've managed to gain their trust. Gavin doctors their sores every week or so."

"Who's Gavin?"

"The vet." He opened the back door and she asked, "Do you want to know who Felix is?"

"No. I sign his damn paycheck. Why isn't he picking up the feed?"

"Felix was busy and I was in town at a board meeting, as you may recall, so I picked it up. No big deal."

As soon as they stepped into the garage, the Dobermans sniffed at their feet.

"Oh, I hate these dogs." Jessie made a face.

"Why?" Again he was curious. She seemed to have an affinity for animals.

"They're trained to kill. I told Daddy I didn't want an animal like that, but he insisted when he went on that trip to Alaska. He was afraid someone would breach the security system while he was gone. And he wanted a surprise for the perpetrator."

Cadde remembered that trip with Roscoe. They were checking out the oil situation, but Roscoe decided it was too damn cold for his Texas blood. Roscoe called Jessie two to three times a day and sometimes more if he was feeling restless and worried. Fear was his constant companion. He never lost the paranoia that someone was going to take Jessie from him.

"Why don't you just get rid of them?" he suggested.

"I tried. No one wants a dog like that. I might see if Gavin can gently put them to sleep. I hate doing that but they kill every animal that comes into their perimeter—squirrels, rabbits, raccoons, possums, birds, anything. There's always something dead in the yard in the mornings."

She took a breath. "And they attacked the man who delivers hay for the horses. He stopped at the house and made the mistake of getting out of his truck. They were on him in a second. Felix was barely able to grab their collars and restrain them so the man could get inside his vehicle. It was very scary. I'm even afraid to go out after dark, and if they attack one of my mistreated animals I would just die."

"Then call your friend Gavin first thing in the morning." He didn't want her living in fear. He wasn't all that fond of the dogs, either.

They walked to the passenger side of his King Ranch truck. Suddenly she turned and he bumped into her. He caught her arms to steady her. Smooth, silky skin tempted his fingers and a delicate fragrance wafted to his nostrils. His heart rate rose like mercury in a thermometer. Oh, God. He released her. This was going to be a long, long evening.

"A couple of days ago Will brought me a baby fawn," Jessie was saying. "Someone had killed her mother."

"Who's Will?" How many men came out here to see Jessie? He knew she was the big selling point. The animals were just an excuse. For the first time jealousy flickered in his gut. It was ridiculous. He'd never had these symptoms with the other women he'd dated. So why was Jessie different?

"The game warden," she replied, and he jerked his attention back to the conversation. "The little thing needed nourishment badly. I have her in a cage in the barn. Since she's a new scent I'm afraid the Dobermans will attack her. I keep a rifle at the barn and one in the house if anything goes awry."

"Jessie, I don't like the sound of this. Call the vet."

She flipped back her long hair. "Are you telling me what to do?"

"Yes," he replied.

In the light from the garage he could see her black eyes flashing. "Just so you know I don't respond well to people telling me what to do."

He met her gaze. "Just so you know, as your husband, I'll be doing that—a lot."

"I figured," she replied in a saucy tone. "Don't expect me to be a dutiful wife."

He opened the passenger door of his white truck. "That's the last thing I expect from you."

She laughed softly and it seemed to clear the tiredness and stress from his mind.

His vehicle was high off the ground and he intended to help her inside, but she hitched up her skirt, showing a long length of smooth thighs, and hopped in without a problem.

Why did Roscoe think Jessie was fragile and helpless? She had as much strength as he had. Why had Roscoe never seen that?

He walked around to the driver's side. Why had *he* never seen that? He just assumed Jessie was as vulnerable as Roscoe had described. They'd both been wrong. Jessie could match his strength any day of the week.

Their marriage would be a test of wills. Who'd be the first to give in, the first to compromise?

As he backed out, he knew one thing. It wasn't going to be him.

CHAPTER FOUR

STUPID! STUPID! JESSIE CURSED silently. Why didn't she let Cadde help her? Her father's paranoia had made her dependent and she'd spent many years staking her independence, proving to everyone, mostly herself, that she was capable of handling her life. Claiming that prize hadn't been easy, but she was tired of being afraid of everything around her. So she faced life head-on, determined to do things on her own. Sometimes, though, she needed to make better judgment calls—like tonight.

Little was said as Cadde drove away from the house. She watched his big hands on the steering wheel: capable, efficient and strong. That described him to a T.

A Shilah Oil coffee cup was in the console along with papers listing oil wells and production numbers. The four-door cab truck was big, but with Cadde's presence it seemed to grow smaller. A woodsy coffee scent tempted her nostrils. She leaned back and let the cool air from the air-conditioning calm her nerves.

When they reached the cutoff to U.S. 290, Cadde stopped the truck. "Where would you like to go?" His tone indicated he didn't care and that irritated her.

"There's a nice Italian restaurant in Brenham," she replied. "It might be more miles, but less traffic."

"Fine." He turned right. He was halfway friendly

earlier. Now he seemed to have nailed that door shut. If he wanted to be temperamental, that was okay with her—up to a point. This evening was about them getting to know each other and he had to make an effort.

They breezed into Brenham, a small town of nearly fifteen thousand, and home to Blue Bell Creamery. As a child, she loved it when her dad would take her to get ice cream. Even though it was one of her fondest memories, it took all of her childish imagination to ignore the guards. She had wanted to run and play with the other kids, but was never allowed.

She switched her attention to the road and gave Cadde directions. He followed them without saying a word. When he stopped at the house that had been converted into a restaurant, he asked, "Is this it?" Clearly, he wasn't impressed.

"Yes. It's very nice and has great food," she informed him.

"Fine," he said again in that clipped tone.

She gritted her teeth and got out. It was pointless to wait for him to help her. She'd already blown that.

As they walked to the front door, a warm breeze ruffled her hair. Tossing it back, she gazed at him and had to admit he'd made an effort in dressing. He wore dark slacks, a white shirt, with his dress boots and Stetson. Every woman in the place was going to be looking at him. He had that air, that presence that drew attention. He'd certainly caught hers and her feelings hadn't changed since the first time she'd met him. She had to wonder, though, if they could build a life on her feelings alone.

They didn't have a reservation, but were able to be seated without waiting. She could just imagine Cadde's ire at having to wait. Their table was by a fireplace, which was unlit because it was the last month of summer. Still, with the muted lighting and a candle flickering in the center of the linen tablecloth, it was very romantic. They had a view of a small courtyard with green plants. The whole ambience was relaxing. She took a deep breath and prepared herself to enjoy the evening.

Cadde laid his hat on a chair as a waiter placed menus in front of them. "May I get you something to drink?" he asked.

"A glass of your best chardonnay," Cadde replied without pausing.

The waiter turned to her. "I'll have the same," she told him.

As the waiter walked away, she opened her menu. "The chicken alfredo is good, and so is the marsala."

"Mmm." He studied the dinner entrées.

The waiter came back with two glasses of wine. Setting them on the white tablecloth with a coaster, he asked, "Are you ready to order?"

Jessie closed her menu and unfolded her linen napkin. "Yes. I'll have the chicken alfredo."

Cadde did likewise. "Parmesan steak. Medium rare."

She should have known he'd order steak. There was just something about Texas men that they had to have steak. Her father had been the same.

She shifted uneasily and thought this would be a good time for them to talk. Straightening her napkin in her lap, she said, "You have two brothers, but I know little else about you or your family."

"I was born in High Cotton, Texas." He took a gulp of the wine. "After our parents died in a car accident, we lived with our aunt and uncle." A flash of resentment crossed his handsome face.

"Your expression changed when you mentioned your parents."

He looked at her for probably the first time since they'd left the house. "I don't know why." His chilling tone issued a warning—*don't pry.*

The silence stretched and she could almost feel a negative vibration coming from him telling her he wasn't in a talkative mood. She was about to ignore all the warnings when their dinners arrived.

Cadde emptied his glass. "Bring the bottle, please."

"Yes, sir."

In a matter of seconds, the waiter was back with the wine.

"Thank you," Cadde replied, filling his glass.

She twirled fettuccine around her fork and watched him cut into his steak with sharp strokes. Between each bite he gulped the wine. After the third glass, she'd had it. She carefully placed her napkin on the table and picked up her purse.

"If you have to drink yourself silly to have dinner with me, then the deal is off." She stood and strolled from the room, but not before she saw the shock on his face.

At the small entry alcove, she asked the lady for a taxi. She didn't even know if Brenham had taxis, but evidently they did since the woman handed her a card with a number. She noted the curious look on the woman's face. After seeing her come in with Cadde, she was probably wondering what was going on.

As she went out the door, she punched the number in on her cell and gave the taxi company her location. Darkness had settled in over the neighborhood, but the outside lights were bright, illuminating her way. The houses were lit up and a couple of boys rode by on bicycles, enjoying the last days of summer. Through some of the windows with open curtains she could see families were sharing their day—loving families. That was something she was never going to have so she might as well face it.

She glanced at her phone for the time. How long did it take a taxi to get here? The cell was suddenly jerked from her hand. She whirled around to find Cadde. He was furious from what she could glimpse in the streetlight. His hat hid most of his expression.

"Give it back to me." She jumped for it, which was ridiculous since he was so much taller.

"You're going home the same way you came here," he snapped.

"Like hell. I'm not going anywhere with a man who has to get drunk to spend a couple of hours with me."

"I'm not drunk."

"Oh, please." She placed her hands on her hips. "Jessie…"

The cab drove up, interrupting him. Cadde opened the door and handed the guy some bills. "Sorry. Thank you."

Jessie was seething. How dare he! She was so angry she was about to burst out of her dress. "Give me my damn phone!"

"You're not getting it." He held it higher and it made her that much angrier. "Listen to me. I'm not drunk, but it's hard for me to adjust to this situation so easily. For years Roscoe told me to never mess with his daughter. You were off-limits. I can't make an about-face overnight."

Some of her anger cooled. "Why would Daddy say that?" She couldn't believe her father would do such a thing, but then again he protected her from life every way he could. He scared most of her men friends away only because he was afraid of her getting hurt. Cadde was different, though. Her father knew him.

"Think about it, Jessie. Roscoe shielded you from everything and everyone."

"That doesn't excuse your insensitive behavior tonight." She wasn't letting him off with that ludicrous explanation. "Give me the phone and we'll call this evening a waste of time and put a big emphasis on my insanity in thinking that we could make this marriage work."

"Jessie..."

She didn't want to hear anything he had to say. Jumping for her phone again, she stumbled in her high heels and fell toward him. His arms went around her and he balanced her against the car that was parked at the curb. Somewhere between the anger and something she couldn't describe, everything changed.

Her breathing became shallow as his head bent toward her. She stood on tiptoes to meet his lips. It wasn't gentle nor did she expect it to be. Her arms slid around his neck and she melted into a kiss fueled by anger but buffeted by emotions that doused every trace of outraged feelings. His lips softened and she went with the flow of discovering Cadde.

He tasted of wine—heady, delicious wine that made her dizzy. She knew he would kiss this way, completely, mindlessly and without any doubt of who was in control. The hair at his nape tickled her fingers, his broad chest felt like a wall she could always lean on for support. Her phone was still in his hand and it rubbed her back in a soothing erotic way. His other hand pressed her closer to his male frame, and she experienced his all-consuming power.

Just when she thought her feet would leave the ground and she'd float around in outer space from the sheer pleasure, he eased his lips to her cheek, to her forehead.

"Let's go home," he whispered in a throaty voice.

She breathed in the heady scent of him, the wine. The moonlight spilled its magic rays upon them and she wanted to explore these feelings, but she also knew she wasn't ready. She needed time to get to know him. Would he understand?

"I'm hungry," she murmured.

"Me, too." He kissed her forehead and her resolve weakened.

She played with a button on his shirt. "I'm hungry for food."

"Jessie," he groaned.

"You ate. I didn't."

He took a step backward and the heat of summer stung her skin—skin that he'd refreshed with his male touch. She felt bereft, wanting his body against hers again. Why was she hesitating? She wanted more than a sexual relationship. She wanted love and trust along with the intimacy. She wanted a marriage that would last a lifetime.

To ease her erratic thoughts, she picked up her purse from the ground where she'd dropped it when she'd stumbled. Her hair fell forward and she flipped it back.

He handed her the cell and stared. The moonlight seemed to draw them closer and closer, not physically, but emotionally. *He understood.* Taking her hand, he led her into the restaurant. "These people are going to think we're nuts."

She laughed and it eased all the doubts in her mind. They needed moments like this to build a foundation for a real marriage.

The lady at the entrance looked surprised and the waiter raised a questioning eyebrow since they were seated at the same table. But being a professional, he asked politely, "Would you like something to drink?"

"Iced tea," Cadde replied, hooking his hat on a chair.

"Me, too," Jessie added. "And I'll have the alfredo again with a house salad."

"Yes, ma'am." The waiter walked away with a curious expression.

Laughter bubbled inside her.

"Don't laugh," Cadde said, as he noticed her struggle to contain her amusement. "He has a right to think we're insane."

She unfolded her napkin. "Don't start again. This evening is about us getting to know each other."

"I certainly know a lot more about you. You're as stubborn as Roscoe."

She bit her tongue to keep sharp words from escaping. Patience was not her forte, but tonight she would try. Just as well the waiter returned with a tray. He placed iced tea on a napkin and a salad in front of her and then served Cadde's drink.

"Thank you," she said, and the waiter walked away with a slight smile.

Soft music played in the background. She hadn't noticed that earlier, but now it seemed to intensify the romantic mood. Picking up her fork, she was determined they'd have a normal conversation, even though she knew she was stepping on some forbidden ground.

"How old were you when your parents died?"

Cadde was staring at his Stetson, but her soft voice drew his undivided attention. Well, partially. He was reeling from the kiss. The off-limits signs were no longer in his head. Jessie had completely demolished them with her passion. He still tasted her lipstick—tasted her. He'd always thought of Jessie as unemotional because she was cool, businesslike. He was wrong—again. Now he was learning about Jessie the hard way—shock after shock. Her lips, her touch he would remember for a long time.

He moved uncomfortably. "I was sixteen." Running his thumb across the rim of the glass, he felt its dampness, its coolness. This wasn't an easy subject for him to talk about, but he couldn't continue to stare at the glass or his hat. He had to share. That's what Jessie wanted. It was time to open the door he kept firmly locked. He wrestled with his thoughts.

"We…were in Austin at the state basketball championship for our district and Kid and I played on the team. Kid was almost fifteen but tall for his age so the coach let him play cause we needed another player. High Cotton had never gone that far in the play-offs and we were determined to win, which we did by one point. We were riding a wave of excitement and someone sneaked beer onto the bus—well, everyone knew it was Kid. He never said how he got it and I didn't want to know. The coach fell asleep in the front seat and the driver's attention was on the road. We celebrated all the way home."

He gripped the cold glass. "When we reached the school, the principal was waiting for Kid and me. We thought it was because of the beer. He took us to the gym and Aunt Etta, Uncle Rufus and Chance were there. Chance had a bruise on his face and arm and his clothes were dirty. The moment I saw him I knew something was terribly wrong." He took a swallow of tea to cool the heated emotions inside him.

"Our aunt put her arms around us, and said, 'Boys, your parents died tonight.' The world we knew suddenly ended. The high of the win was replaced with a gut-wrenching low. We stood there holding on to each other until Dane Belle walked in."

"I'm so sorry." As she placed her hand on his forearm, his eyes were drawn to her long slim fingers. He wasn't sure what to say and all he could feel was her soothing comfort. He never talked about this to anyone but his brothers.

"Who's Dane Belle?" she asked, and that broke the headlock on his emotions.

"The owner of the High Five ranch and the nicest man you'd ever want to meet. Aunt Etta, my dad's sister, and Uncle Rufus worked for him. He moved us into my aunt and uncle's house, which is on High Five. Dane was there to help us every step of the way. He literally stepped into our dad's shoes."

She removed her hand to continue eating and he felt a moment of disappointment. He was the strong one, never needing anyone's comfort, but her soft supportive touch got to him.

"I can't imagine anyone taking Daddy's place." She pushed the salad aside as the waiter brought her entrée.

"He didn't replace him. He just filled this big empty void in me, Kid and Chance." Leaning back, he fiddled with the napkin and the words seem to gush out of him like one of his oil wells when they hit pure Texas gold. "You'd have to know Dane to understand. He was a gambler, a drinker, but he had a big heart that he gave to everyone. He never met a stranger and he made the Hardin boys feel right at home. We spent all our holidays with them. Chance still does. Kid and I have a harder time getting home. We always seem to be hundreds of miles away."

"Does Dane have children?"

"Oh, yeah." He took another swallow of tea. "Three

beautiful daughters by three different mothers. Dane was also a ladies' man, a charmer, sort of like Kid."

"No one is like Kid." She lifted an eyebrow. "So you grew up with his daughters?"

"Yeah. We lived down the road from High Five and then we relocated to their backyard. Summers were fun because all the girls were home."

"What do you mean?"

"Caitlyn was raised on the ranch because her mother died in childbirth. Madison and Skylar lived with their mothers. There was a clause in the divorce papers that Dane got the girls during the summer and Christmas, that way their lives weren't disrupted during the school year." He felt a smile tug at his lips. "I'm surprised Kid survived those summers because the sisters knocked him for more loops than I can count. He was always teasing and picking on them. We usually baled hay in the summer and the girls were always there, even though Dane and Miss Dorie, their grandmother, didn't want them to be. They wanted them to be proper la-dies." Cadde suppressed a laugh. "You'd have to meet them to understand that one. Caitlyn is bossy and re-sponsible. She tried her damnedest to be the boy Dane had always wanted. Madison is like a lollipop—she's so sweet you just want to lick her, which Kid has done on more than one occasion. And Skylar, well, she's the wild sister, the one Dane worried about the most. They certainly kept Dane on his toes."

Cadde leaned back as memories seemed to grip him. "After baling hay under a hot Texas sun, we'd pull off our hats, boots and shirts and jump into Crooked Creek to cool off. Sometimes the girls would join us. One time Kid dove in and snuck up behind Caitlyn and pinched her butt. She slapped him and he sank like a rock. We thought she'd killed him. We kept diving trying to find him, even Dane got in the water. Kid came up downstream, laughing. Caitlyn chased him all the way to the barn. He hid from her for two days."

"Sounds as if you had a happy life on High Five."

"Yeah." He twisted his glass, knowing Dane and the sisters had given them a reason to keep going, to keep living. "I still miss Dane."

"He passed away?"

"His drinking finally got him."

There was silence for a moment.

"You haven't said anything about your parents."

Glancing up, he saw her gazing at him with dark, concerned eyes. While he'd been talking, she'd finished eating. "That's not an easy subject."

He could feel the gusher of words being capped, his throat closing. Then she laid her hand on his arm again and her gentle touch freed his emotions.

"Dad said they were high school sweethearts and married after graduation. They were happy…"

"They weren't."

"What?"

"I'd rather talk about Dane and the sisters. Those are good memories. My parents…"

She squeezed his arm. "What happened?"

He could do this. He could handle anything. From somewhere deep inside him he heard the word *liar*. Talking about his parents was something he didn't do, except with his brothers. They understood. Jessie wanted him to talk, to share. Could he?

She rubbed his arm and it eased the grip on his throat, and the words came gushing out once again. "My…dad…is the reason I'm in the oil business. He preached education and how we should be bosses, not roughnecks. He taught us family values and about trust and faith, but in the end it was all a lie."

"Why?"

"Seems my dad told my mom he was leaving her. It had just happened and all that kind of stuff. My mother wanted to know who the woman was, and he wouldn't tell her. She started hitting him and he lost control of the car." He swallowed. "On the biggest night of his young sons' lives we were going to come home to find that our father had left us. I thought he'd meet us at the gym and he'd tell us how proud he was. Instead, we came home to find that our father had really left us… for good."

Both her hands gripped his arm. "Cadde, I'm sorry."

The waiter poured more tea and removed the plates. "Would you like dessert?" he asked.

"No, thanks," Jessie replied.

"My mother didn't deserve that," Cadde murmured as if the waiter hadn't interrupted them. "She was the nicest person."

The words had come from a deep personal well inside him and Cadde thought he'd done enough sharing. "How about your mother?"

Jessie removed her hands and folded them in her lap. "I never knew her."

"Not ever?"

"She left when I was a baby. Whenever I asked about her, Daddy would say that she left us and I had him. That was all I needed."

"But you know who she is?"

She fidgeted in her chair. "I didn't until I was older and snuck into Dad's study and found my birth certificate." She paused. "Her name is Angela Martinez."

The spotlight was now turned on her, and by the thinning of her lips Cadde knew she didn't like it. Sharing was hard for her, too.

"And?" he persisted.

"Okay." She reached for her tea glass and took a swallow. "I called every Martinez in the Houston phone book, and believe me, there were a lot. I found a lot of kind people, but not my mother."

"Did Roscoe know you did this?"

Her eyes darkened. "I would never hurt him like that." She placed her napkin on the table. "I just wanted to talk to her."

"About what?"

"I was fifteen. I didn't have a plan." She cocked a dark eyebrow. "Are you trying to make me angry?"

"Not intentionally."

"Good." She took another sip of tea.

He watched her. "But you do get a little heated when you talk about your mother."

Her eyes narrowed to slits of fire and he knew a whole lot of stubborn was coming his way.

"Have you ever asked Rosa about her?" He tried to sidetrack her.

"Rosa and Felix didn't come to work for us until after Crissy was kidnapped." Her temper seemed to cool instantly.

"I didn't realize that."

"I'd had a normal childhood until then. Crissy and I were like sisters. Aunt Helen would take us to school and to our ballet and soccer classes. Life was fun. Suddenly it all changed."

Dark emotions clouded her face and he wanted to comfort her in some way, but he wasn't good at that. "You lived in Houston at that time?" he found himself asking.

She nodded. "Two blocks from Crissy. The kidnapper came in through her window and carried her away to his car. The police said that's when she woke up and started to fight. She scratched his face and his hands. While he was trying to restrain her he broke her neck." Jessie took a deep breath. "He stuffed her into a culvert at the end of the street and covered her with leaves. It was two days before they found her."

"I'm sorry, Jessie," was all he could say, and it seemed to be enough.

"Life became hell. Daddy carried a gun and hired Rosa and Felix to watch me. Felix had a gun, too. Daddy took me out of school and hired a tutor. I never went back."

"But you went to college."

She tossed her long hair over her shoulder. "Now that was a fight."

Knowing her and Roscoe's temperaments, he could imagine. "You won."

"In a way." She shrugged. "The college had to be up north where no one had ever heard of Roscoe Murdock, and the guards had to go with me. It was difficult to make friends with big, burly guys hanging around, but I managed. I missed Daddy, Rosa, Felix and Myra so much. I'd never admit it, though."

"Never," he joked.

She made a face at him.

The warm vibes stoked a flame deep in his groin. He cleared his throat. "Myra is Rosa and Felix's daughter?"

"Yes. She works for Houston's district attorney's office, a very tough lawyer." Her face became thoughtful. "I can see what you meant about Dane now. Myra is two years older than me and she sort of took Crissy's place. She was someone to play with, talk to, share secrets and giggle with. She's my very best friend."

He was glad she had Myra so she could vent her frustrations. He had Kid. A fight with Kid spiked his blood pressure more than a five-mile run. And Kid knew him better than anyone.

"Sadly, though—" she was saying "—no matter how much I told Daddy I could take care of myself, he never lost that fear of someone kidnapping me."

"I know."

Her eyes caught his. "That's why I'm married to you."

A tangible silence followed and Cadde seemed to lose his balance in the darkness of her eyes.

The waiter laid their bill in a vinyl folder on the table. "Can I get you anything else?"

"No, that's fine," Cadde replied, dragging his gaze from Jessie's to reach for his wallet. He placed a hundred dollar bill in the folder. "Keep the change."

"Thank you, sir."

Cadde glanced around the restaurant. "Looks like we've closed down the place." The tables were empty and one area completely dark.

Jessie leaned over and whispered, "They're waiting for us to leave."

Waiters and the hostess stood at the entrance, trying very hard not to stare at them.

Jessie picked up her purse. "We better go."

Cadde followed her out and placed his hat on his head. "Good night," he said to the group in the alcove.

"Have a good evening," they chorused.

Once outside, the warm night air embraced them. Instinctively, Jessie reached for his hand. He gripped hers with his strong fingers and they walked to his truck. Darkness now ruled the neighborhood. Very few lights were on, but the streetlight provided ample illumination.

They moved to the passenger side of the vehicle. Cadde pushed a button on his key ring and the doors unlocked with a click. Opening the door, he helped her inside. She smiled. Oh, yeah, this was the way it was supposed to be done.

In a second, Cadde was in the driver's seat and they sped away. Jessie leaned against the headrest. "It was a nice evening, wasn't it?"

"Touch and go at first, though," he remarked.

"That's because you made me mad."

"I have a feeling you get mad a lot."

Jessie watched the night slip by in waves of blackness, punctuated with a light here and there. "I don't... really."

"But you have a temper," he added in a teasing way that didn't offend her.

"Yes," she admitted. "I always thought I got that from Daddy, but I'm not sure."

"You got it from Roscoe," Cadde assured her. "That man had a temper. I remember one time he lit into a tool pusher for letting a guy who was clearly intoxicated on a rig. He yelled so much he bit his cigar in two. You know how he was always chomping on a cigar."

"Yeah. And the angrier he got the more he chomped."

"Mmm."

Jessie relaxed in the loving memories of her father. She and Cadde shared that—the connection that held them together. Could there be more?

Glancing at Cadde, she wondered how he expected this evening to end. Well, she knew—in the bedroom. She was the one who had asked to take their relationship further and she didn't want to tease him. That would be cruel, but again she hesitated. And she knew why. She wanted more.

He drove around to the garages and pushed a button on his sun visor. The garage door went up. Lights came on. While he guided the truck into his spot, the Dobermans barked, eager to confront their visitors.

"Down, boys," Cadde said as he got out and walked around to her side.

The Dobermans sniffed her. "Good grief," she complained, sliding out. "You'd think they'd know me by now."

"Just instinct, I suppose," he said, and they went into the house. The dogs darted away to the front, on guard.

Cadde pushed buttons on the wall, closing the garage door and setting the alarm system. Rosa had left the kitchen light on and there was another light on in her bedroom and the foyer. Coming into a dark house was not one of Jessie's favorite things. Rosa knew her phobias.

They walked through the kitchen, dining room and living room to the large foyer. Jessie's nerves were taut, and she turned quickly to talk to Cadde. His arms went around her waist and she forgot what she was going to say. He took her lips gently this time and, unable to stop herself, she returned his ardor. His hands trailed from her back to her hair, and desire, raw and potent, shot through her.

Breathing heavily, she whispered, "Cadde, could we talk?"

He sagged against her. "Jessie…" he groaned.

"Like you said—" she rushed into speech "—this is too fast. I need a little time." She held her thumb and forefinger close together. "Just a little."

"More rules, huh?" His voice held a note of complacency rather than anger.

She kissed his cheek. "Thank you," she murmured, and ran up the stairs.

"This is not how you get a baby, Jessie," he called after her.

CHAPTER FIVE

JESSIE HURRIED INTO HER ROOM, smiling. Somehow, she'd known behind that hard exterior Cadde Hardin was a nice man. He was giving her time. Touching her lips, she still felt the heady sensation of his kiss. She fell across the bed and closed her eyes.

Something wet touched her cheek and that euphoric feeling vanished. She reached out, pulling Mirry into the crook of her arm. "Miss me?"

The dog snuggled closer, and Jessie could see dog hair clinging to her black dress. Oh, well, it was going to the cleaners anyway. Her cell buzzed. She grabbed her purse and fished it out. Seeing the name, she clicked on.

"Hi, Myra."

"I called Mama earlier and she said you were out with Mr. Cadde." Myra dragged out the last part.

"Yes, and I had a great time."

There was a long pause. "So he agreed to the deal?" Myra was the only person she'd told about her plans, and she was vehemently against it. But Jessie had listened to her heart.

"Yes." Jessie bit her lip, trying not to react to the disapproval in Myra's voice.

"Just like that?"

"No, but we worked it out." Jessie scooted up against the headboard, the dress sliding up to her hips.

"With strings, I'm sure, to his benefit."

Jessie gave up on being tolerant. "Myrie, I'm not talking to you if you keep being so critical."

"I'm just worried about you."

"Don't be. I could use my friend's support."

"Cadde Hardin is wrong for you."

And the conversation went like so many in the past— Myra in her misguided wisdom was always trying to protect Jessie, and Jessie inevitably lost her cool. Why couldn't the people closest to her understand that she had to live life—her way?

"You don't know him."

"I know his type."

"And what is that?" Jessie stroked Mirry to calm herself.

"Strong, powerful, determined and in control…always. I see his type in the courtroom all the time."

"Cadde's not like that." Well, that probably wasn't true. Jessie barely knew Cadde, but she was trying to make a point.

"You've known him, what? Ten years or more? And ninety-nine percent of that time he's ignored you. He was sucking up to your father for a big chunk of Shilah."

"I didn't meet him until I came home from college and that hasn't been ten years. If you don't apologize, I'm done talking to you."

A tense pause. "Okay, I'm sorry, but he's going to hurt you."

"I might hurt him. Have you thought of that?"

"Since you're besotted with the guy it hasn't crossed my mind."

Jessie sighed. "Myrie, I'm not that little girl you used to lead around by the hand. I can make my own decisions and handle the consequences." She stuffed a pillow behind her back with more force than necessary. "I recall a certain lawyer I know who dated a man for nine months and then found out he was married. She cried for three days."

Another pause. "Okay, I'm a lousy judge of men."

"Yes, you are, so let me make my own mistakes."

"That's hard to do."

"Try."

Myra laughed. "Tell me about your evening."

"No. It's private."

"You're kidding."

Jessie kicked off her heels and they landed with a thud on the carpet. "He's my husband and I'm not telling tales about our relationship." And it would be a whopping tale. She could embellish with the best, but the truth was they were both feeling their way and she wasn't giving Myra details. She wasn't a teenager.

"Wow! This is serious. We talk about everything."

"Not my husband, though."

A long pause.

"Wanna hear about this lawyer who's been giving me the eye?"

"Oh, no. Not another one." Jessie settled back to hear the rest of the story.

CADDE FLUNG HIS HAT ACROSS Roscoe's study and it landed somewhere behind the brown leather sofa. He needed something strong. Opening the liquor cabinet, he pulled out a bottle of Scotch. He didn't bother with a glass. He wasn't going to need one.

Unscrewing the top, he set the Scotch on the coffee table and plopped onto the sofa. Jessie needed time. She'd started this whole charade and now she wanted to wait. He didn't get that, but then he didn't get a lot about women. Maybe that's why he was still…

Single?

He wasn't single. He'd been married eighteen months—without sex.

He reached for the bottle and took a sip, wincing as it went down. Damn! The stuff was potent. Taking a breath, he noticed the lights were on all over the house. What was that about? Rosa and Felix had gone to bed long ago. Many nights he came in late and the lights were always on. Why? He upped the bottle again.

Rules! Jessie had rules. As much as he wanted to be irritated, he somehow understood. At his age he had come to realize that men and women were different in more ways than the obvious ones. Compliments, flowers, open hearts and love reached a woman faster than a bullet could strike a moving target. The first two most men handled without a problem. The last one…love… proved to be the stumbling block.

He was no different. He wasn't even sure what love was. His parents were supposed to love each other and look how that had turned out—tragically. But their defunct marriage wasn't the reason he was single all these years. He hadn't really known about his dad's affair until recently.

Deep down he must have known. He came home from school early one day and found his mother crying. She said she'd had some sad news about a friend. She'd lied to cover up...for him. And then his dad had worked a lot of overtime. He was rarely home. There were signs, but as a kid he didn't recognize them.

He tipped up the bottle again.

Cadde loved his brothers, his aunt and uncle, Dane and the Belle sisters. Those relationships were permanent, solid. They'd never change. Even though there were disagreements at times, the bond still remained.

Marriage was different. He took another swig. How did he make it work without straying? How would he stay faithful to his wife and commitment year after year? So many others had tried and failed. What hope was there for two people who weren't in love?

He only knew one thing for sure—he wasn't going to be like his father. Straightforwardness and honesty was his plan. As he raised the bottle again, he wondered what Jessie expected from him...besides a baby. Did she expect him to love her?

Oh, God. His head hurt. Was it the Scotch? Or thoughts of Jessie? Another drink might help.

He should be at Shilah working. Now, the oil business he understood. He set the bottle on the coffee table and reached for the phone on his belt. Being out of contact this long wasn't like him. He'd turned off his cell because he knew Jessie would get mad if he took calls during dinner.

Reading through his messages he saw he had one from the engineer, the geologist, three from Kid and two from Chance. He closed his cell. They could wait until morning. Right now he couldn't focus enough to reply.

He grabbed the bottle. Jessie had given him a shock when she'd left the restaurant. He didn't expect her to do that. He didn't expect her to do a lot of things. Through the haze of Scotch he realized Jessie had manipulated him and he'd bowed to her every whim. She was in control, as always.

But maybe not.

As he stood, the room seemed to sway. "O-o-oh." He'd reached his limit. The coffee table was in front of him, but every time he tried to set the bottle on it, the damn thing moved. What the hell, he'd take it with him.

He needed to go to bed.

JESSIE QUICKLY UNDRESSED and slipped on short pajama bottoms and a tank top. After scrubbing her face, she applied moisturizer. Myra had talked on and on and it was past Jessie's bedtime.

It was ironic that for someone who was a brilliant attorney, Myra's personal life was a mess. If anyone should be giving out advice on men, it should be Jessie instead of Myra. Jessie knew what she wanted. Myra did not. The fact they were brutally honest with each other was just part of their relationship.

But Jessie hadn't told Myra everything. Her secret was her own and she planned to keep it that way.

Rinsing her hands, she froze. Someone had opened

her door. She tiptoed to the bathroom doorway and peered around the frame.

It was Cadde!

He stumbled to the left side of the bed. He had something in his hand—a bottle, which he tried to set on the nightstand. After the third try, he managed it. He'd been drinking. That was more than evident, but what was he doing in her room?

I'm moving into that big master bedroom.

His words came back to her and she trembled. What did he plan to do?

He sank onto the bed and yanked off his boots and then he stood and unbuttoned his shirt, sending it sailing toward her bay window. He seemed to sway. How drunk was he?

Since the light was on she saw him clearly. Broad, naked shoulders met her eyes, followed by swirls of dark chest hairs that arrowed down his lean stomach into his slacks. She swallowed, but otherwise remained perfectly still, which was difficult because her pulse hammered loudly in her ears. He undid his belt and removed his pants, revealing black Jockey shorts.

By now she was deaf. She couldn't do anything but stare at the male body in front of her. Where did those gorgeous muscles come from? Cadde sat at a desk all day. Evidently he worked out. When? He spent every waking moment at Shilah. Or so she'd thought. Something else she didn't know about him.

He staggered for a moment and then threw the top sheet aside, crawling into the bed.

Was he out?

He sighed and she jumped back. Taking a deep breath, she glanced around the corner. He'd maneuvered his long body to the right side. That was her place. She always slept on the right. Damn!

She slid to the floor and pulled up her knees. Mirry hopped into her lap. "Shh," she whispered into Mirry's nub of an ear. "We have a man in our room."

Mirry cocked her head, as if she understood.

Jessie could sleep in a guest room, but her stubborn pride wouldn't let her. On the other hand, she didn't want to have drunken sex, either. She peered around the door again. He was out.

With Mirry in her arms, she walked into the bedroom. Cadde didn't stir. His breathing was heavy and there was a faint scent of Scotch in the room. Placing Mirry in her bed, Jessie flicked off the light and waited. Still he didn't move.

Frowning, she moved as quietly as possible to the left side. Cadde had most of the ecru sheet wrapped around him. The room was cool from the air-conditioning and she needed something to cover herself. Grabbing the peach comforter from a chair, she spread it out and eased beneath it.

How was she going to sleep here? It wasn't natural to her. She turned onto her right, hoping to get comfortable. It didn't work. She heard a whine and looked down. Mirry stood on her hind legs, her paws on the mattress. The poor thing was confused because Jessie wasn't sleeping in her normal spot near Mirry's bed.

Jessie scooped her in beside her and tried to get some sleep. And she must have. When she awoke she knew it was morning even though it was still dark. She pushed hair away from her face and sat up to look at the clock on her nightstand. The light was on in her bathroom and she could see clearly. Five o'clock.

Cadde was still sleeping, inches from her in the king-size bed. His brown hair fell across his forehead and she wanted to smooth it back, to feel his skin and...shock him out of his mind probably. Enough time for that later. At present he was going to have a gigantic headache.

Unable to resist, she studied his features. Dark eyebrows feathered away from his eyes, not too thick or thin, just manly. His eyelashes were long and sexy for a man, and his straight nose and curved lips were, again, sexy for a man. Dark stubble covered the lower part of his face. Her stomach quivered in awareness.

Handsome was too generic of a word to describe him. *Damn pulse-throbbing good-looking* suited him better and she could just imagine the hearts he'd broken over the years.

And she was dawdling. She didn't want him to catch her staring at him. Easing from the bed with Mirry in her arms, she noticed the Scotch bottle on the nightstand. She grabbed it, not wanting Rosa to find it. Rosa had a thing about drinking. She'd given her father a few lectures on the subject. Once he'd fired her, but Rosa wouldn't budge.

She'd said she wasn't leaving Jessie in the hands of a drunk and slammed the door in his face. Her father chomped on his cigar until it almost disappeared. He never again drank in front of Jessie or Rosa, though. He did that in his study or at the apartment at Shilah.

It was the only time she'd ever seen her father make a concession to another human being. But he knew Rosa would take care of Jessie if anything happened to him.

Quickly dressing in jeans and a T-shirt, she headed downstairs with the bottle. Looking down, she noticed Mirry wasn't there. She glanced back to see her curled up in her bed. Too early for Mirry, she thought.

And for her. Oh, God. She needed coffee.

Not knowing what else to do with the evidence, she put it back in the liquor cabinet. But it made her think. Did Cadde drink a lot? He'd had wine at dinner and then almost killed a bottle of Scotch. He was an astute businessman and that thinking wasn't fueled by liquor. Maybe she'd made him imbibe. Now there was a sobering thought.

She went into the kitchen to start a pot of coffee. Rosa had it set to come on at six. How did she change the damn thing? She studied the control panel.

"Miss Jessie…"

Jessie almost jumped out of her skin at Rosa's voice. She thought she was still sleeping.

With a hand to her chest, she said, "You scared the life out of me."

"What are you doing up so early?" Rosa walked to the coffee machine, poked a couple of buttons and it came on. Since Rosa was in a cotton robe and slippers, she must have just gotten up.

"Thanks. I…I couldn't sleep."

"After your late night, I thought you'd sleep in."

"No, I…"

"Rosa, have you seen my hat?" Cadde walked in,

fully dressed in jeans and a white shirt. His hair was still damp from the shower. How did he do that so fast?

"No, Mr. Cadde, I haven't seen it."

"Dammit, where did I put it?" He turned and left the room.

He didn't appear to have a hangover, just a touch of grouchiness. The coffee machine beeped and she grabbed a cup and filled it, adding cream and sugar. As she sipped it, she realized Rosa was staring at her.

"Why are you so nervous?"

"I'm…"

"And your hair is everywhere. Did you brush it?"

Oh, damn. In her haste, she'd forgotten to brush her hair. She touched it with one hand. "My hair's fine." She went to the refrigerator for yogurt and fruit.

"I'll get your breakfast, Miss Jessie," Rosa said before she could open the door. "You sit or you're going to fall asleep on your feet."

"Rosa…"

"Go." Rosa gave her a slight push. She sat at the breakfast table and while Rosa's head was in the fridge she ran her fingers through her hair, hoping that would help.

Cadde came back with his hat in his hand.

"Oh, Mr. Cadde," Rosa said. "You found it."

"Yeah." He placed the Stetson on the bar, grabbed a cup of coffee and took a seat across from her.

"What do you want for breakfast?" Rosa asked, placing yogurt and fruit in front of Jessie.

"Bacon and eggs and some of those good biscuits you make."

"Oh. That will take a while, but if you have time."

Cadde glanced at his watch. "Actually, I don't. I need to run. How about toast instead of biscuits?"

"Coming right up."

Cadde sipped his coffee, and she could feel his eyes on her. "Rosa, why were the lights on last night?"

Jessie paused with the spoon halfway to her mouth. Rosa rattled the dishes more than necessary. "Ah...I don't like Miss Jessie coming into a dark house. And just a few were on."

Cadde didn't say anything else for a moment, and then he glanced directly at Jessie. "You left the bathroom light on last night."

"Really?" She licked her spoon just to do something to avoid that keen gaze. "I hadn't noticed."

Rosa placed his food in front of him and dropped the fork and knife on the floor. "I'm sorry." She quickly scooped them up. "I'll get more."

Cadde continued to gaze at Jessie. "Aren't you up awfully early? You're never up when I leave for work."

Jessie shrugged as Rosa laid another fork and knife on the table with a napkin. Cadde dug into his food and Jessie let out a long breath. She couldn't figure out why he wasn't holding his head with both hands. Instead, he looked spry and ready to face the day.

The buzz of his cell interrupted the silence. He reached for it on his belt. "Yes, Kid, I'm leaving in a few minutes." No sooner than he clicked off, it buzzed again. With a sigh, he answered, "I'm on my way, Chance."

He pushed back his chair and moved to get his hat from the bar. "Thanks, Rosa." His eyes caught hers.

"I'll see you tonight." The way he said *tonight* made her think of him in nothing but his Jockey shorts, and a wave of heat warmed her skin.

"What time?" she asked to maintain some of her dignity.

"Seven, eight." He leaned over and whispered, "Tonight we play by my rules."

She coughed as a piece of strawberry went down like a jalapeño pepper—hot and startling.

He grinned and walked out.

How dare he? Her temper simmered just below the surface and nudged her wide-awake. If he thought…

"Miss Jessie, what's Mr. Cadde doing in your room?" The scolding tone hit Jessie the wrong way.

"He's my husband."

"He didn't…"

Rosa had a hard time finishing the sentence so Jessie finished it for her. "Force himself on me?"

Rosa gasped.

"You've known Cadde for years and you know he's not that type of man. It was my decision to take our marriage further. Mine, Rosa. And I can handle the consequences." She threw her napkin on the table and stood. How many times did she have to say that? "So please, please stop smothering me and let me have a life, a life of my choosing." She strolled toward the door and stopped. Jessie knew Rosa meant well, just like Myra, and Jessie couldn't hurt her this way.

She turned. "That was harsh. I'm sorry." Cadde's parting words had her nervous and snappy.

Rosa pointed a finger at her. "You talk to Myra too

much. You're getting her attitude." The relationship between Rosa and Myra wasn't good. They argued all the time, mostly about Myra's career and her single status. Rosa wanted grandbabies.

She walked back and hugged Rosa. "Myra has to make her own decisions and so do I. Please let me be an adult. Let me get hurt and feel the pain. Let me have a life."

"I just want you to be happy, my *niña*." Rosa touched her cheek.

"I'm planning to build a life with Cadde, have babies to fill this big, lonely house, to feel safe and secure and not sleep with the light on anymore."

"Oh, Miss Jessie, a baby?" Rosa put her hands over her mouth in awe. That was the only word Rosa had heard. *Baby.* The word could light up Rosa's face like a diamond ring could light up a young girl's.

The thought made her look at her platinum wedding band. Cadde's matched hers. She didn't know if her father had bought them or Cadde. The rings were just there when the minister had performed the ceremony. She preferred to think that Cadde had purchased them. And it would stay on her finger until he took it off.

"Not yet." She kissed Rosa's cheek. "Now I'm going upstairs to brush my hair and if I don't return, well, I'll be asleep."

WHEN CADDE REACHED HIS OFFICE, Kid and Chance were waiting for him. He sat in his chair without saying a word.

"How come you didn't answer your phone?" Kid asked, his feet propped on Cadde's desk.

"I do have a personal life." Cadde pulled a large folder forward.

Kid formed a steeple with his fingers. "How's that going?"

"None of your business," Cadde retorted, and knocked Kid's boots off his desk. "I don't know why I share anything with you guys."

Chance looked up. "Hey, I haven't said anything."

"And I appreciate it."

Cadde opened the folder, trying not to wince at the pounding in his head. He knew his limit. He knew when to stop. What had possessed him to down almost a whole bottle of Scotch?

Jessie.

"From where I'm sitting I'd say big brother had no sex last night."

Chance frowned at Kid. "Could you use a little tact?"

"Tact?" Kid drew back. "It's Cadde. I'm not wasting my manners on him."

"You don't waste them on anybody," Chance told him.

"That's not true. Mom said I had the best manners of the three of us."

Chance laughed. "She was your mother. She had to say nice things about you, and it was a stretch because you were in trouble all the time."

"I was not."

Cadde thought it was great they could talk about their mother without mind-numbing silence. This wasn't the time, though. He'd clap his hands to get their attention, but the sound might paralyze him. Instead, he unfolded a map and pointed to a spot.

"These are our leases in Caddo Parish. They're small tracts and the problem is we don't have enough acreage to drill a well. That's maybe why Roscoe never drilled there. Kid—" he drew papers from the folder "—here's the land we lease and owners' names and some notes on adjoining properties. Your job is to find out who owns the mineral rights. If an oil company already has a lease, we need to know when that contract expires. We need more land and it's up to you to get it."

"So Jessie gave the go-ahead?"

Cadde sighed, not wanting to discuss Jessie. "There's a lot of paperwork and legwork to be done before I can call a board meeting." He'd realized this last night when he'd been going over the leases. The tracts were small, smaller than he'd thought. He couldn't investigate further because he had to meet Jessie.

He pushed those thoughts from his bruised mind. "Chance, get an estimate on the cost of renting a rig versus moving one of ours. I'd like to keep our rigs in Texas but I need to see the figures first."

Chance stood. "I'm on it."

"Remember, we have a meeting with Joel, Tim and Bob at eight to discuss this further." He rose to his feet. "Now I need coffee."

"I made some in my office," Chance said. "I'll bring you a cup."

"Thanks. Make it a big one."

After Chance left, he could feel Kid's eyes on him,

and he hated that. Kid had a way of seeing beyond the surface. Maybe that's why he was so popular with women. They liked it when a man could tune into their feelings. God, he was hopeless in that department. He had no idea what Jessie was thinking.

"Are you okay?" Kid asked, and Cadde felt sucker punched. Was it that obvious?

"If I didn't know any better," Kid went on, "I'd say you have a hangover, but that couldn't be right. You can hold your liquor. You're known for that. Right?"

Cadde muttered under his breath, and if Kid could gauge what he was thinking, he'd take a step backward and leave, which he did, after he picked up the map and papers.

Chance brought back a thermos of coffee and didn't say a word. That was Chance—not intrusive, but a soothing, calm presence.

After a couple of swallows, he forced himself to think about last night. He remembered sitting in Roscoe's study drinking and agonizing over Jessie having the upper hand. Bits and pieces flittered through his mind; soft, smooth sheets with lace on the pillowcases, the bathroom light blinding at times.

His next recollection was waking up in Jessie's bed. As he tried to recharge his memory, she'd stirred. He'd pretended to be asleep, but he sensed her watching him for a moment before she'd slipped out of bed and dressed quickly.

He let out a long breath.

This morning he tried to appear as normal as possible, even testing the waters to see if she was upset. She wasn't. Oh, God, she looked like every man's fantasy, dark hair tousled all around her and her eyes had that just-woken-up sleepy gaze. Sexy as hell.

That picture made him needle her about tonight. Having the last word could become a habit. He could still feel the fire in her eyes.

He flexed his shoulders and wanted to go work out in the room down the hall he'd turned into his own personal gym. But he didn't have time. He had a meeting and his day was full.

Finishing off the coffee, he knew he and Jessie had to talk—again. They had to discuss what she expected from him without a power play in this business deal of a marriage. She wanted time. Why? And how much time did she need? She was making him nuts and his head had to be clear to run Shilah. That's what was important—Shilah.

Or was it?

CHAPTER SIX

JESSIE WOKE UP AT NINE and scrambled to her feet. Good grief, she had to get moving. She brushed her hair and clipped it back. Hurrying out of the bathroom, she noticed the clothes Cadde had strewn on the floor last night were gone. A man who picked up after himself— how novel. Her father had never picked up a thing.

Pushing thoughts of Cadde aside, she went down the stairs. Mirry followed, making pitiful little grunting sounds. Jessie knew she needed to go outside. This was always a problem with the Dobermans. She heard the vacuum system going, so Rosa was busy and Felix was at the barn. After filling a bowl with dog food, Jessie carried it to the garage. She then went back inside and put the garage door up. The Dobermans shot in to devour the food. She put the door down. The dogs were trapped for a while.

Mirry did her business in the front yard and Jessie let her play for a bit. But not long. Jessie left Mirry in her bed in the breakfast room and then put up the garage door. The dogs bolted out. Smelling the scent in the front yard, they'd circle the house for about an hour, trying to find their foe. It was a daily routine for Jessie and she was tired of it. She'd call Gavin as soon as she got back to the house.

"Mornin', Miss Jessie," Felix called as she entered the barn. He was in the small kitchen she'd had installed. "I was fixin' the fawn something to eat." In worn jeans and boots, Felix was just a little taller than her with a weather-worn face and calloused hands. *Good* was the word to describe Felix. If he wasn't sleeping, he was working. He was an expert welder. He'd built all the pipe fences on the place. There was nothing he wouldn't do for her. He was her number one protector and a rifle was never very far away.

"How is she this morning?"

The scent of alfalfa, dust and manure filled her nostrils. The barn was her place. After getting a business degree, she intended to work at Shilah with her father. She should have consulted him first because he axed it immediately. She would sit on the board, but she wouldn't work. He'd added that he'd worked enough for both of them.

She'd thought of looking for work elsewhere. That was an absurd idea with a guard hovering around her. No matter how much she'd begged and pleaded, her father wouldn't relent about her security. When she'd managed to escape a few times, all hell had broken loose. The guard was fired, she got a lecture about her behavior and then she'd threatened to run away and never come back. That had brought tears to her father's eyes. Soon Jessie was the one relenting. She couldn't hurt him that way. She'd put up with a guard as long as he was alive, but now she was on her own.

"Still weak."

Absorbed in her thoughts, Jessie wasn't sure what

Felix was talking about. She placed the powdered milk back in the cabinet, her thoughts drifting. The barn had been built with the house, but no one used it except Felix for welding. While she was trying to figure out the rest of her life, her father had bought her a horse, Lady— her first taste of freedom. She loved flying through the woods by herself.

Lady got an infection in her hoof and that was how she'd met Gavin, who had a friend at the Houston SPCA. He'd tell her awful stories about animal abuse and she found herself getting involved. It kept her busy. That and her volunteer work at a women's shelter. She'd often thought she had a kindred spirit for abused animals and people. And on that thought followed another—did she feel abused by her confinement? The answer still eluded her.

Jessie realized Felix was staring at her and she took the baby bottle from him. "I'll feed her. I'm running behind this morning."

"You were out late last night," he said. "I'm glad Mr. Cadde was with you."

Jessie patted his shoulder. "Stop worrying."

"I wish you hadn't fired those guards." Felix's words of concern followed her.

So many people worried about her. She just wanted to breathe and feel free without someone looking over her shoulder. Was that too much to ask?

"Please, let's not have this conversation again."

"Yes, ma'am."

Guilt nudged her at his woeful tone. "I'm fine, Felix."

He nodded, his floppy straw hat covering his expression.

She knelt in front of the cage that Felix had built and opened the door. The little fawn looked at her, fear in her big brown eyes.

"She's better, huh?" Felix asked.

Jessie scooted in and put an arm around the fragile neck, stroking the tan-and-white-spotted body. "It's okay. I'm not going to hurt you." While talking, Jessie tempted the fawn's mouth with the nipple. She trembled and then licked and took the bottle greedily.

"Oh, yeah, she's much better. Yesterday I had to practically force her to suck."

The fawn downed the bottle in no time and Jessie crawled out, smiling. "We need to give her a name."

"Mmm."

"Bambi," Jessie decided. "We'll call her Bambi."

"Sounds good." Felix trailed behind her as she went through the door to the corral. "I already gave the horses a round bale of hay."

She leaned on the fence, watching the horses.

"They look good, too, huh?" Felix asked beside her.

The horses gathered in the middle of the corral, munching on big chunks of coastal. Their sores, welts and infections had healed and they were gaining weight. When she'd first gotten them, they'd been so thin.

"Yeah," she murmured, thinking about Lady. She'd gotten the hoof infection again and died about two years ago. Jessie missed her and she missed riding. These horses were broken to ride. She might give it a whirl when they were healthier. But then she had a lot on her plate right now and she didn't want to get thrown on her butt.

She felt a gentle nudge and turned to see the donkey, not so patiently waiting for feed. He'd lost one eye from infection, and it always seemed as if he was winking at her, so she'd called him Winky.

The ram, not wanting to miss any attention, joined them. She petted both. The ram she called Dopey. At mealtime he was always trying to hook Winky with his horn, which wasn't there anymore. The crazy thing didn't seem to know that.

"Come on, you two, I'll give you some sweet feed."

After tending to them Jessie glanced at her watch and realized she was running late. She'd promised Fran at the shelter that she would come in today.

"I've got to run, Felix." She wiped her hands on her jeans. "Would you mind giving Bambi a bottle about one? I'll pick up some cream to add to her milk and feed her again when I get back."

"Okay, but I don't like you driving around out there by yourself. Sure wish you had a guard."

Jessie just shook her head.

"I got the feed out of your Suburban," Felix called after her. "I left the back open so it can air out a bit."

"Thanks."

She ran to the house, ignoring the Dobermans. The August sun was already hot, her clothes were sticking to her and she smelled faintly of manure. Good grief! A quick shower and she'd be on her way.

As she darted through the kitchen, Rosa was preparing lunch.

"Miss Jessie—"

"Not now, Rosa, I have to go to the shelter."

"Why? Why do you have to go to that place?"

Jessie put her hands over her ears, not wanting to hear one more word about her safety. Why did everyone treat her as if she was helpless? Cadde had never done that. The highlight of her life was sitting on the other end of the table at board meetings watching him glare at her. He treated her as an equal, though, not sucking up to her like Hooter Caldwell and Hubert Gillespie, two of her father's old cronies.

Before each board meeting, Cadde would want to talk. He'd explained what was going to be discussed. Not once had he come out and asked for her vote. He'd leaned heavily in that direction, but he never crossed that line.

If he had said, "Jessie, please," she wouldn't have been able to refuse. She admired that he let her make her own decisions. If she had bowed to his wishes, she would have become helpless in his eyes as she was in everyone else's. She wasn't letting that happen. Maybe she had a thing about control.

She wanted Cadde to see her as a mature woman able to handle life with as much strength as he did. It had taken enormous strength to overcome the death of his parents and then later to find out about his father's affair. He never faltered at the almost insurmountable obstacles in his life.

Her mind spun with chaotic thoughts. Mainly to avoid thinking about the night. Cadde would sleep in her bed and their marriage would become real. He'd alluded to that this morning. It was what she wanted. Her stomach cramped in denial, which she ignored.

After showering, she slipped into black lightweight linen pants and a sleeveless matching top. She adjusted several silver chains around her neck and pushed her feet into heeled sandals.

Mirry lay on the carpet, her face on her paws, watching her.

"What do you think?" Jessie held out her arms.

Mirry barked. The dog had a funny bark, very low and deep in her throat as if she was afraid to really let out a loud sound.

Jessie placed her hands on her knees and bent down. "I'm going to be gone for a while. Do you want to stay up here or downstairs with Rosa?"

Mirry trotted to her bed and curled up into a ball. Maybe the dog could understand.

JESSIE HAD A HARD TIME getting past Rosa without eating something. Finally, she was on her way. The Suburban was still a little smelly. She would rethink putting feed in her vehicle. Her dad's Cadillac and truck were in the garage and she could use one of them, but she hadn't been able to—too many memories.

On the drive in, she called Gavin and he said he would come out tomorrow and take care of the dogs. She'd put the decision off long enough and she felt a sense of relief that she had actually done it.

The noonday traffic was hectic once she reached Houston. Luckily the shelter wasn't far off U.S. 290. It was well hidden in a strip center. On the front door it read B&B Accounting. Under that was a big closed sign. To protect the women everything was top secret.

The place was known as Rachel's House. Rachel was a woman who had made the decision to leave her abusive husband. With her parents' help, she filed for a divorce, but the husband eventually found her and beat her to death. The biggest supporter of Rachel's House were Rachel's parents. They owned the strip center and offered the space rent free.

She parked in the allotted area, walked to the side door and knocked. Fran Turlock, the director, opened it. Fran was a gray-haired ball of energy.

"She's back," Fran said as she locked the door again with quick sure movements.

Jessie knew who she was talking about. Nina Lynch. She'd been in the center seven times in the past year.

"What happened?" Jessie asked as she followed Fran into her office.

"Same story. Vernon had one too many beers and started blaming Nina for everything wrong in his life, which led to a fist in her face and stomach. The neighbors called police and they arrested Vernon." Fran sank into her chair. "What do you think the odds are of her pressing charges?"

Fran was a social worker and devoted to the women who came here, but there were just so many ways to excuse stupid.

"Is she okay?"

"She's asking for you." Fran reached into a drawer and pulled out Jessie's ID badge. It had Jessie on it and Counselor beneath. Here they only went by first names.

Jessie clipped it to her blouse and picked up Nina's file off the desk. "I'll talk to her."

"Jessie…"

She looked back.

"He hit the little boy this time. He's four years old and was trying to protect his mother."

"Oh, my God."

"Yeah. They've been checked out in the E.R. and along with the bruises Nina has some fractured ribs. The left side of Toby's face is blue, but physically he's okay. Mentally, that's another matter."

A knot formed in Jessie's stomach. The women who came here just wanted someone to listen, to be supportive and caring. She didn't know if she could do that now. A child's safety was at stake. Nina had resisted all help, but time after time she came back to the shelter for protection. She could only listen and try her best to steer Nina in the right direction.

"This is probably going to be out of Nina's hands now," Fran was saying. "I'm almost positive the state will step in to protect the children."

"Does Nina know?"

"No. I thought it would be best coming from you."

"Gee, thanks." She walked down the hall with a resolve to make Nina see reason. Children's paintings covered the walls, all done by kids who had stayed here. Outside the place looked drab, but inside it was very colorful, with calming baby-blue walls. A family room was the center of activity with two big TVs that had been donated. Small bedrooms flanked it on both sides with bathrooms situated between every couple of rooms. A courtyard was out back surrounded by a wood fence. Children could run and play there while their mothers sorted out their lives.

Comfy chairs and pillows were scattered about the big living area. Some women were watching TV, their kids huddled close to them. The children who came here were usually quiet and well-behaved. Maybe, like Mirry, they were afraid of being hit. Sometimes it just broke her heart, but she had to concentrate on making their mothers see a better way of life. And most important to build their self-esteem.

She spotted Nina sitting in a rocker, clutching her two children. Pulling a chair forward, Jessie took a seat close to her. Nina didn't move a muscle, her face was pressed against Toby.

"Are you okay?" Jessie asked, knowing she couldn't talk to Nina in front of the children. That was a big no-no.

Sonia, one of the other women, came to her rescue. "Toby, would you like to play with Ben? There are lots of toys."

Toby raised his head to look at Nina and Jessie had to restrain herself from gasping. The left side of his face was blue and one spot by his eye was almost black. How could Nina look at her son and not want to get as far away from Vernon as possible?

"Go ahead, sweetie," Nina urged, wiping at her bruised eyes with a tissue. "Take your baby sister with you." The two kids scooted down and went with Sonia.

"I'm a mess." Nina wadded the tissue into a tighter ball. "No one understands."

"Explain it to me."

"Vernon's a good man and…"

Jessie placed a hand on Nina's forearm. "Look at Toby's face. Do you see good there?"

"He got in the way," Nina sobbed. "Vern didn't mean to hit him so hard."

Jessie squeezed her arm. "Vernon hit Toby. It wasn't an accident. It's all in the police report."

Nina jerked her arm away. "He didn't mean to. I thought you understood but you don't. How could you? You're rich and have everything you want."

Jessie drew back. How did Nina know that? How did she know anything about her?

"Why do you say that?"

"Just look at the way you dress. And you have that refined air. I'm a big fat slob."

Jessie let the first part slide. She wasn't talking about her life. "Is that what Vernon tells you?"

"All the time."

"Do you believe him?"

"Don't you?"

Nina came from a troubled home. Her parents argued constantly. Eventually, the mother divorced the father and quickly remarried, as did the father. Nina was shuffled back and forth. When siblings arrived, Nina was left out in the cold. She got into trouble doing drugs at school and then got pregnant. After that everything had spiraled out of control. Jessie felt for her, but Nina had to face reality.

"I see a pretty and intelligent woman fighting to maintain her dignity, her pride. A woman who has leaned on others, but now has to stand up and make the right choices for herself…and her children."

"I'm not that strong." Nina rocked back and forth.

"You have to be," Jessie told her. "It's not just about you and Vernon anymore. You can press charges or not. That's your choice, but the state will step in to protect your children."

"What do you mean?"

Jessie swallowed. "They'll take them away."

"What!" Nina stopped rocking and stared at her in disbelief. "No! No!" She grabbed Jessie's hands. "Please don't let them do that. You can stop it, right?"

"No," she replied with honesty. "You're the only one who can stop it. You have to show them you'll not put your children in danger and you'll provide a safe home for them."

"How am I supposed to do that? I don't have an education. My parents won't help me. I've already tried that. They said I was twenty-one and could make it on my own."

"How about the aunt you mentioned? The one who sends you something for your birthday and Christmas every year."

"Aunt Lois?" Nina frowned. "She's old and lives in Amarillo."

"How old is she?"

"Fifty-something."

Jessie sighed. "Call her."

Nina glanced toward her children. Toby was pushing a toy truck around on the area rug, his gaze going to Nina every few seconds. "He looks so sad."

"Call your aunt," Jessie persisted.

"Aunt Lois's never been married and she doesn't have any children. I don't even know if she likes kids. She's a librarian and my dad said she was odd. Oh, God, I need a cigarette."

"Child Protective Services and the police will be here to talk to you and the children. You need to have answers about your future when they do. I'm urging you to call your aunt."

"I…I…"

"No excuses, Nina. Make the right choice." Jessie patted her arm and stood.

"Will you be here tomorrow?" Nina asked.

"I'm not sure, but Wilma and Opal will be." Jessie had no idea what her life would be like tomorrow.

"I can't lose my children. They're all I have."

"It's up to you, Nina." Jessie walked down the hall to Fran's office.

"How did it go?" Fran asked.

Jessie took the seat across from her, balanced Nina's file on her lap and began to scribble notes. "She's still making excuses for him."

"Even after you told her she might lose her kids?"

"No. That was the stimulus that finally cleared her brain. Do you know anything about her aunt Lois?"

Fran shrugged. "When Nina first came here, she didn't want her parents notified if anything happened to her. She listed an aunt on the form." She turned toward her computer. "I'll check." After a few clicks, Fran added, "Yep. Lois Winslow from Amarillo. She may be Nina's only hope."

"If she calls her." Jessie placed the file on Fran's desk.

Fran shrugged again. "If she doesn't, it's out of our hands."

"Yeah." Jessie stood. "Sorry, I don't have much time today."

"That's okay, Jessie, we appreciate your help."

At the door, Jessie paused. She wanted Nina to have every opportunity. "Fran, I'll pay for their airline tickets to Amarillo and new clothes and whatever it takes to make her feel good about herself. Anonymously, of course."

"Jessie, you've donated so much to this shelter and it's more than welcomed, but CPS and the police will have a lot to say in this."

"Please let me know the outcome."

Fran nodded.

Now they waited for Nina to make all the right choices.

Jessie sped home to wait for Cadde and tried to leave the sadness behind her. The truth was, though, her whole life was an album of sadness. Maybe, along with Cadde, a little happiness was waiting for her, too.

CADDE PACED IN HIS OFFICE. It was barely four o'clock and he couldn't concentrate. Nothing sidetracked his interest from the oil business. *But Jessie.* They had to talk and get their arrangement clear without either of them losing their temper. Maybe she'd changed her mind. Maybe that's why she was hesitant. Maybe they could come to an agreement about Shilah.

Maybe, maybe, maybe wasn't easing his frustration

or giving him any concrete answers. And that's what he needed—answers. He grabbed his hat and headed for the door.

In his secretary's office, he said, "If you need me, you can reach me on my cell."

"You're leaving?" Barbara asked in a shocked tone. "It's just four o'clock."

He stopped to stare at her and he didn't have to say a word.

"Oh, oh, I'm sorry."

"If Kid or Chance is looking for me, tell them I'll see them in the morning. Early."

"Yes, sir."

The August heat was suffocating. Sweat peppered his skin and he turned up the air-conditioning full blast. The Houston traffic was crazy this time of day and it took all of his concentration to navigate through it. Finally he hit U.S. 290 and sped toward home.

He should have called Jessie, but he was sure she was there. What else did she have to do?

When he reached the entrance, he had a funny feeling in his stomach. He couldn't explain it. It was just an uneasiness.

At the garages, he slammed on the brakes. Mirry shot out of the open doors and Rosa ran after her, shouting something. It was too late, though. The Dobermans were on Mirry.

Shit! Cadde reached for his Smith & Wesson pistol in the console. He never used the gun, but Roscoe had insisted he carry one. Jumping out, he jammed the clip in place. Out of the corner of his eye he saw a movement. Jessie was flying toward the dogs. One Doberman's teeth latched around Mirry's neck in a death grip. The other one leaped into the air, trying to snatch Mirry from him. Felix lumbered behind Jessie, firing a rifle. The loud blast didn't faze them. The dogs never let go of their prey and Jessie never paused in her flight to save Mirry.

"No, Jessie, no," he screamed.

The Dobermans had tasted blood. They'd kill her.

CHAPTER SEVEN

"Jessie!" As Cadde screamed her name, a growling Doberman leaped for her, knocking her down, his teeth digging into her neck. Jessie struggled to get away, her arms flailing at the dog.

Cadde bolted forward, blood pounding in his ears. He had to fire without hitting Jessie. Seconds ticked by like minutes. The dog flung his head, snarling, trying to lock his powerful jaws into her skin, but was unable to because Jessie was fighting with everything in her. When he got a clear shot, he pulled the trigger at point-blank range. The Doberman writhed and lay limp. He swung to the other one and fired again. The dog jerked and then dropped backward. Dead. Mirry fell to the ground, unmoving, covered in blood.

An unnerving and gut-wrenching silence followed the gunshots. He quickly laid the gun on the grass and knelt by Jessie's still body. Her face was so white, her scattered dark hair making it look even paler. Teeth marks oozed blood on her neck. "Jessie." His voice came out sounding hoarse. Was she dead? She couldn't be. She was fighting just a second ago. Oh, God!

Felix and Rosa fell down beside her.

"My *niña.* My *niña!*" Rosa cried.

Felix was silent, but his hands shook on the rifle.

Cadde reached for the soft skin under her hair, and in that moment, he knew Jessie meant more to him than a business deal. He didn't have time to analyze the thought, nor did he want to. Like Felix, his hand shook, but he felt a pulse—a strong one. She was alive. Relief eased the grip on his heart.

"Rosa, let me have your apron." He had to stop the bleeding.

Rosa whipped it off and he looped it around Jessie's neck and applied pressure. The cotton soaked up the blood immediately. "Get some towels. We have to go to an E.R."

Rosa flew to the house and Felix asked, "What can I do?"

"Pray."

As he continued to apply pressure, Jessie stirred, muttering, "Mir-ry."

"Lie still," he instructed.

"Mirry." Jessie pushed against him and sat up, looking at the dead Dobermans on the green summer grass. Her gaze searched for the little dog and then she found her. "Oh, my God! Mirry!"

"Jessie, no!" He tried to block her view, but Jessie tore away and crawled on her hands and knees to the bloody mess. Cadde realized he couldn't stop her. He couldn't shield her from the pain. His heart stopped at the actual thought that he wanted to.

She scooped up Mirry and cradled her against her chest. "Mirry, I'm sorry. Mirry." She rocked to and fro and his heart took another hit.

Rushing back with an armful of towels, Rosa halted when she saw Jessie and Mirry. Tears welled in her eyes.

Cadde stood, taking them from her. He knelt by Jessie once again and looped a towel over Mirry in her arms.

Wrapping it around the bloody dog, Jessie said, "Call Gavin."

He pushed hair from her face. "You've been hurt. We have to go to an E.R."

"No." She tried to pull away from him. "Felix, call Gavin."

Cadde shook his head at Felix. He was sure the dog was dead, but how did he tell her? There were no words to ease her pain.

Jessie staggered to her feet and reached down for the phone that had fallen out of her pocket. Jerking it out of her hand would be too cruel so he let her make the call.

"Gavin, Mirry's been hurt. I'm bringing her in."

What? She wasn't driving. He did the only thing he could. He lifted her into his arms and rushed to his truck.

"Cadde, put me down. I can drive."

Oh, yeah, she was back and in full fighting mode. God, she was one stubborn woman.

Felix held the passenger door open. Cadde placed Jessie on the seat and buckled her seat belt.

Rosa wrapped more towels around the bloody dog in Jessie's arms. She stroked Jessie's face. "Listen to Mr. Cadde, please."

"Rosa." Jessie's voice cracked.

"I'm sorry, my *niña*. Mirry was making those funny sounds when she has to go to pee. I opened the door to call you and she shot out. I couldn't stop her. I'm sorry."

"It's okay," Jessie murmured.

He closed the door and walked around to the driver's side. "Take care of those dogs, Felix."

"Yes, sir. I will. Just look after Miss Jessie."

Backing out, he glanced at her sitting there covered in blood and looking so forlorn. Mirry was something she poured her love into, just like she would a baby. *Someone to love.* She'd told him that yesterday. Had it only been yesterday? Seemed as if they'd more than discovered each other in a few short hours. But maybe they'd already known the important stuff—the stuff that counted.

"We're going to Gavin's," she said.

"Jessie."

"Mirry needs a vet."

Once again he couldn't tell her what he suspected. He had to pamper her so she could accept the truth.

"Okay. Okay." He turned onto the blacktop road that led to U.S. 290. "We'll take Mirry to Gavin and then we're going to the emergency room."

She didn't answer and he recognized the tactic—the one that tested his patience. Every time he tried to talk to her about a board meeting, she employed the silent technique. And that meant Jessie was going to do exactly what she wanted. She might not know her mother, but she'd certainly inherited a lot of Roscoe's traits.

"Oh, oh, oh," Jessie squealed.

"What? Are you hurting?"

"I feel a heartbeat, Cadde," she cried excitedly. "She's alive!"

"Are you sure?" He didn't think that was possible.

"Give me your hand."

She took his right hand while he steered with his left and put it beneath the towel on the bloody, damp fur. "Just wait a second," she said, and he felt a faint throb against his fingers.

"Hot damn, there is a heartbeat."

"Yes! Hurry! Hurry!" Her eyes met his and a closeness, a newness passed between them. They'd connected. Out of this horrible dark day the glimpse of sunshine was blinding.

He swerved in and out of traffic as she gave directions. Gavin's clinic wasn't far from downtown in a renovated house on a corner off Montrose. Before he could turn off the engine in a parking area, Jessie unbuckled her seat belt and got out. He followed. A man with sandy-blond hair and blue eyes opened the door.

Gavin looked at Jessie covered in blood. "What happened?"

"The Dobermans attacked Mirry."

"Oh, my God!" Gavin rubbed Jessie's shoulder. That was just a little too friendly to Cadde's way of thinking. Or he could be overacting.

"One attacked Jessie, too. She needs to go to an emergency room."

"What!" Gavin paled, and Cadde could see there was more than concern on his face.

"Gavin, this is my…husband, Cadde." She paused

before *husband* and he wondered why. Was there something between the vet and Jessie?

"Nice to meet you." They shook hands and Cadde realized he was taller than Gavin. Why did that please him? He wasn't in high school.

Gavin turned back to Jessie. "I'm sorry. I should have come out there today, but your...husband is right. You need to see a doctor." Again with the pause before *husband.* What was it with these two?

"I'm fine," Jessie said, and lifted the bundle in her arms. "But Mirry is not."

"Bring her inside." They made their way into a sterile-looking room with a stainless-steel examining table. Jessie laid her bundle on it. Her T-shirt was soaked with blood and Rosa's apron was still looped around her neck.

Gavin partially removed the towel. "Oh, Jessie. That dog did a number on Mirry. Her neck is chewed severely and there are long gashes on her body that'll need stitching. I'll do X-rays and anesthetize her to deal with her injuries. There also might be some internal bleeding. I'll have to keep her in the clinic for a few days to monitor her."

"But she's going to make it?"

"You know I'll do my best." Gavin patted her arm again. "Noel," he called.

A young college student came in.

"Take Mirry and flush her wounds. I'll start an IV shortly."

"Yes, sir." The boy gathered the bloody dog and disappeared into another room.

Gavin pushed the stained apron aside. "One of those bites looks deep. Go see a doctor with…"

"Her husband. Cadde Hardin." The words came out before he could stop them.

Jessie glared at him, and it seemed as if Gavin had more to say. "I didn't realize you lived with Jessie."

"I do," Cadde stated clearly, and a palpable tension crept into the room like a mosquito everyone wanted to swat.

Jessie stepped between them. "I don't want to leave Mirry."

"She'll be out." Gavin's gaze slowly shifted back to Jessie. "She won't know if you're here or not and she's in a lot of pain."

"Oh." Jessie put a hand to her mouth.

"I'll sedate her to keep her comfortable," Gavin assured her. "Now go."

"I'll call as soon as I get out of the E.R.," Jessie blurted out as Cadde led her away.

In the truck, Jessie said, "Sometimes you can be rude."

"And sometimes you can be stubborn. Damn stubborn. Over-the-top stubborn." He sucked in a breath while darting through traffic. "How long have you known this guy?"

"Five or six years. I met him at a fundraiser for the Houston SPCA. I had a horse then and he came to look at her hoof even though he's a small-animal vet."

"I'll bet. I'd say he has a thing for you."

"We're friends. That's it." He could feel her eyes

pinned on him like an AK-47 and she was fixing to fire off a few rounds.

"Then why did you pause before *husband?*"

"I…I…"

"What have you told him about me? About our marriage?"

"He knows it was an arranged marriage, okay?"

"If you wanted a child so much, why didn't you ask Gavin?"

"I'm not married to Gavin!" she shouted. "If you want to fight, Cadde, we'll fight." She leaned her head against the headrest. "But I'm so tired."

He felt like a heel. She'd been through a traumatic experience and he was grilling her like a jealous man.

The stress of the day was finally catching up with her. She deflated like a balloon, all her energy gone. He sped toward Ben Taub Hospital. It took about an hour in the emergency room. They called Gavin to get the immunization status of the Dobermans. Their shots were up-to-date so there was no rabies scare.

The doctor said Jessie was fine. Removing her bloody T-shirt and bra, she slipped on a hospital gown. Jessie was docile through the whole thing, which must have been a first. They cleaned the bites and the doctor reported the dog's teeth hadn't hit a vein and hadn't damaged a muscle. But one bite was a gash that he was afraid would open. He numbed the right side of her neck and put a stitch in and added two strips of surgical tape, hoping it wouldn't leave a noticeable scar.

He gave her an antibiotic injection and something to help her rest. He told her she needed to follow up with her doctor so the wounds could be watched for infection.

Leaving the hospital, he could see the shot was already beginning to affect Jessie. She yawned and snuggled into the seat. Since he knew she would insist on seeing Mirry first thing in the morning, he took her to the apartment. It was closest. Jessie didn't resist.

On the ride up in the elevator, she said in a sleepy voice, "I have to call Gavin."

"Let's wait a minute." Once inside, he handed her his phone. Hers was either in the truck or on the ground at the house.

She punched in Gavin's number. She knew it by heart so she must have called him often. That relationship still puzzled him. After a moment, she clicked off and gave him the phone.

"Mirry's out of surgery and resting comfortably. Gavin said the Doberman almost bit off her neck. He had to do a lot of repair work and now we wait to see if she'll survive. Oh, my poor Mirry." She sagged against him and began to cry low pitiful sounds.

He held her. "She'll make it." He stroked soft unbelievably smooth skin through the opening on the back of the gown. Just when his emotions were spiraling in another direction, she pulled away.

"What am I wearing?"

"A hospital gown."

"Where's my T-shirt and bra?" She felt her breasts and he tried to look anywhere but at the rounded flesh pushing against the cotton. He failed.

He exhaled. "The nurse threw them out. They were ruined with blood stains."

"Oh."

"Come on. You're asleep on your feet." He led her down the hall and flipped on the lights. Pulling back the brown comforter and tan sheet, he guided her forward. She plopped onto the side of the four-poster bed, her chin bobbing on her chest.

He knelt in front of her and removed her blood-spotted sneakers.

She raised her head. "I've always wondered about the women you brought here."

"Have you?" He glanced into her sleep-filled eyes.

"Mmm. Now I'm here."

"You're my wife," he said, puzzling himself. But he never imagined she thought of him at all. Much less whom he dated before their marriage.

She scrunched up her face. "Does that make a difference?"

That didn't require an answer because he had a feeling she wasn't aware of what she was saying or asking.

"We have to get your jeans off," he told her. "Lie down. It might be easier."

"Okeydokey." She leaned back, her arms above her head.

He meant for her to help him, but evidently that wasn't going to happen. Undoing the button and zipper, he said. "Raise your hips."

"Okeydokey." She lifted her hips.

What was in that medication the doctor had given her? She wasn't acting like prim and proper Jessie. He yanked from the hem and they slipped off. She wore white bikini panties with a lace trim. Somehow he knew they'd be white, not that he'd thought about it. Much.

"Get straight in the bed."

"Where's the bed?"

He smiled, feeling cocky that he'd seen Jessie with her guard down, no defense or attitude anywhere in sight. "You're on it," he replied, and helped her to scoot under the sheet.

"Cadde," she murmured.

He pushed her hair away from her face, his fingers lingering for a moment on the taped skin on her neck. Thank God he'd gotten there in time. "Sweet dreams, Jessie."

His cell buzzed and he reached for it. It was Rosa.

"Mr. Cadde, you haven't called and we're worried sick."

He walked out of the bedroom to the living area, not wanting to disturb Jessie. "Jessie's fine. She's asleep."

"Asleep? Where?"

He could hear the anger in Rosa's voice and he let it go because he knew she was concerned. Drawing a patient breath, he explained what had happened.

"Bring Miss Jessie home. I've been taking care of her since she was seven years old."

"She's asleep, Rosa, and I'm not disturbing her."

"Then I'll come there and I'll take her to see Mirry tomorrow."

Cadde's patience only stretched so far. "Stay there and make sure Felix feeds Jessie's animals. She stays here with me. I hope we're clear on that."

There was a slight pause. "Yes, sir."

"If you want to do something, you can bring her some clothes in the morning. They had to throw away her T-shirt and bra."

"I'll be there at eight."

Cadde clicked off and thought how Jessie must feel with two people hovering around her at all times. Was it similar to being a bird in a cage, unable to fly, unable to experience freedom? No wonder she had fired the guards.

Running his hands over his face, he wondered where his Stetson was. It had to be in the truck. Lately, he had a hard time keeping up with his hat. Facing forty was doing a number on his memory.

Or was it Jessie?

Flipping off the lights, he went down the hall to the bedroom. Jessie was out. He sat at the foot of the bed and removed his boots and socks. Taking a deep breath, he stood and whipped off his shirt and jeans. After turning off the light, he slipped beneath the sheet on the other side of Jessie.

He was dog tired and surprised he was even functioning after the dreaded hangover from last night. A few hours of sleep and he'd be as good as new. Somewhere between that deep abyss of complete relaxation and consciousness he heard Jessie scream.

"Cadde!" She sat bolt upright. "There's no light. There's no light."

What was she talking about? He scooted closer and

pulled her back into the bed. "It's okay. You're just having a bad dream." Or at least that's what he hoped it was.

"I can't sleep without the light, Cadde. I can't."

So that was it, and the reason the lights were always on at the house. Jessie still had fears from her childhood. He wasn't good at consoling or any of that stuff. He was an action man, anything to keep from opening his heart. His mother had said that she hoped he found an understanding woman who could reach his sensitive side.

He let out a long breath. "I'm here, Jessie. We don't need a light."

She snuggled into him, a hand on his bare chest. That wasn't what he had in mind, but she felt good. Maybe too good.

Before he knew it, she was asleep again, one leg looped over his. Luckily, he was too tired for the sensation to ignite other parts of his body. He did what any man would do. He held her. Maybe that was all she needed—to know that someone was there. That someone cared.

CADDE WOKE UP AT FIVE and crawled out of bed, careful not to wake Jessie. After a shower, he shaved and then changed into jeans and a white shirt. Jessie was still out. He left a light on in the bathroom just in case she woke up before dawn. He didn't want her to be afraid.

In the kitchen, he made a pot of coffee and searched for food. There wasn't any. With all the trauma, they hadn't eaten last night. He could go and get something, but Jessie might wake up and he needed to be here. His other option was Kid or Chance. Chance had a family so he called Kid. The call went to voice mail. Damn!

Another option was Barbara. She was used to his early calls. Within thirty minutes Barbara knocked on the door. That was the good thing about having a middle-aged secretary. They were dependable, responsible and always up before dawn. There would be a bonus in her paycheck.

He pulled the food from the bag. A double order of scrambled eggs, sausage and biscuits were in a foam take-out container. Yogurt, strawberries, blueberries and a cantaloupe were in a bag. He just stared. He thought the fruit would be cut up on a tray. Well, he could handle this. It wasn't like drilling an oil well.

After washing the strawberries and blueberries, he drained them on paper towels and tackled the cantaloupe. His mother had cut them all the time, but he'd never watched. It just magically appeared on the table. How hard could it be? He took a knife and split it open and cleaned the seeds from the inside. Then he started cutting slices.

The door opened and Kid burst in. "You called? What's up?"

Cadde kept cutting. "Why didn't you answer?"

"I was busy, okay?"

"And you just assumed I'd be at the apartment."

"Hell, no. I came into the office and saw a light down here."

Cadde continued to slice the cantaloupe.

"What are you doing?" Kid asked.

"Cutting up fruit."

"You're supposed to peel it first."

He knew there had to be an easier way, but he wouldn't admit that to Kid. "So? This is how I do it."

Kid frowned. "Why did you call?"

"To pick up breakfast."

Kid snorted. "I'm not peeling fruit for you, and why in the hell are you eating a cantaloupe?"

"It's not for me. It's for Jessie. She's asleep down the hall so keep your voice down."

"What?"

Cadde told him about the Dobermans. Just as he finished, Chance breezed in.

"I saw a light down here. What's going on?" His eyes went to the mess on the counter. "You're supposed to peel it first. Momma did it that way unless we were taking it outside to eat and then she'd leave the rind on."

He thought how great it was that his brothers were happy to impart their knowledge.

Pointing the knife at them, he said, "Go to work."

"Jessie's here," Kid whispered, and then told Chance about the Dobermans.

"Is she okay?" Chance asked, his sensitive antenna up and working. Chance got all the sensitivity in their family. Most of Kid's was below his belt.

"She's fine. Go to work."

Kid snatched a piece of cantaloupe. "I'm going to Louisiana for a few days to check at the courthouse to see who really has the mineral rights on several of those properties."

"Then why are you still here?"

"I'm gone." Kid strolled toward the door.

Chance reached for a slice. "I have the numbers on leasing a rig when you're ready."

"I'll be in my office later."

"Later, then." Chance followed Kid.

Cadde carefully arranged the fruit on a plate and set it on the wood table. He placed the yogurt beside it. Pouring a cup of coffee, he leaned against the counter, sipping it. His life had been turned upside down for the past two days. He needed to be in his office. He had a company to run.

"Cadde, where are my clothes?"

Suddenly, he forgot about work and strolled down the hall. Jessie held her jeans in her hands, her hair falling around her face. He felt a familiar kick in his lower abdomen. *Work. Work.* He had to keep work on his mind and not the half-naked woman in front of him.

"Don't you remember?"

"Oh." Her eyes held a faraway look and he knew she was remembering the awful evening. She sank onto the tumbled bed. "I have to see Mirry and go to Rachel's House this afternoon."

"Who's Rachel?"

She glanced up. "It's a shelter for abused women."

"Abused animals. Abused women. Who are you?"

"What?"

"This is not the daughter Roscoe portrayed to me."

Those dark eyes pinned him to the wall, like a target. "How did Daddy portray me?"

"I got the impression you were very vulnerable, a woman who needed protecting—a woman who sat in that big house reading fashion magazines and eating decadent chocolates or something."

She flipped back her hair. "Is that how Daddy described me? Or is it how you see me?"

He held up his hands. "Let's not argue. I'm just taken aback that you have a life that your father never mentioned."

"Daddy tended to see me one way—as his helpless little girl. He tolerated my 'fun activities' as he called them."

He folded his arms across his chest and leaned against the doorjamb. "What do you do at the shelter?"

"Counseling, but mostly I listen. These women have been browbeaten by their husbands into thinking they're worthless and deserve to be beaten."

"And you need to see someone this afternoon?"

"Yes." She stood. "And I need clothes."

He glanced at his watch. "Rosa's bringing you some at eight. If you call, you might catch her before she leaves." He nodded toward the phone on the nightstand.

She twisted the jeans she still held in her hands. "Thank you for what you did yesterday. I don't know what we would have done if you hadn't arrived."

"Felix would have handled it."

"I'm not sure. He wasn't as calm as you were. He was really worried about me."

"Don't you think I was?"

Her eyes held his. "Were you?"

"More than I ever thought I would be." He turned and went back to the kitchen. The emotional mushy stuff was hard this early in the morning. Hell, it wasn't easy late at night, either. A couple of relationships had ended because of his hesitance to confess his undying love. He wanted Jessie to know he cared for her.

That was enough for now.

The business deal was getting personal.

CHAPTER EIGHT

JESSIE PLOPPED ONTO the bed, holding the jeans to her racing heart. *He cared.* And it hadn't required any manipulation on her part. It had been a natural progression of them getting to know each other. Yesterday Cadde had saved her and Mirry and she'd always be grateful for that. He'd taken control. It was nice to have him worry about her—just like a husband would.

Cadde Hardin was a special man.

And jealous.

She knew Gavin cared for her in more than in a friendly way. She'd gone out with him a couple of times, but then stopped when it became clear his feelings were different from hers. They remained friends. Although she realized Gavin was waiting for her to end her sham of a marriage. That wasn't happening. Not now.

It was strange how she never reacted to Gavin like she had to Cadde. From the moment she'd looked into his intense brown eyes, it seemed he'd literally reached in and snatched her heart. If her father hadn't been so protective of her, they might have connected a long time ago.

Or maybe not. He might never care for her the way she wanted.

The sobering thought caused a needling sadness to settle in her.

Glancing at the bedside clock, she jumped up and grabbed the phone. It took her five minutes to assure Rosa she was okay. After hanging up, she went into the kitchen in the hospital gown. That was her limited wardrobe.

Cadde leaned against the counter, sipping a cup of coffee, his feet crossed at the ankles. He looked relaxed in jeans and a pressed white shirt. Her breath caught in her throat at his tall lean frame. Obviously, he was ready for work.

When he saw her, he straightened. "Would you like breakfast?"

Two plates were on the table. One had eggs, sausages and biscuits; the other had a pile of strawberries and blueberries and slices of cantaloupe that looked as if they'd been cut with a chain saw. Beside the fruit was a small carton of yogurt.

"Where did you get this?"

"I had my secretary bring it over." Barbara was in her late fifties and happily married, so Jessie knew she didn't have a problem with unrequited love in that area. She was almost positive Barbara hadn't cut the cantaloupe, which meant Cadde had—for her. A warm feeling suffused her and it had nothing to do with the high temperature outside.

"Which is mine?" she asked, just to tease.

Pouring her a cup of coffee, he frowned. "Don't you like fruit and yogurt?"

"Yes, but I'm hungry. We didn't eat last night." She

bit her lip in thought. "We'll share," she decided, and reached for a plate in the cabinet. She felt a cool breeze to her back…and more. "Are you staring at my butt?"

"It's kind of hard not to…with the gown open like that."

Good grief. She gathered the back with one hand and carried the plate to the table. "These things are not made for privacy."

"Mmm." A smirk followed the sound.

She used a fork to scoop eggs, a sausage and biscuit onto her plate. Taking a seat, she jumped up again. "I forgot cream and sugar for my coffee." She knew where the packets were because she'd eaten here many times with her father. She managed to hold her gown closed.

As she took a sip, she could feel his eyes on her. "After what you've been through, you're very spry this morning. How's the neck?"

"Kind of sore on the right, but I'm fine." She dug into the eggs. "And I have a lot to do today."

"Jessie, you were attacked by a dog. It's okay to just rest."

Again, she was almost positive Cadde never said things like that and she could tell she was right by the shocked look on his face.

He picked up his fork. "Remember you have to see your doctor."

"I'll work it in." She munched on the fruit. "Oh, I don't have a vehicle. What's your schedule like?"

"I have several meetings."

"Here at Shilah?"

"Yes," he replied slowly, looking at her.

"Good, then I'll take your truck."

"What?" He almost spit coffee on the table. "No. No. I'll share my breakfast, but I'm not sharing my truck."

She made a face at him.

"Can you even drive a truck?"

"Yes, Cadde. We have one at the barn that I use all the time." At the expression on his face, she relented, but not nicely. "Okay, I'll get Rosa to chauffeur me." She carried her plate to the sink.

The only sound was the clatter of the dishes.

"You can take the truck," he said in a quiet tone.

She swung around. "Really?"

"Yes." He stood and fished out the keys from his pocket. "Just be careful."

"Thank you." She reached up and kissed his smooth-shaven cheek, a fresh manly scent tempted her nostrils, her senses.

His hands went to her hair. He threaded his fingers through it, holding her head. Waves of dizzying plea-sure made her feel weak and she stood on tiptoe to meet his kiss. His lips tasted hers briefly. Enticing. Invit-ing. Suddenly he drew back. She felt deprived, want-ing more.

"Get some rest today. Now I have to go to work." His hand lingered on her neck for a moment and then he strolled past her. "Don't wreck my truck," he called over his shoulder.

Jessie whirled around the kitchen, feeling free. Feel-ing euphoric. It was just him and her in an apartment, alone. Like a normal couple—in love. She paused in her happy dance. They weren't a normal couple. She pushed back her long hair, her scalp tingling from his touch. It may not be the real thing but it was something and she could live with that.

After covering the fruit with plastic wrap, she put it in the refrigerator. She quickly rinsed the dishes and placed them in the dishwasher. As the appliance clicked on, she heard a knock on the door. Rosa came in with a brown leather overnight case, a bag and her purse.

"Oh, Miss Jessie, just look at you." Rosa gave her the once-over. "Why are you in that gown?"

Jessie hugged her. "It's all I had to wear from the hospital."

"Oh, your neck." Rosa touched Jessie's sore skin. "Go get in bed. I'll take care of you and I brought breakfast."

She held up her hands. "I'm fine, Rosa, and I've already eaten."

"I'll put these in the refrigerator then. I made some breakfast tacos." Rosa walked into the kitchen and Jessie picked up the leather case.

"I have to shower and get dressed," Jessie said. "I want to check on Mirry."

"I'll drive you." Rosa hitched her purse high on her arm.

Jessie stopped in the hall doorway. "No, Rosa. I have Cadde's truck."

"Now, Miss Jessie, you've been through a terrifying ordeal and you don't need to be driving." Rosa shook her head. "It was awful, just awful, and we were lucky Mr. Cadde arrived when he did. The Dobermans attacked the one person they were trained to protect. We should have gotten rid of them long ago."

Sadly, Jessie knew the truth of those words. She should have dealt with the dogs after her dad had died, but she kept putting it off. Now Mirry had to pay for her procrastination.

"I'm fine and hopefully Mirry will be, too."

"I'm sorry. It all happened so quickly."

"It's okay," Jessie assured her. "It was an accident. I just thought Mirry would never leave the house without me."

"After you left to go to the barn, she was fussing around and started making those noises. I opened the door a crack and she shot out. The Dobermans were on her so fast I almost had a heart attack."

"We don't have to worry about that anymore."

"No." Rosa waved a hand. "Get dressed and we'll go see Mirry."

Jessie sighed and walked farther into the room. "Rosa, I told you I have Cadde's truck and I'm staying in Houston as long as Mirry is in the clinic."

Rosa's features became stern. "Miss Jessie, you need to come home."

Jessie stood her ground. "I'm not seven years old anymore. I'm a grown woman and I can take care of myself."

"I promised Mr. Roscoe."

Her hand tightened on the leather handle. "Daddy is dead." She took a breath because it always hurt to say the words. "Rosa, please let go. You and Felix have to allow me some freedom."

"We worry so much."

"I know and I appreciate all your concerns, but I have a husband now. My life is changing." Jessie didn't give Rosa time to argue. She turned toward the hallway. "Bye. I'll call you later."

She held her breath until she heard the door close. Sometimes it was hard being an adult. She had to hurt the people she loved, but if she didn't, they'd cripple her emotionally.

In less than an hour she'd showered, brushed her hair and coiled it into a rope, clipping it behind her head. Dressing in white slacks and sandals, she slipped on a lime-green sleeveless blouse that gathered at the waist with a silver chain. By nine she was sitting in Cadde's truck. It took a while to adjust the seat. He had it pushed far back to accommodate his long legs. Once she was comfortable, she started the engine. It burred to life.

Backing out of the CEO's parking spot, she realized the truck was big. She'd never driven anything this huge, but she'd manage. First, she adjusted the mirrors so she could see traffic and then she donned her sunglasses. The August sun was blinding. A car honked and she became aware she was in the middle of the parking lot. She pressed the gas pedal and shot out for the ride of her life.

Luckily she made it to Gavin's without anyone honking at her again. Her heart stopped when she saw Mirry. She was lying in a basket, covered in a multicolored cotton blanket inside a kennel. An IV was in her taped-up right paw and liquid dripped from a bag. Her swollen body had several long stitched-up wounds, as did her neck. Around her neck was a rubber ring that looked like a doughnut.

"She's better," Gavin told her. "I know it doesn't look like it, but her pulse was very low last night. This morning it's stronger."

"Can I sit with her for a while?"

"Sure." Gavin brought her a chair and she sat talking to the unconscious dog. It was hard to explain her attachment to Mirry. But Mirry needed someone and Jessie desperately needed someone, too.

"I'm sorry, Mirry. Gavin's going to make you all better," she was saying as Gavin walked in over an hour later. "She's not waking up."

"I have her heavily sedated. I don't want her trying to move her neck."

She reached for her purse on the floor and stood. Thank God Rosa had put her purse and phone in the case. She'd hate to drive that big truck without a license. "Thank you, Gavin. I appreciate everything you've done."

He glanced at his watch. "If you'll wait thirty minutes, we can have lunch together."

"I can't." She hated these conversations. "I'm scheduled at the women's shelter and I have to see my doctor about my dog bites."

His eyes lingered over her. "You look great."

"Thank you," she replied, wanting to slither away. She didn't like hurting Gavin. "I was lucky Cadde arrived when he did. The dog didn't have a chance to get a good grip on me before Cadde shot him."

"The hero, huh?" Gavin said in a cold voice she'd

never heard before, and she thought it was time to tell Gavin the truth.

"Cadde and I are trying to make our marriage work."

"I figured that out last night. He's a take-control type of guy…the kind women like."

She wasn't discussing Cadde with Gavin. She hugged Gavin briefly. "Thank you for everything."

"Jessie," he called as she walked toward the door.

She looked back.

"When he breaks your heart, I'll be waiting."

"Please don't do that," she said, and left feeling as low as pond scum. Why did no one ever listen to her? She'd told Gavin two years ago there was nothing romantic between them, but he always let his feelings show. She'd have to find another vet.

Putting Gavin out of her mind, she called her medical doctor and the receptionist said they could work her in at three. She stopped for a hamburger and ate it in the truck. A spot of mustard on the leather steering wheel caught her eye. Oh, no! As hard as she rubbed with a paper napkin, she couldn't get the stain out completely. She licked the napkin and rubbed again. There still was a slight smudge. Maybe Cadde wouldn't notice. Maybe men didn't notice things like that. It was a truck, she told herself. Men in Texas equate their trucks with their identity. And Cadde's had a smudge on his. He would notice.

She made her way to the women's shelter, watching the traffic carefully. Fran let her in and they walked to her office. Fran didn't say anything, just fiddled with papers on her desk.

"How did it go with Nina's aunt?"

Fran grunted. "The woman has a three-bedroom house and was happy to offer Nina and the kids a home."

"That's…wait…was? What happened?"

Fran removed her glasses and rubbed her eyes in a tired way. "A caseworker from CPS talked with Nina yesterday as did the police. The worker also visited Vernon in jail. He was allowed to call Nina."

"What?"

"Yeah." Fran shoved her glasses back on. "CPS is working to keep the family intact. Vernon has agreed to counseling with Nina once a week and a CPS worker will drop by unexpectedly to check on things."

"Nina agreed to this?"

"Oh, yeah. You know she's always spouting what an excellent provider Vernon is, what a good person he is and how he gives her money for the kids. I think she has a file folder of excuses for Vernon."

"I can't believe it." Jessie was flabbergasted. Nina had a chance at a new life and she'd turned it down.

"Once she talked to Vernon, any other resolution was over. I don't understand it, but it's CPS's worry now."

"Nina's afraid of making it on her own without an education. She's more afraid of that than Vernon hitting her and the kids. We know it's an insane decision, but we'll never convince her of that."

"Let's be positive. Counseling might help Vernon. He knows this is his last chance."

Jessie heaved a sigh and got to her feet. "I'll talk to Nina."

"She doesn't want to see you," Fran said.

"Why?"

Fran shrugged. "She knows she's making a bad choice, but she doesn't want anyone to talk her out of it."

"I've always just listened and tried to show her better options."

"I know that and you know that. Nina's feeling a little guilty right now. She's returning to their apartment later this afternoon, but if she comes back, we'll take her in and offer her shelter. That's all we can do now."

Jessie had a bad feeling about this. A habitual hitter wasn't going to change, but she understood that CPS had to give them a chance to be a family. She just hoped they protected those kids.

Fran peered at her neck. "What happened to you?"

"I was mauled by a dog."

"Oh, no! Are you okay?"

"Yes. My husband shot the animal before he could do any real damage."

Fran leaned back in her chair. "How's the marriage going?"

"Great." Jessie didn't want to talk about her personal life. "I have a couple hours to kill. Do you need any help?"

"Why don't you go home and rest."

"I can't." Jessie winced. "I have a doctor's appointment at three."

"Well, then." Fran leaned forward. "I could use an extra pair of hands in this office."

For the next hour, Jessie did filing and typed counselors' notes into the computer. She thought how much easier it would be if counselors had laptops, could access the shelter's network and type in their own information. She'd speak to Fran about that later. A big donation would help Fran to make a decision. Of course it had to be presented to the board for approval, but if someone was willing to pay for them, she didn't see a problem.

As Jessie left she had to restrain herself from going into the family room to visit Nina. But Nina had made her decision, right or wrong, and Jessie had to respect it. Just as Jessie wished the people around her would respect her own wishes.

She checked on Mirry again. Gavin was out but the tech let her sit with the dog for a while. The little thing was so swollen, and Jessie realized it would probably take a long time for Mirry to be well again. She was alive, though, and Jessie clung to that.

The doctor's appointment went smoothly. There were no signs of infection, but he wanted to see her again in a week. When she got out of his office, her energy level dropped considerably. She needed a nap so she went back to the apartment and fell into a deep sleep.

CADDE HADN'T HEARD FROM Jessie all day and he wondered if she was okay. Had he made a mistake letting her take his truck? Was it too big for her to handle? This morning she'd sounded so miserable when he'd refused and it was clear she didn't want Rosa to drive her around. He could feel her fight for independence. Before he knew it he was giving her his keys.

At the oddest times today when he was in meetings

and people were expecting his undivided attention he found himself glancing at his watch, waiting for quitting time. There was no such thing to him before. He worked long hours and never watched a clock. But now he was thinking about seeing Jessie again.

On impulse he went down the hall to the apartment. The lights were on and Jessie was sprawled across the bed, asleep in her clothes. The night had finally caught up with her.

He backed out, not wanting to disturb her. In the living room he saw her purse on the sofa and retrieved his keys. He had to pick up something for dinner.

JESSIE SCRAMBLED OUT of bed and glanced at the clock. It was almost six. Where was Cadde? They hadn't made any plans for the evening so she assumed they'd meet back here. He might plan on working late, but she had his truck. That worked in her favor.

After taking a quick shower, Jessie searched through her case for her shorty pj's. They weren't there. Of course not. Rosa hadn't expected her to spend another night in the apartment. Now what? She wasn't sleeping in that hospital gown again.

She opened the closet and saw a row of color coordinated shirts; white, pale yellow and light blue—all solid colors, no plaids or prints or checks. Next to the shirts were three pairs of Wrangler jeans and two pairs of slacks, black and khaki. At the top were two Stetson boxes and at the bottom two pairs of boots, black and brown. He had this same wardrobe at the house. What did this say about Cadde? That he was organized and knew what he wanted and what he liked. Yeah, that described him. He wasn't wishy-washy or indecisive.

Her father had told her ever since Cadde was a kid his focus had been the oil business. Through the years that had never changed. And his personal life was much the same. She'd bet that he bought his clothes at the same store, wore one brand of boots and jeans, wore a certain kind of Stetson and had his hair cut at the same place. Cadde Hardin was a creature of habit. He was orderly and had probably never been late for an appointment in his life.

As for her, she'd been lobbying for change since she was seven. And inside a mall she could have a ball. She wondered if Cadde had ever been in a mall. She'd guess not, because the image didn't fit. His territory was an office or an oil field.

One white shirt was pushed to the end of the rack and she pulled it out. It wasn't pressed and she wondered why. Then saw the tear on the sleeve. Even though she knew it was too big for her, she slipped it on and rolled up the sleeves, the rip disappearing in the folds. Buttoning it up, she thought it would be perfect to sleep in, soft and comfy.

The entry door opened and she tensed, a reflex action she couldn't control. "Cadde," she called.

"Yeah," he answered. "I brought supper."

She hurried into the living room and Cadde just stared at her, a bag in one hand.

The silence stretched. She became self-conscious and rushed into speech. "I hope you don't mind I borrowed your shirt." She tugged at the hem that came almost to her knees. "Rosa didn't expect me to spend another night and she didn't pack anything to sleep in."

"No, it's fine." He walked into the kitchen and placed the bag on the table.

What was wrong? He wasn't this stiff or unfriendly this morning. Maybe he was just tired.

"How are you?" he asked, his eyes on her.

"Fine. No infection, but I have to see the doctor again next week."

"And Mirry?"

"Oh, Cadde." She sat in one of the wood chairs, feeling more self-conscious than ever. "She looks bad. Gavin had to do a lot of repair work and Mirry's in terrible pain. I could hardly stand it. I want to take her home, but that's probably not going to happen for a while."

"She'll get better. Give her some time." His voice relaxed and so did Cadde.

Jessie felt the tension in the room tiptoe away. "What's for dinner?"

"Chicken fried steaks, baked potatoes and salads. I got us the same thing so you don't have to eat off my plate." He pulled take-out containers from the bag.

She tilted her head. "That's no guarantee."

He lifted an eyebrow but the only sound that came out of his mouth was, "Mmm."

She stood and made ice water for them to drink. Opening the lid on her salad, she asked, "You sent Barbara out for food again."

"No, I went."

"How did you go?" She took her seat and poured ranch dressing over her salad.

"In my truck."

She looked up. Had he seen the smudge? Was that the reason he was so standoffish when he'd first arrived? "Do you have an extra pair of keys?"

"Yes, but I didn't use them," he replied, opening the containers. "I came in here earlier and you were asleep. I got my keys out of your purse."

"Oh." She hadn't even heard him.

Cadde grabbed forks and knives out of a drawer and sat across from her. "Funny thing, there's a discoloration on my steering wheel. Have no idea what caused it, but it wasn't there last night."

"Oh." Feigning innocence was the best plan, she decided.

"Any thoughts on how it got there?"

"Okay. Okay. I ate a hamburger for lunch and got mustard on the steering wheel. I rubbed it off immediately. It's only a tiny smudge."

"You ate in my truck?" he asked in a horrified tone, much as if he'd been asking if she'd killed someone.

She leaned over and whispered, "Is it against the law?"

He tensed and then his face relaxed into a grin. "No."

"I'll try to get it out tomorrow. Whatever to make you happy."

"Don't worry about it." He cut into his steak. "I can live with a smudge."

"I don't think so." She took a bite of salad. "Your

closet looks like something out of a magazine, everything in its place."

"When you've lived in a twelve-by-twelve room with two sloppy brothers, you learn to be organized. Our mother always picked up our clothes from the floor and they just magically appeared in our closet. But Aunt Etta was different. If you didn't put your laundry in the basket, they didn't get washed or ironed. Kid didn't get the knack of it until he had to wear dirty clothes to school. From then on he knew Aunt Etta was serious."

"How did he get the name Kid?" She covered her potato with toppings.

"When my dad was small he used to watch *The Cisco Kid,* an old Western. He wanted to name me Cisco, but Mom wouldn't hear of it so Kid got stuck with it. Chance teases him that he should have been named Poncho, the sidekick."

They continued to talk as they ate, but Jessie knew they were skirting around the main topic—the night. How did she bring it up? How did she tell him she was ready to make love? She trailed her fork through her potato and stuck with an easy subject. "All three of you have unusual names. How did Chance get his?"

"After two boys, my mother wanted a girl. There were some complications with the delivery and she knew she wouldn't be able to have any more children. It was her last chance for a girl and that's what she called him."

"And you?"

"It's my grandfather's name. My parents were just teenagers when they got married and they lived with him. My grandmother had died long ago. When I was eight, he passed away and he was so proud I carried on his name."

Cadde took the remains to the trash and Jessie helped. "How did you get yours?" he asked.

She paused in picking up a container. "I have no idea. I guess it was a name my dad liked. When I was in first and second grade, the teachers kept trying to put Jessica on my papers. But it's simply Jessie—Jessie Marie."

Cadde leaned against the counter. "We don't have middle names."

"Really?" Her elbow brushed his arm as she rinsed the forks and knives. He instantly moved away.

"I have to go back to the office. You get some rest."

What?

"Cadde!"

He stopped with his hand on the door.

"Don't treat me like a fragile, helpless woman."

"I never think of you as fragile or helpless. You can ruin my day faster than anyone I know, including Kid."

"I don't want to ruin your day," she said with as much finesse as she could without blurting out, "have sex with me."

He got the message. "You were attacked by a dog yesterday. That alone was traumatic and you said the other night you weren't ready. I don't think…"

"I'm ready."

CHAPTER NINE

"Jessie…"

"Let's have a glass of wine," she suggested, never dreaming it would be this hard to, well, seduce him.

He walked farther into the room. "You got mad the last time I drank wine."

"That's because you were guzzling it." She opened the built-in liquor cabinet. Her father had always kept it well stocked, but she didn't know how it was now. There were several bottles. Evidently Cadde had continued the tradition. "How about a merlot?"

"Fine."

She handed him the bottle and their hands touched, and the sexual tension was a thing she could feel—pent-up sexual tension, in him and in her.

Suddenly he set the bottle on the coffee table. "I don't need wine to sleep with you." His eyes roamed over her. "All I have to do is look at you in that shirt with your hair mussed up like you just got out of bed and every male muscle in me kicks in."

She stepped closer to him, so close she could feel the heat from his body. "Then why were you leaving?"

"Because…"

She trailed her hands up the front of his shirt and felt the solid wall of his chest. As she slipped a button through a hole, his arms snaked out and grabbed her around the waist, pulling her even closer until there was nothing left to the imagination. Her soft curves welcomed the hardness of his body.

His lips tentatively kissed the hollow of her neck and paused over the tape for a brief second, then moved to her ear, her cheek. She gasped from the sheer satisfaction when he finally took her lips. Slowly, he kissed her, their tongues tasting, exploring and needing more. He groaned as his mouth moved over hers in urgent need. She didn't know much, but she knew this was the real thing. Real emotions. Real sexual desires. He wanted her.

He swung her into his arms and carried her into the bedroom. The room was in darkness but the bathroom light was on, heightening the romantic mood. Cadde made fast work of the buttons on her shirt, his fingers caressing her soft flesh. She scooted back on the bed and removed her panties.

The muscles across his broad chest rippled as he removed his clothes and boots in record time. Without losing a second, he yanked off his Jockey shorts. She could only stare at his perfect male body. At the sight of his full arousal, her stomach lurched in anticipation and moisture pooled between her legs.

With one knee on the mattress, he hovered above her and then gathered her into his arms in the most powerful embrace she'd ever felt; gentle, loving and exhilarating. Her feminine body pressing against his hardness was an erotic sensation. Her mind swirled as she got lost in his masculine touch.

"What's that scent?" he asked, his lips against her skin.

"It's…cherry blossom…lotion."

His lips trailed from her neck to her breasts and pin-points of heat permeated her body. Unable to resist, her hand went to hard muscles and thus began a ritual of them really getting to know each other intimately. He moaned at her tentative efforts. She became bolder, holding and stroking him.

After tasting every part of her until she wanted to scream from the unabashed pleasure, he took her lips once again, deeply, riveting. She couldn't even think. She just craved him.

He rolled onto her and she instinctively opened her legs, needing him in a way she didn't quite understand. At his first thrust, she stiffened. She didn't want to do that, but it was natural and she had to get past it. Breathing heavily, Cadde paused and his body stilled.

Tightening her arms around him, she whispered, "Please, Cadde."

He moaned. "Jessie."

She wrapped her legs around him, refusing to let him stop. He moaned again and thrust inside her. Slow and easy, he kept up the rhythm and her body welcomed him, needing every thrust in a way that surprised her. The pain was forgotten as every nerve ending came alive in her. Slow and easy became fast and furious and she enjoyed the delicious rocking vibe. Her body convulsed in waves of unimaginable gratification.

It shook everything she'd ever thought about sex. About men. There was no way to describe what she was feeling. She felt as if she was falling off a mountain top and sailing into clean, fresh air, buffeted only by Cadde's arms.

His body shuttered in release and she kept holding on, hoping this moment would never end—the moment she'd found out everything she'd ever wanted to know about sex with a man she loved.

"You lied," he breathed into her neck.

"Yes," she admitted without one ounce of shame, running her fingers through his hair.

He rolled away and her body felt bereft of his warm skin. "You should have told me."

"Why?" She propped up on one elbow.

"Just because..." He turned to look at her. "Are you okay?"

She took his hand and placed it on her face. "Feel that smile. It's from ear to ear. You did that." She scooted closer and laid her head on his shoulder, her palm on his chest. "Now I'm tired and sleepy."

Cadde stayed awake long after Jessie had fallen into a deep slumber. *She was a virgin.* All the signs were there but he never saw them. She wanted to wait. Well, there'd been a reason for that—a good reason.

He thought once again how sheltered her world had been with guards and guns. She didn't have a life and maybe now she was going a little too fast. Running a hand over his face, he sighed. He'd wanted to stop, but she wouldn't let him and the honest truth was he didn't know if he could. Heartfelt emotions were exploding all around him and he just wanted her, virgin or not. He hadn't had sex in a while so that could be the reason. Or it could be Jessie.

She knew how to push his buttons and she knew how to make his body respond. At the last she'd really gotten into it and he had a hard time keeping them on the bed. *Wild virgin Jessie.* If it got any better, he didn't know if his heart could take it. But he was willing to find out.

Slipping out of bed, he went down the hall to turn out the lights, doing the same in the bathroom. He crawled back in beside Jessie and pulled the sheet over them. Making a soft whimpering sound, she snuggled into him as if they'd been sleeping together all their lives.

For some reason sleep evaded him. The business deal kept tempting his mind. He'd fulfilled his end of the agreement. Now she had to do the same. Shilah— that's what was important to him. But no matter how he tried to slice it in Shilah's favor, he knew something special had happened tonight.

AROUND FIVE JESSIE WOKE UP. "Cadde, the light is off."

"I know," he mumbled. "Go back to sleep. I'm here."

She kissed his neck. "I'm not sleepy." Her lips moved to his shoulder, his chest and every muscle in him came to full attention and saluted.

"Jessie."

"Hmm." She slid one leg across him and sat on his stomach, her hair falling forward. "Don't say you don't want to have sex because you'd be lying. A man can't hide that and you really can't this morning without a stitch of clothes on."

He leaned up and wrapped his tongue around one tempting nipple. "For someone so inexperienced you're very wild in bed, do you know that?"

"I read a lot," she murmured, and slid her body over his, her soft breasts pressing into his chest. He cupped her face, threaded his fingers through her long hair and kissed her. The emotions from last night fired to life. He rolled her onto her back and she giggled. It was the only sound in the room, beside sighs and moans, for some time.

A pounding on the door woke them from a lethargic sleep. "What the hell?" Cadde crawled from the bed and jerked on his jeans. "Kid's supposed to be in Louisiana, but if that's him, I'm going to wring his damn neck." Kid was known for not knocking, though.

Cadde yanked opened the door and a dark-haired woman pushed past him.

"Where is she? Mama said she didn't come home last night. What have you done to her?" She pointed a long finger at him. "Just so you know I have connections to the police."

Cadde frowned. "Who are you?"

"Myra," Jessie gasped from the doorway, wearing nothing but his white shirt. "What are you doing here?"

"Mama's worried sick. You didn't come home."

"I told Rosa I wasn't."

"Oh." Myra brushed aside her hair and looked at him and then back to Jessie. "Mama forgot to mention that part."

"How did you get into the building?" Cadde asked, a little concerned that a maniac could walk right in.

"A good-looking guy let me in after I told him who I was."

Chance. Cadde knew without a doubt.

"And who are you?"

"Myra Delgado. Rosa and Felix's daughter."

She didn't extend a hand in greeting and that was fine with him. "I'll go shave and shower and leave you two to…whatever."

As he strolled away, Jessie clenched her hands into fists. "What are you doing?"

Myra shrugged. "Mama called at four, five, six and then again at eight. I promised I'd check on you. She's worried."

"If I hear *worried* one more time, I'm going to scream. Do you hear me, Myra?"

"I'm not deaf. You're shouting."

Jessie expelled a long breath. "Please let me live my life."

Myra glanced toward the hallway. "He's not bad, kind of ruggedly handsome in a brooding sort of way."

"I would have introduced you, but you were acting like a real bitch."

"I have that reputation, you know."

"Yes. Use it in the courtroom but not in my life."

Myra hugged her. "Gotcha. Have fun playing house."

"Myra." Jessie stopped her at the door. "Don't come back unless you're invited."

"Now that's damn cold."

"It's not meant to be. I want some privacy."

"I'm starting a murder trial so I'll be scarce for a while." Myra winked. "Call if you need me, kiddo."

Jessie went back into the bedroom. The bed was tumbled from a very active night. She wrapped her arms around her waist, still living in the moment. Last night was perfect—better than she'd ever dreamed or fantasized about. And under Cadde's tutelage she'd gotten a lot of years of frustration out of her system and acted boldly, even brazenly. She couldn't have done that with anyone else but Cadde.

Thinking of him, she moved toward the bathroom. He stood at a sink, shaving, a towel wrapped around his waist. There wasn't an ounce of fat on him and she knew because last night she'd touched every inch of his marble-crafted body.

With smooth quick strokes he swiped away his morning stubble. She could still feel it rubbing against her sensitive skin in an erotic, almost sinful way, igniting more suppressed emotions in her.

He noticed her. "The she-devil gone?"

She smiled. "She means well."

"If you say so." He wiped his face and leaned against the vanity, facing her. "I was thinking I'd call an emergency board meeting for Monday. Before I do any more work on the Louisiana deal, I'm going to need their approval."

And just like that her bubble of happiness burst into a million little pieces, each one attached to her heart. But what did she expect? They had a deal—a business deal that did not include any words of love. Just sex—procreation.

"Fine," she said, and walked into the bedroom to straighten the bed with strong jerky movements.

He followed with a scowl. "You're not doing another about-face, are you?"

Could he be any more insensitive? "No. You lived

up to your end and I'll honor mine." She jammed a fist into a pillow and slammed it against the headboard.

"The comforter is short on this side," he pointed out.

"I like it that way." She turned and went to the kitchen where she wanted to lay her head down and just cry. But she didn't. Instead, she made coffee and set about fixing breakfast.

She warmed up the tacos for Cadde and pulled out the fruit and yogurt she hadn't eaten yesterday. As she lifted the spoon to her mouth, he walked in all dressed for the day as if the night had never happened. She spooned so fast the yogurt went down the wrong way and she coughed.

"Are you okay?" he asked, pouring a cup of coffee.

"I'm fine." She coughed again and reached for her mug.

"Are you upset?"

"No."

"You seem upset."

"I'm fine." She wrapped the remaining fruit and put it back in the refrigerator. "I have to shower and change," she muttered. "I want to see Mirry as soon as I can."

Cadde sat there with his mouth open. What had just happened? What could Myra have said to her to make her so upset? He knew talking to Jessie was not the answer. She was mad, mad, mad! Once she cooled off, they would talk.

Wolfing down the tacos, he followed them with coffee and headed for the door. He had work to do. His hand went to his head. He still hadn't found his hat. It was probably at the house and he hadn't been back there yet. The thought of getting one from the bedroom was tempting, but not that tempting. Jessie clearly needed some time alone.

He had consecutive meetings all morning. At the last one lunch was brought in. He picked at his food, not able to get Jessie out of his mind. What was she so mad about?

Back in his office, he went through permits and licenses they would need in Louisiana. Chance breezed in.

"Did you know Uncle Ru's been down with the flu for over a week?"

Cadde looked up. "No. I haven't talked to them lately."

"Someone should have called us." Chance sank into a leather chair.

"Why didn't they?"

"Sky said Aunt Etta didn't want to bother us." Chance placed his elbows on his knees. "I don't like not being there. Shay and I were talking and we're thinking of moving back. The kids in school are always picking on Darcy because of her big glasses and because she's so thin. I want her to grow up feeling good about herself and I think that can happen in High Cotton. Shay's getting her teaching certificate, and landing a position in High Cotton's schools will be much easier than hoping for one in Houston."

Cadde nodded. "Sounds as if your mind is made up."

"Yep. I'd like to build a house on Mom and Dad's land, in the left front corner facing the road, but Aunt

Etta owns half of that three-hundred-acre tract. She always says it's ours. I just don't want to step on any toes."

"Build your house, Chance, I don't foresee any problems. But we need to talk to Aunt Etta to get everything clear and on paper."

Chance stood. "I'm going home this weekend. I'll talk to her."

"She'll be happy you're coming home." Cadde reached for his pen on the desk. "You're not quitting Shilah, are you?"

"Hell, no, every penny I have is invested here. I'll use the chopper to travel back and forth."

"Good. Tell Aunt Etta and Uncle Ru I said hi and I'll get home as soon as I can. Right now my life is a..." Cadde pointed his pen at Chance. "Don't allow anyone into this building unless you call me first."

"What?" Chance seemed puzzled at the quick change of topic.

"You let Myra Delgado in this morning."

"Yeah. She's an assistant D.A. and Rosa and Felix's daughter."

"I don't care. You call first."

"Okay. What happened?"

"She...uh...interrupted us, and said something to upset Jessie."

"How do you know that?"

"Because after she left Jessie was acting weird... mad."

"Maybe you said something to upset her."

"What!" Cadde threw his pen onto the desk. "Just

because Kid is away doesn't mean you can pick up his habit of annoying the crap out of me."

Chance held up his hands. "I'm just trying to help you. You didn't say anything to her after Myra left?"

"No. I…oh, no!" His mind clicked with the reality of his own actions. He'd mentioned the board meeting. After what had happened last night between them, he knew that was a big no-no in Jessie's eyes. But Shilah was an important part of their business deal. Even as the thought zapped through his mind, he knew it was wrong. It negated everything they'd shared last night and made it business, functionally, not emotionally. Oh, God, he had to see Jessie.

He shoved back his chair. "I've got to go."

"Cadde."

His phone rang and Barbara's voice came on, "Mr. Hardin, Arnie called from accounting. You're ten minutes late for your appointment."

Cadde sighed. "Tell him I'll be right there."

At the meeting, Arnie reviewed labor, material and rig costs of drilling in Louisiana. Cadde had to know if they could even afford this venture, but the numbers went right over his head. He couldn't concentrate. Something beside business had his full attention—Jessie.

He stood. "I really have to run. Get all the figures to me. I'll go over them in the morning."

"Um…okay."

Cadde hurried down the hallway. Jessie should be back from seeing Mirry by now. He stopped dead. The truck keys were in his pocket. With the way she was acting this morning, he'd forgotten to give them to her. Dammit!

Hurriedly, he unlocked the apartment door. Inside, everything was dark, not a light on anywhere. The bedroom was the same. No sign of Jessie. All her things were missing, but the scent of cherry blossoms lingered, as it did on his tongue.

But Jessie was gone.

CHAPTER TEN

CADDE HEADED OUT OF HOUSTON. Jessie had to be home by now. His guess was she'd called Rosa to pick her up and that had probably taken a slice of her independent pride. He was lousy at reading the signals. Still, they shouldn't have to read each other's mind. She should have said that he'd hurt her feelings and then they could have talked about it. But oh, no, she'd closed up tighter than a turtle poked by a stick.

That was Jessie, though, stubborn as hell, and she wasn't sinking her pride. He knew how long she'd fought to keep it.

As he negotiated traffic, his thoughts shifted to Chance. He was going home. Family had always meant a lot to Chance. That's what Cadde wanted with Jessie—a family, but their deal was there between them like a slap in the face. It stung. Somehow they had to get beyond that. She had to understand Shilah had to move forward. That didn't diminish them as a couple, as a family. How did he explain that without hurting her feelings? How did he explain it to himself? All he knew was that he wanted her in his life.

He drove up to the garages and got out. Instead of going to the house, he walked toward the barn. He paused in the entry. Jessie sat in loose hay holding a bottle so a baby deer could suckle.

She cooed softly. "You're so much better, Bambi. Drink all you want."

A one-eyed donkey stuck his head through an open window.

"Go away, Winky, you're not getting any more food."

The donkey brayed in disagreement and Jessie's face lit up like he'd never seen before. She was happy here in this musty barn with her animals. This was her world— a world she carved away from the aggressive protection of the people in her life.

Felix walked in from the back door. "She's stronger, huh, Miss Jessie?"

"Much stronger." Jessie stroked the deer. "Since the Dobermans are no longer here, she can roam free in the barn. But I would like her to get some sunshine."

"I'm building a small pen with an eight-foot fence around it."

Jessie jumped up and hugged Felix. "Thank you. Now she'll have lots of sunshine."

"Mr. Cadde." Felix finally spotted him.

Jessie didn't acknowledge his presence. She went into a small makeshift kitchen. To say she was still mad was like saying water was wet.

"Mr. Cadde, your gun and hat are at the house."

"Thank you, Felix."

He turned to Jessie. "Could we talk for a minute?"

"I'm busy," she replied, and rinsed the baby bottle.

"It will only take a minute."

"Fine," she snapped in that clipped tone he was beginning to know well.

"Not here. In private."

"Sorry, I'm busy." She made to walk past him and he caught her arm, leading her out of the barn.

She tried to wiggle away from him. "Let me go."

"No," he told her. "We're talking…now."

She ceased her struggle to get away, but he didn't loosen his grip. They went through the garage into the kitchen.

A startled Rosa stopped peeling potatoes. "Miss Jessie…"

"She's fine," Cadde replied. "We just need a few minutes alone."

Once inside the bedroom, Cadde closed and locked the door.

Jessie placed her hands on her hips. "This had better be good."

He took a deep breath, gauging every word. "After last night, it was crass of me to mention the board meeting."

"Yes, it was." She sat on the foot of the bed. "Being new at this I let my emotions get involved. That won't happen again."

"Really?" he mocked her.

"Yes." She stood in a restless movement. "I could be pregnant and if I am then we won't need to have sex again. If not, well, I guess we'll have to."

She made to walk past him and he caught her arm again. "No, no, no, that's not how it's going to be. A real marriage…that's what it says in the agreement. I'm sorry if bringing that up upsets you, but we're having a real marriage with sex every night or however much we want." He took a breath. "Do you know how long it's been since I've had sex?"

"This morning," she quipped.

"Before that."

"Last night."

He smiled. She smiled. Suddenly the tension wasn't there.

"Longer than that…a long time, so last night was special for me, too." He rubbed her forearm and knew it smelled of cherry blossoms. "But there's something you need to know about me. I'm not good at the emotional stuff. Chance is. Kid was born with it. They had to yank him out with tongs and he still came out smiling. I'm the serious, responsible brother. I know everything there is to know about the oil business, but I know absolutely nothing about women. Last night was awesome and I want to build on that. I want you. That's about all I have to say."

"It's enough." Her eyes sparkled so maybe he was getting something right.

She stepped closer to him and he stepped back. Was he insane? But he had something to get off his chest. "I don't want a kid of mine born as part of a business deal and I don't want that agreement hanging between us. It just creates bad feelings. I'd rather we start out better than that."

"What about the transfer of the share giving you control?"

He jammed his hands through his hair and pushed

everything he'd ever dreamed about to the side burner. What he said now would shape their marriage and he was very aware of that. "I hope you'll listen to my plans for Shilah and vote with your head, vote for what you think is right for this oil company. We have to build this marriage on trust and honesty."

Jessie walked to her dresser. Opening a drawer, she pulled out a folder and laid it on the bed. "There's the agreement. I haven't taken it to the lawyer yet."

He grabbed the document from the folder and ripped it into several pieces. He then threw them into the air and as they fluttered around them, Jessie jumped into his arms, wrapping her legs around his waist, her arms tight around his neck.

He held on and he knew their relationship had just changed. Turning, he fell backward on the bed, cradling her in his arms. She raised up and whipped her T-shirt over her head, throwing it on the floor. Her bra followed.

As he was giving one breast his full attention a knock sounded at the door.

"Miss Jessie, are you okay?" Rosa called.

Jessie smiled, the biggest smile he'd never seen. "I'm fine, Rosa. I'm really, really fine." And then she started to unbutton his shirt.

Jessie understood he wasn't always going to get it right, but he was trying. A part of him wondered if he'd just made the worst decision of his life. His child would not be born under a business agreement, though. And Jessie's feelings were important. That shocked him the most. He didn't want to see that hurt look in her eyes again.

As he took her sweet lips he knew she was in control, but this time it didn't bother him.

THEY SPENT THE WEEKEND in bed or in the pool with sporadic trips into Houston to see Mirry. It was the most relaxing two days Cadde could recall. He didn't go into the office, not once, and he even took the time to call his aunt and uncle. That was usually Chance's department, but family was important to him, too.

On Monday morning he was up early and dressed for work. Jessie was still asleep. He leaned over and kissed her cheek. "I'm leaving."

"Mmm," she mumbled, but she didn't wake up.

He walked to the door, wondering if he should remind her of the board meeting at ten. But he chose not to. She knew about it and the decision was hers. Shilah's future was in her hands.

Chance rushed into his office at fifteen minutes to ten. "Ready?"

"Yeah." Cadde glanced at his watch. "We have a few minutes. How's everything in High Cotton?"

"Great. Uncle Ru is back cowboying."

"I know. I called."

"Aunt Etta told me and I guess she told you she doesn't want the land. She's leaving it to us, her heirs."

"Yep." Cadde reached for his jacket. "I promised her I'd get one of the lawyers to draw up the papers, but we still need to do something about our parents' house."

"Maybe when Kid gets back."

Once again, they put off the dreaded task.

He picked up his briefcase. "Let's go."

"This is just a business formality, right?" Chance asked as they walked out of Cadde's office. "I mean, you have the agreement with Jessie."

Cadde shook his head. "No. We tore it up."

"What? But…"

"I'm going to trust Jessie to do the right thing. Isn't that what marriage is about?"

"Yes, but you've talked to her, right?"

"No, the decision is hers."

"What!" Chance followed him like a pesky mosquito. "I'm not understanding any of this."

"We're trying to build a marriage on trust. Do you understand that?"

"Well, yes, but if we needed votes we should have waited for Kid."

Cadde stopped and faced him. "Relax. I'll handle the board meeting."

They walked in and took their seats. Jessie's seat was vacant. But all of Roscoe's cronies were there: Percival, better known as Hooter Caldwell, Hubert Gillespie, Owen McGrew, Hank Parker, J. T. Hardeson and George Pettibone.

Hooter Caldwell chomped on his cigar. "What's this meeting about, Cadde? We just had a board meeting."

"Yeah," Owen McGrew piped up, "you're not bringing up those Louisiana leases again, are you?"

Cadde scooted his chair forward. "Roscoe held on to those leases for a reason, have you ever thought of that?"

"Roscoe was plumb crazy and I never understood him most of the time."

"But you understood it when he made you money?"

"Hell, yeah."

"Jessie's not here," Hooter commented. "Has she been notified of the meeting?"

"Yes," Cadde replied with all the patience he had. "I live with her, remember?"

"That don't amount to a plank of wood on a cold, freezing night."

Cadde placed his hands on the table and stood, every muscle in him ready to pounce on Hooter as if he were no more than a cockroach. Everyone but Chance seemed to move their chairs back.

"I didn't mean a thing." Hooter chomped a little harder on his cigar. "I have a twisted sense of humor."

"Yeah, Cadde, Hoot just flew in from Vegas and his mind's a little muddled." Hub Gillespie tried to smooth things over.

Cadde wasn't letting it drop, though. "Because of Roscoe I'm honor bound to respect your positions on this board, but if another crack like that is made I'll find a way to get your ass off this board. Roscoe left a lot of loopholes in your agreements—for his benefit, and I inherited them when I became CEO. I can bring in investors as I see fit and if I feel there is any insubordination by a board member, I have the power to remove him. If you don't think I can, try me. Am I clear, Hooter?"

The man coughed and sputtered, as if he were choking. Owen hit him on the back and the cigar shot out onto the table. Without a word, Hooter reached for his handkerchief, wiped the table, and positioned the cigar back in his mouth.

"We're clear, Cadde, mighty clear."

Before Cadde could say another word, the door opened and Jessie walked in. Dressed in a dark business suit, heels, her hair pulled back into a knot, she looked like an entirely different person. But he knew her. He knew her body. Now he had to trust her.

"Sorry I'm late. I got caught in traffic." She removed her sunglasses and took her seat across the table from him. "What are we talking about?"

"Cadde hasn't said anything yet," Hooter replied, placing a hand on Jessie's arm. "And may I say, my dear, you look lovely."

"Thank you," Jessie said, easing her arm away.

Lecherous old man! Keep your hands off my wife.

"Let's listen to what Cadde has to say then."

He blinked, losing the gist of the conversation. All he wanted to do was punch Hooter, but he quickly collected himself and went into his spiel adding a lot about Roscoe and his way of doing business.

Complete silence followed his speech. The only sound was Barbara tapping away on her laptop, recording the minutes.

"I think this is something Daddy would do." Jessie was the first to speak. "I vote yes."

"Are you sure, Jessie?" Hooter asked, and reached for her arm again, but Jessie evaded him by standing.

"I'm very sure, and now I have to run." She picked up her sunglasses and walked out of the room.

Cadde pushed to his feet. "Chance, take the vote. I have to speak to my wife."

"What?" Chance was confused, but only for a second.

As Cadde strolled away, he heard Chance's voice, "Anyone opposed to the proposal?" There was a slight pause and not a whimper of opposition. "Okay, boys, we're invading Louisiana."

Cadde hurried toward the elevator to catch Jessie, but she wasn't there. She didn't have time to go anywhere but... *The apartment.* He opened the door and there she was dressed in his white shirt. He closed the door and locked it, smiling.

All it had taken was trust...and honesty.

JESSIE LIVED IN A DREAMLIKE state. She was happier than she'd ever been in her life as they settled into marriage. At night the lights went off and she didn't mind. She had Cadde's arms around her. That was all she needed. They never mentioned the *L* word and she was okay with that, too. Their relationship had evolved and she had hopes it would continue to do so.

What surprised her the most was that Cadde was usually home by six and he spent weekends with her. He talked on the phone, used his laptop, but he was there and she didn't feel so alone.

After two weeks Mirry came home. She still wore the doughnut thing and she was able to eat and drink. Mirry could stand but she didn't move from the pillow Jessie had her on in her room. Gavin had said that she would eventually start walking again. It would take time.

In the past Gavin had never sent her a bill. She always mailed a check, though, hoping it covered his expenses. This time she received an enormous bill for Mirry's operation and her stay at the clinic. She paid it. Maybe Gavin had finally gotten her message.

One morning she heard a whimpering sound.

She reached for the bedside lamp and turned it on. Mirry stood on all fours looking up at her. "Cadde." She crawled out of bed, completely naked, and walked around the room. Mirry slowly followed. "Cadde, look, she's walking."

Cadde pushed up on his elbows. "Damn beautiful sight, too." He was looking at her, not Mirry.

She gave him a long kiss. "I'm taking Mirry outside. She has to go pee."

He frowned. "It's barely five in the morning."

"I know." She reached for her cotton robe and slipped it on, tying the sash. "We won't be long."

Jessie carried Mirry downstairs and sat on the step while the dog did her business. Mirry sniffed the grass, the air and seemed to enjoy the warm early morning.

Suddenly, Cadde sat beside her.

She pushed back her hair. "Don't you have to go to work?"

"Mmm." He put his arm around her and she laid her head on his shoulder. "Just thought it wouldn't hurt to witness a miracle."

"She's better, Cadde. She's better."

He stroked her hair. "And so are we."

"Yeah."

Cadde may not get the flowery words right, but he

more than made up for it in his actions. If she loved him any more she was actually going to hurt. There was a softness in him that was hard to reach, but once it was exposed he was like a soft cuddle bear. She had a feeling the softness came from his mother.

She wondered like so many times in the past what qualities she got from her mother. She'd never know. Why was she thinking about it now when she was so happy?

Resting against Cadde, she felt at peace for the first time in forever. They watched Mirry taking awkward, sure steps in the grass.

Just like they were.

CADDE WAS KNEE-DEEP IN figures when Kid strolled into his office and slapped folders onto his desk. "All done, big brother, signed, sealed and delivered."

"You got the leases signed that we needed?"

"Yep. Took some legwork and going through the deeds at the courthouse, but every owner I approached was willing to sign. Times are tough everywhere and the hope of extra money is a welcome green light."

"Did you get them at the price we discussed?"

"Yep. No one asked for more." Kid placed a book on the desk. "Here's the draft book."

"You did a great job, Kid."

"Hell, yeah, I did." Kid plopped into a chair and propped his boots on the desk. "And what the hell am I doing running around busting my ass on these leases while you're tearing up the agreement with Jessie?"

Cadde leaned back. "Chance told you?"

"Yes, and I can't believe you jeopardized this whole project."

"I didn't want to start our marriage with that agreement hanging over our heads. I had to trust Jessie to make the right decision for herself and for Shilah."

"What?"

"It's called trust, Kid."

"Who the hell are you?" Kid jumped to his feet. "Where's Cadde, my brother whose focus is the oil business and only the oil business?"

Cadde leaned forward. "I've changed. My priorities are split between family and business."

"Oh, God, I need a drink. I can't take this on a sober stomach."

Cadde picked up his pen. "I'm sure you can find someone to keep you company."

"It used to be my brothers, but now all they talk about is marriage, babies and trust. God, I need a stiff one."

"Have fun. You've earned it."

"You bet I have and this night is not going to be about trust. It's going to be about having one helluva good time."

"I never thought otherwise."

With his hand on the door, Kid paused and turned back. "I've been eating crawfish with beer three times a day in Louisiana so I might be a little punch-drunk already. But I'm happy you and Jessie have found some sort of balance."

"Thanks, Kid."

Cadde shook his head, wondering if Kid would ever

grow up. And if there was a woman alive who could put up with him on a daily basis.

Smiling, he reached for the draft book and unlocked the bottom drawer on his desk. Placing it inside, he spotted a brown folder at the back. He'd never noticed that before and he pulled it out. A pink string held it together.

What was this?

Slowly, he undid the bowknot and opened the folder. An eight-by-ten glossy photo of a woman in a string bikini jumped out at him. Her long dark hair flowed over her shoulder and her olive complexion was smooth and silky. *Jessie.* She looked like Jessie but Cadde knew it wasn't. Jessie was much more beautiful.

More photos followed of Roscoe and the woman, the woman and Roscoe with a baby and more of just the woman and a baby. Without a doubt, he knew this was Jessie's mother. As he turned over the last photo, he found a sticky note. On it was written: *Cadde, use this information as you see fit. Roscoe.*

What the hell?

Then he began to read what looked like a letter to Jessie.

You've asked me so many times about your mother and I couldn't tell you the truth. I just couldn't, but I couldn't die with that lie on my conscience.

I met your mother in Vegas. Her name is Angela Martinez. She was the most beautiful woman I'd ever seen. She was also a stripper. After spending a week with her, I offered her fifty thousand dollars if she would give me a child. I was forty-seven years old and she was twenty-one, but that didn't matter. I wanted a child. She took the money and we came back to Texas. Her family was poor and she was stripping to pay the rent. I knew the money would be a temptation she couldn't resist.

She became pregnant almost immediately. The day you were born was the happiest day of my life. I believe Angela was happy, too. But then her family started calling. They needed money. To keep Angela with us, I sent them twenty thousand more dollars. That didn't last long. They were calling again. I told Angela she had to choose—us or her no good family. She left the next day with you. The moment I found out I was on a plane to Vegas to get you. She would not take you from me.

But she tried once again to steal you when you were eighteen months old. Aunt Helen kept you while Al and I worked. Angela somehow snatched you while you slept and Helen was in another room. I once again flew to Vegas and this time I told Angela if she ever came back to Texas I would kill her and she knew I meant it.

I never heard from her again and that's just as well. You're my kid and no way on God's green earth was she taking you from me. When Crissy was kidnapped, I feared it was Angela trying to get back at me. But the police checked and Crissy wasn't with Angela. The police said she'd married. I guess she moved on without us.

Every day of your life I feared Angela was going to take you from me. The guards had a lot to do with Crissy but a lot to do with Angela, too. No way was I letting her have any contact with you. She wasn't taking the one thing I treasured most on this earth.

A lot of what I did was wrong, but I wasn't letting you live in a run-down neighborhood with a stripper for a mother. Sometimes we have to make choices and I stand by every one I made. I love you, baby, and I know you'll forgive me because that's just the way you are. I know you've wondered many times about qualities you got from your mother. Your love of animals you got from her. I had to pay to bring a mangy dog and cat from Vegas and she treated them like babies.

I wish I could have told you this when I was alive, but, baby, talking about Angela was not an easy subject for me. I know I manipulated the situation to my benefit and I also got the greatest reward—you. That, Jessie, I will never regret. Love, with all my heart, Daddy.

Cadde just stared at the words on the paper, unable to do anything but think about how this was going to affect Jessie. He'd never understood the tight security on Jessie after so many years. Now he knew. Roscoe did not want Angela to take Jessie, and if Jessie was older she might choose her mother over Roscoe.

Good God! How did he deal with this? How did he tell Jessie? How could he not? A marriage based on trust wasn't going anywhere if he kept things from her. And Jessie craved information about her mother.

He reached for his cell and punched in a number. "Chip, I need all the information you can get me on Angela Martinez from Las Vegas, Nevada." Chip was a computer whiz kid who worked for Shilah. He'd find whatever Cadde needed to know about Jessie's mother.

Now he waited.

CHAPTER ELEVEN

JESSIE OPENED THE BOX and read the instructions. It had been a month since she and Cadde had had sex for the first time. She was fudging…a little. Three weeks and four days was more accurate, but she couldn't wait any longer. She'd bought a pregnancy test.

Mirry looked up at her. "I have to pee on a stick, Mirry, so you might not want to watch this."

The dog slowly made her way back to her soft pillow.

Jessie did the test and laid it flat on the bathroom vanity. Staring at the result window, she crossed her fingers and hoped for two pink lines.

"Jessie." She heard Cadde calling. "Where are you?"

"Upstairs!" she shouted.

"Come down. I need to talk to you."

What! There was something serious in his deep voice that hadn't been there this morning. She was torn between hurrying down to see Cadde and waiting the appropriate time for the test results.

"Can it wait a minute?"

"No. It's important."

That didn't sound good. She gave the test one last look and ran downstairs.

She found Cadde in her father's study, pacing. By

the scowl on his handsome face she knew something was wrong. It had to be about Shilah and it had to be the reason he was home so early.

To soothe her jittery nerves, she went into his arms and hugged him. Smiling, she glanced up at him. "What is it?"

He took her lips in a long kiss and she sighed in contentment. How could she love one person so much? She ached when he wasn't with her.

Suddenly, he stepped back. "I'm getting sidetracked. We have to talk."

She wrinkled her nose at him. "Getting sidetracked is much more fun."

"Yeah, but…"

"Did something go wrong with the Louisiana leases?"

"No, everything is moving forward."

She stared at his hatless head. "Did you lose your hat again?"

"No. It's in the truck."

"Come on, Cadde, you're scaring me. What is it?"

"Okay." He held up both hands. "I found something that your father meant for me to find."

The jittery nerves returned full force. "What?"

"It's more or less a letter to you."

Her panic eased a little. "When I was small and he was away for any length of time, he'd write me letters. Is it a letter that got lost in the mail?"

"No. This is serious." Cadde took her hand and led her around the big desk and gently pushed her into her father's chair. The putrid scent of cigars lingered—a reminder of her father.

A brown folder tied with a pink string lay in front of her. Cadde touched it. "This is what I found."

She reached for the string and Cadde caught her hand once again. "Please read what's inside with an open mind."

Her stomach clenched. There was no doubt that the contents were going to change her life. A part of her wanted to not open it, the other part had her reaching for the string. She jumped back in the chair as an almost nude woman stared at her.

"Who is that?"

"Your mother," Cadde replied, and confirmed what she already suspected.

"Oh, my God! Oh, my God!" She held her hands against her mouth in shock. Recovering quickly, she rifled through the other photos, hardly able to take her eyes off the smiling dark-haired woman. Her stomach clenched tighter as she read the letter.

For so many years she'd wondered and the truth was nothing like she'd imagined. Her mother was a stripper who her father had paid to have his child. She was that child. All the protection, the sheltering and smothering was to keep her from having any contact with Angela—her mother. And...and...

She quickly closed the folder, snatched it up and ran from the room.

"Jessie!"

She didn't stop. She rushed into her room, slammed

the door and locked it. Sliding to the floor, she held the folder to her chest.

The doorknob turned. "Jessie, open this door."

"No."

"Jessie, please."

His voice washed over her like warm soothing water. Why wasn't he running in the other direction? She was the daughter of a stripper who was paid to have her? And…she couldn't even say the rest in her head. It was too awful.

"Jessie, please."

Oh, that strong, compelling voice had her. Getting to her feet, she unlocked the door, crawled into the middle of the bed and sat cross-legged, the folder clutched against her chest.

As Cadde entered, she said, "Please go away."

He sat on the bed, facing her. "I'm not going anywhere."

"Why?" She brushed away a tear and held out the folder. "Haven't you read this?"

"Yes. You now know the circumstances of your birth and who your mother is. Why would that affect me other than to be concerned for you?"

"Because I'm just like *him*."

He frowned. "What?"

"He paid Angela for a baby and I tricked you into having one. I'm a horrible, horrible person just like my father." She dissolved into tears and couldn't seem to stop them.

"Jessie, stop crying." He tucked strands of her hair behind her ear and she wanted to absorb herself into him, not caring that the letter had clearly pointed out her selfish inherited faults. "Our situation is completely different from Roscoe's and Angela's. We're married and building a life together and you didn't trick me into anything. I went into our marriage with my eyes wide-open."

"But you didn't want a baby." For her own sanity she had to point that out.

"I do now. And we tore up the agreement, remember?" He stroked her wet cheek and once again she burst into tears. He was so gentle, so kind and she didn't deserve it.

"Jessie, please…wait, I'll get you some tissues."

As he walked into the bathroom, she tried to stop the tears, but couldn't. The more she wiped them away, the more they flowed.

"Jessie," Cadde called. "There's a pregnancy test on the vanity and there's two pink lines in the window. What does that mean?"

"What? Oh…oh!" She'd forgotten about the test. She leaped from the bed and frightened Mirry. "It's okay, Mirry," she reassured the dog, and dashed into the bathroom to gaze at the results.

"What does that mean?" Cadde asked again.

"It means I'm…uh…we're pregnant. We're pregnant!" She jumped up and down in excitement.

Cadde grabbed her and swung her round and round. "We're pregnant," he said in awe.

The wonder in his voice brought on more tears and she sank to the floor in a blubbering heap, totally confused with her reaction.

He squatted in front of her. "Why are you crying?"

"I don't know!" she wailed.

"I'm happy. You're happy, right?"

"Yes!" she wailed louder.

He scooped her into his arms and carried her into the bedroom. Gently depositing her on the bed, he lay beside her, boots and all. Pulling her against his side, he said, "Cry all you want."

And she did just that. She could hear this insane woman boohooing and she thought it surely couldn't be her. But it was. All the heartache from her past ebbed from her system. It was replaced with the bright glow of the future.

She rubbed her wet face on his white shirt. "We're having a baby."

"Yes," he replied, and she felt him stiffen.

"Why did you do that?"

"I'm waiting for more tears. I've heard pregnant women get emotional."

She wiped her face against him again. "I'm through crying."

"Good." He pulled her closer.

"I look like my mother," she murmured, playing with a button on his shirt.

"Yes. She's beautiful, but you're more beautiful."

She turned her head to see his face. "You think so?" That sounded as if she was fishing for a compliment and she wasn't. He'd said it many times when they were naked, but never when they weren't.

"Most definitely." He kissed her forehead and that touch, that reassurance, made her feel better.

"I wonder where she is now."

"I had my computer guy do a background check on her."

She sat up on her knees, eager for any news about her mother. She didn't understand it, but that thirst for information was there.

"And?"

He pushed into a sitting position. "She died when you were nine years old."

"Oh." Her hands fluttered against her mouth as a poignant moment of sadness hit her.

"All the security and protection was for nothing, but Roscoe never checked. I guess his pride wouldn't let him."

She fiddled with the hem of her shorts. "How did she die?"

"She married a guy named Juan Ruiz who was a member of a gang and crazy jealous. One night as Angela was stripping, a guy tried to touch her. Juan pulled a knife, confronting him. Angela jumped off the stage to stop the fight and Juan accidentally stabbed her. He spent five years in prison for her death."

"Oh, my."

"Chip was able to locate him. He's back in Vegas, remarried with a family and no longer a member of a gang. Chip had a phone number, so I called. It's amazing what people will tell you over the phone."

She looked up. "What did he say?"

"Angela married him because he promised her that he and some of his gang members would help her steal you."

"Oh, no."

"Yes. The plan was to take you to Mexico to hide you from Roscoe. They tried three times, but the guards prevented them from getting anywhere near you."

"What guards? I didn't have any guards until after Crissy was kidnapped."

"You had guards, Jessie. You just didn't see them."

Could that be true? She was just a kid and never sensed anyone was watching her. "How do you know this?"

"When Juan mentioned guards, I thought he was confused so I had Arnie check the payroll records from back then. Roscoe started paying guards when you were eighteen months old."

She shook her head. "I never knew."

"Juan said the first time they just walked up to the front door of Al's house, intending to kick the door in and take you. Before they even made it to the door, two men were on them with guns. They managed to get away. The second time they attempted to break into your window at Roscoe's. Once again the guards stopped them. The third time they tried to snatch you from a playground. Again, they were detected, and that time they went to jail. The cops didn't have any evidence so they had to let them go. But Roscoe was very aware that Angela was still trying to abduct you."

"Did they try once we moved here?"

"No." Cadde glanced around the room. "This fortress was too high-tech for uneducated gang members. But Angela kept planning to get you back...until her death."

She sank back on her heels. "I guess that was the main reason for all the tight security. I can't even imagine what my life would have been like had they succeeded."

"Not good," he said with his usual honesty, and she had to admit he was right.

She flipped back her long hair. "And I probably wouldn't have been a thirty-year-old virgin."

"And I'm really, really grateful for that." He caressed her thigh.

Linking her fingers with his, she said, "It feels kind of strange that my life could have turned out so differently and it makes me angry at both of them for subjecting me, an innocent child, to that type of custody hell."

His hand gripped hers. "It's over."

"I know, but it's hard to take all this in." She stroked his hand with her other one. "Daddy said my mother came from a poor family. Did she have any siblings? Any family?"

"Your grandparents are dead. Your grandfather was Mexican and your grandmother was white."

Jessie touched her hair. "Since my father was also white, I guess that's why I'm not as dark as my mother."

"Probably."

"Do I have any siblings?"

"No."

"And my mother?"

"She had two brothers and two sisters."

"Are they living?" That kernel of interest was still there.

"The brothers are dead. One was a member of a gang and he introduced Juan to Angela. He was killed in a gang fight. The other worked in a casino and was a dealer in a back room high-stakes poker game. Something went wrong and he was shot." He lifted her chin. "Guess what the middle sister's occupation is?"

"A hooker." She grimaced.

"No. A nun."

"What?"

"She works in an orphanage in Italy."

"And the other sister?"

"She was also a stripper and got involved in drugs and prostitution. When she was arrested, her sister, the nun, came from Italy and the police released her into her sister's care. She works at the orphanage now, helping take care of kids who have no one."

"Is she a nun, too?"

"Chip couldn't find anything to confirm that. But she lives with the nuns and has done so for the past fifteen years." He kissed her forehead. "Maybe one day we'll go to Italy so you can meet them."

She poked him in the chest. "You will never be able to stay away from Shilah that long."

He gathered her into his arms. "You never know." Stroking her hair, he asked, "Are you okay?"

"It's like sleeping with the light off. As long as you're here, I can do it. As long as you're here, I can handle anything."

He turned her face to look at him. "Please never ask me to leave again."

"I won't," she said, smiling. "We're having a baby."

"Mmm." He took her lips and nothing was said for some time. All the bits and pieces from her past fit together like squares of a quilt to make it complete. And that's the way she felt—complete in a way that surprised her. There was no wonder anymore. She knew exactly who she was and the enormous price her father had paid to have her. His life was fraught with fear and that was the biggest price of all.

It was her life now and fear was not a part of it. She had Cadde and a baby on the way. That was what real life was about—loving and living. Against her will, a niggling doubt surfaced. Cadde hadn't said that he loved her. It hadn't ever bothered her before so why was it bothering her now?

A baby changed everything and she wanted it all, just like a fairy tale. She held on to what she had, though—Cadde in her arms and in her life. Would their marriage be like her parents' relationship? Would Cadde be unable to love her the way Angela couldn't love her father? No, Cadde had said they were different and they were.

But the niggling doubt remained.

THE NEXT DAY THE PREGNANCY was confirmed. Jessie and Cadde were beside themselves with joy. The baby was due in early May. Jessie was unprepared for Rosa's reaction. She screamed, she cried, she laughed and immediately went to town to buy yarn to start knitting baby things. Even Myra was happy for them. Jessie lived in a bubble of happiness and nothing and no one was going to burst it. Not even her doubts.

Mirry was much better and Gavin removed the doughnut. It gave them a chance to talk.

"I'm sorry, Jessie, about the bill. It got mailed by mistake."

"It's fine, Gavin. You saved Mirry's life."

"I shouldn't have said what I did about your husband. I was way out of line and I apologize."

"Thank you, but I was thinking, for all concerned, that I need to find another vet."

"Jessie, please don't do that."

She looked into his worried eyes. "I have to. Please understand."

He sighed. "I do." They hugged briefly. "I wish you all the best, and I hope we can remain friends."

"That would be nice."

They parted as friends and Jessie was happy about that.

TWO WEEKS LATER SHE WAS in town and stopped by Cadde's office, as she often did. Chance and Kid were with him.

"Oh, sorry, I didn't mean to interrupt."

"You're not interrupting," Cadde said, and got up and kissed her.

Kid snapped his fingers. "Wait a minute, Jessie, I have something for you."

Cadde groaned, his arm tightening around Jessie. "I don't even want to imagine what that might be."

Kid came rushing back. "I thought you could put this on your Suburban." He handed her a bumper sticker.

Jessie stared at it. In big blue letters was written:

Baby and Boobs on Board. For a moment she was speechless.

Cadde jerked it out of her hand. "She's not putting that on her vehicle, you idiot."

"Why not?" Kid wanted to know. "It's fun. It's a laugh. Doesn't anyone around here laugh anymore?"

Chance looped an arm over his brother's shoulder. "Let's go and I'll explain tact versus tacky to you."

Jessie took the sticker from Cadde, walked over and kissed Kid's cheek. "I'll think about it, and thank you for thinking of me, boobs and all."

"Now there's humor." Kid pointed a finger at Cadde.

For the first time Jessie felt like a Hardin, a real member of the family.

After the brothers left, Cadde said, "You're not putting that on your vehicle."

She lifted an eyebrow at his stern tone.

"Please don't put that ridiculous sticker on your car."

"That's better." She went into his arms and his hands trailed from her back to her pinned-up hair. "Oh, no, mister, I have a lot to do today." She pulled back. "I have to decide on a color for the baby's room. I'm thinking creamy pale yellow. What do…" Her hair tumbled down her back and Cadde's lips blazed a path from her ear to the corner of her mouth. "Cadde, oh…Cadde."

She forgot about colors. She forgot about everything, but the man holding her, kissing her, driving her crazy. As she gave herself up to a fun afternoon she thought there had to be love in this much happiness.

There just had to be.

SEPTEMBER FADED INTO OCTOBER. Cadde asked that she think about stopping her volunteer work at the center until after the baby was born. She agreed. She didn't want any stress in her life.

She felt she owed it to Fran to tell her in person. As she suspected, Fran was happy for her and wished her only the best. Jessie stopped short when she was leaving Fran's office. Nina stood in the hallway, within earshot of Fran's door. Had she heard what Jessie had told Fran?

"It's not what you think." Nina immediately went on the defensive.

"I'm not thinking anything. I'm just surprised to see you."

Fran came up behind Jessie. "The counselor that Nina and Vernon are working with told Nina to leave when Vernon gets in one of his moods."

"That's what I did," Nina said rather hotly. "He didn't hit me and he wasn't drunk."

"I'm glad you found a way to work things out."

"No, you're not," Nina snapped. "You have no idea what my life is like."

Fran intervened. "Jessie has been nothing but nice to you. What's with the attitude? Every time you come in here you ask for Jessie."

"I'm sorry." Nina wrapped her arms around her waist and Jessie saw she was trembling. "I'm on edge. I need a cigarette."

"Cathy might have one, but you know the rules. You can't smoke in here. You'll have to use the patio."

Nina turned and walked off.

"What did I do?" Jessie asked, rather befuddled at Nina's reaction. "She seems to hate me."

"I think she's jealous because you seem to have it all."

"Me?" Jessie asked, more confused than ever. "She doesn't know anything about my life."

"She wants to be like you, beautiful, composed and in control."

Jessie wanted to laugh at the description. She wasn't in control of anything and any composure she had was pure strength of will.

Fran turned her toward the door. "Go home and don't worry. You know the women here have big problems."

But Jessie did worry and she discussed it with Cadde. He was just glad she wasn't going back to the center. As the days passed she forgot about Nina and concentrated on getting ready for the baby. Cadde kept saying it was too early and she needed to slow down. Against every instinct in her, she took his advice. But she couldn't resist the occasional outfit or toy. Mainly because she spent a lot of time in baby stores. Rosa had knitted enough blankets to last the baby's lifetime.

Cadde and Kid painted the baby's room. She wasn't allowed to smell the fumes. One wall was a soft yellow and another a pale mint-green. They had to paint the yellow wall four times before they got it the color she wanted.

Kid pointed the roller at her. "This is it, woman. I'm beginning to look a little yellow."

They all laughed and Jessie knew this was what it was like to be a part of a family—a real family.

NOVEMBER ARRIVED BEFORE they knew it. Cadde wanted to spend Thanksgiving at High Five ranch so she could meet all of his extended family. Rosa and Felix went to visit Felix's sister in San Antonio. They hadn't seen their families in years. Myra reluctantly agreed to go with them.

Meeting so many people at one time was overwhelming, in a good way. Everyone was so nice, especially Aunt Etta and Uncle Rufus. They made her feel welcome. They made her feel at home. She met Chance's wife, Shay, for the first time and they instantly formed a connection. They planned to meet for lunch one day.

She was drawn to the kids like a magnet and she carried Skylar's and Cooper's one-year-old son around as long as he would let her. Soon he wiggled out of her arms to play with his cousins.

She wondered what her and Cadde's child would be like. Would he or she be a little terror like Caitlyn's twins? Or angels like Maddie's kids? Or sweet and adorable like Skylar's daughter Kira? Or spunky like Darcy?

At that moment she caught Cadde's eyes across the room. He smiled, walked over and kissed her cheek. She yearned to hear "I love you" but what he said was, "Having a good time?"

She couldn't believe how much the lack of three little words could hurt. It wasn't important, she told herself.

But she couldn't explain it to her heart.

CHAPTER TWELVE

CADDE HATED SHOPPING. He bought his shirts, jeans and boots from the same store. It was easier that way. These days he found himself shopping more than usual, mostly in a jewelry store. He was buying Jessie an engagement ring for Christmas and it had to be the right one. After looking until his head was spinning, he settled on a platinum round cut diamond to match her wedding band.

While he was looking, he couldn't help but notice all the Christmas decorations and an idea came to him. This Christmas would be special.

He walked through the back door with a smile on his face. "Rosa, where's Jessie?"

Rosa closed the oven and wiped her hands on her apron. "In the living room. We're having pot roast for supper."

"Smells good."

Rosa stared at the silver wrapped gift in his hand. "It's a little early for Christmas."

"It's never too early."

Rosa's eyes narrowed. "You two aren't going to miss supper again, are you?"

They'd gotten caught up in the moment a lot of evenings and missed suppertime. Then they'd sneak downstairs to eat what they could find—just the two of them. He found he liked it that way.

"If we're…busy, you and Felix go ahead and eat. We'll eat later."

"Whatever makes you and Miss Jessie happy. I'm just so excited about the baby." She reached for something on the counter. "Look what I made today."

Cadde gazed at the tiny yellow booties. "That's very small."

"Baby's feet are tiny like a doll's."

He didn't know. He'd never been around babies, especially newborns. Not for the first time he realized how fast his life was changing and soon he would be trying to put his son's or daughter's feet into those booties. The thought was a little frightening and the magnitude of what he and Jessie had created hit him—a life—a tiny helpless baby who would depend on them totally.

"Yeah," he murmured. "That's a little scary."

"Pooh." Rosa waved his nervousness aside. "After a couple of days, you'll handle that baby like a pro."

Cadde nodded and walked through the dining room to the living room. Jessie was standing in front of the big windows, her arms outstretched. Stepping off several spaces, Mirry under her feet, she turned and stretched out her arms again. Her stomach pushed against her knit top. Her clothes were getting tight but he thought she never looked more beautiful. She was absolutely glowing.

"What are you doing?"

"Cadde. You're home early." She rushed to him and

he looped one arm around her, the other he held behind his back. He kissed her slow, taking his time.

She ran her fingers through his hair. "Now that's a welcome home kiss."

"What are you doing?"

"Oh." She glanced toward the window. "I'm trying to figure out how big of a tree we can get in here. We have an artificial one in the attic that Rosa and I put up every year. After Daddy died, I didn't even bother, but this holiday I want a huge live one, maybe seven, eight or nine feet tall." She poked him in the chest. "And you and I are going to pick it out tomorrow so we can get it up early. What do you think?"

"Sounds good to me." He held out the gift. "I bought something we can put on it."

Her eyes opened wide and she sat on the sofa, ripping off the paper with a you-shouldn't-have look. He sat beside her. When she saw the silver baby ornament her mouth formed a big O.

"Read what it says on it." He could hardly contain his own excitement.

"Baby's First Christmas in Mommy's Tummy. Love, Mommy and Daddy." A tear slipped from her eye.

"Jessie."

"I'm not going to cry." She swiped at her cheek. "This is so beautiful and…wait a minute. Did Barbara buy this or did you?"

"I did and I had the jeweler engrave those words on it."

"Oh, oh." More tears followed.

He pulled her into his arms and kissed her forehead. "Are you okay?"

"Yes. Why?"

"You haven't been weepy for days and I'm concerned because you haven't said a lot about your mother."

She sat up. "There's nothing to say and I can't do anything to change the past. So I've decided not to stress over it."

He touched her cheek, needing to reassure her that he was always here for her.

Fingering the ornament, she said, "We're going to put this at the top of the tree right under the angel because it's so special."

"Mmm."

"Do you think we can get the tree tomorrow?"

"Sure. I'll come home about four."

She looked at him with those black eyes, so deep, so gorgeous. "You're coming home early a lot these days."

"Chance and Kid are taking up the slack."

They were finally drilling in Louisiana after a ton of paperwork and permits. Kid was at the site and Chance flew over every couple of days. Cadde wasn't on the phone constantly wanting news and he wasn't fretting about the cost or the probability that they could hit a dry hole. He had more important things on his mind.

"Really?" She arched a dark eyebrow.

"They need to get more involved because I'm taking time off when the baby comes."

The eyebrow lifted higher. "You're joking."

"No. I mean, we're going to have a newborn in the house. Have you ever held a baby?"

Her eyes grew thoughtful. "No."

"I haven't, either. We're going to have to take classes or something."

"I have some dolls in the attic. I can get one down and we can practice."

"I'm not playing with a doll."

"Oh, please," she begged, mischief in her voice. "I could take a picture for Chance and Kid, even the board. Wouldn't that be lovely?"

"No." He tickled her rib cage and she lay back, laughing and squirming. He pressed her into the cushions and supper was forgotten once again.

THE NEXT MORNING, JESSIE FED Bambi and watched her for a while. The fawn was getting big and fat. She needed to cut back on the cream. Her animals were all fat because she wanted them to be well cared for. The horses were in the pasture and when they saw her they would trot to the barn for feed. Her animals had always brought her so much joy, but now her interest was elsewhere. She wasn't planning on taking on any new ones just yet. Her focus was on Cadde and the baby.

After lunch she had Felix get Christmas decorations out of the attic. She sat in the living room sorting through them. Pausing over ornaments in a box, she wondered if her mother had wanted to buy her a first Christmas ornament. Probably not. Her father hadn't, either. They were too busy thinking of ways to claim her.

Jessie sat back on her heels. That sounded bitter and maybe she was—just a little. What type of woman had a baby for money? Those who desperately needed it, she answered her own question. And some no doubt had changed their minds, like Angela. Once giving birth and holding her child, she couldn't let go. Jessie understood that.

But there was still a niggling doubt. What if Cadde…

Her cell buzzed and she quickly clicked on when she saw the caller ID. "Hey." His strong, familiar voice buffeted all the concerns in her head. "What are you doing?"

"Sorting through decorations to put on the tree."

"I'll be home earlier than four."

"Ah, you can't wait to see me."

"That's about it." She heard him laugh. "Bundle up. It's getting cold outside."

She clicked off and leaned against the sofa. Cadde had told her he wasn't good at voicing his feelings, so she was going to take him at his word and go on the way he made her feel—over-the-top crazily happy in love. The doubts were just because she was so inexperienced. She felt Cadde's love in his touch, his kiss and in the way he held her. It was there and it was enough.

Picking out a Christmas tree was going to be so much fun. She'd try her best to not be too indecisive. She… Her cell buzzed again.

Her heart skipped a beat because she thought it was Cadde again. It wasn't. She clicked on.

"Hi, Fran."

"Jessie, I hate to bother you."

"It's no bother. Is anything wrong?"

"Nina's been here for over a week. Vernon beat her up pretty bad. Toby has bruises, too."

"Oh, no."

"Nina's reached the end of the line and she had to make choices she didn't want to. She met with a lawyer who does work for the center. She filed for divorce. We're trying to get her and the kids to her aunt's. Is that plane ticket offer still on the table?"

"Sure. I'll get my credit card." She scooped up Mirry and headed for the stairs.

"Vernon's lawyer got him out of jail this morning and he was served with divorce papers. I want Nina out of the way before he goes into another rage."

"Why can't they keep him locked up?"

"He has rights and just happened to get a lawyer who's a bigger slime than he is."

Jessie found her purse, fished out her credit card and gave Fran the information she needed.

"Thanks, Jessie." A long pause ensued. "Nina asked for you."

"Fran, I don't think…"

"I know, sweetie, don't worry about it. I'm getting her out of Houston as fast as I can."

Jessie sat on the bed for a minute and wondered how someone's life could get so screwed up. She could only hope Nina made better choices for her children's sakes.

Her cell buzzed and she clicked on with a smile.

"I just passed a Christmas tree lot and they have big trees. Want me to get one?"

"No."

He must have heard the sadness in her voice. "What's wrong?"

She told him about Nina. One of the things she loved about their relationship was that they could talk about anything.

"Put it out of your mind because it seems as if the authorities have it handled."

"Okay."

"I'll be there soon."

Noticing the time, she changed into heavier jeans, but found she couldn't button them. "You're really growing, my precious," she said to her stomach, and reached for a maternity pair she'd bought. They felt much better.

She slipped on a white cashmere turtleneck sweater, socks and leather boots. That should be warm enough.

Mirry lay on her pillow and Jessie leaned down. "Cadde and I are going to get a Christmas tree. I'll be back later."

Mirry gave a low bark.

"Okay." Jessie went into the bathroom for soft dog biscuits and gave Mirry two. The dog would chew on those for a couple of hours.

When she reached the kitchen, Rosa gave her the once-over. "You look so happy."

"I am." Jessie smiled.

"I bought a quilting frame at the craft store. I'm going to set it up and see if I can make a quilt for the baby."

Jessie didn't know how to tell her that Aunt Etta was also making a quilt, so she didn't. She placed a hand on her stomach. This kid was going to be one warm baby.

"Felix is at the barn and I'll close my door so you and Mr. Cadde can have time alone."

"Thanks, Rosa, but Cadde and I are leaving as soon as he gets here."

"Oh, then I'll have lots of time."

Jessie went into the living room to continue sorting the decorations. Myra interrupted her.

"Hey, kiddo, how's happy-ever-after going?"

"Great. We're getting a tree this afternoon."

"You got the big guy to go Christmas tree shopping?"

"Yes, and don't say anything rude."

"I'm not, and I personally want to thank you and Cadde for getting Mama off my back about marriage and babies."

"You're welcome, but love is really wonderful. You should try it."

"Please." Myra dragged out the word. Jessie could see her with her hands on her hips and that kick-ass expression on her face. "I'll pass. Oh, I have to go, court is reconvening. Call when you're in town and we'll do lunch."

After she clicked off, she thought about the *L* word again and wished she hadn't. Placing her hand over her stomach, she refused to think negative thoughts. She wasn't letting anything ruin this day.

Studying the decorations, she decided to do the tree in red and silver to match the ornament Cadde had bought. They would have to stop for some ribbon. He was going to love that.

As she pushed boxes aside with her foot, there was a knock at the door. It had to be Cadde. He must have bought a tree. If he did, she was going to be so mad. She swung open the door with a smile, not even looking through the peephole. A man she didn't recognize stood there and he reeked of alcohol.

"Are you Jessie Hardin?"

"Who are you?" she asked instead of answering, and had a sinking feeling this wasn't good. She tried to slam the door, but the man pushed it aside.

"Please leave," she said, backing up.

He followed. "Where's my wife?"

"Who?"

"My wife, Nina."

Everything clicked into place. This was Vernon, but Jessie didn't know how he'd found her or why. "Please leave," she said again.

Before she realized his intention, he slammed a fist into her stomach. Pain ripped through her and she staggered backward. "Rosa!" she screamed.

"I'll teach you to mess with other people's lives. Nina's a bitch stealing money out of my wallet for cigarettes. The house is a mess and when I say anything she spouts nonsense about her rights. Nonsense she got from you. She has no rights, you bitch," he yelled, his face red. "I'm gonna teach you a lesson."

Jessie kicked him in the shin and tried to get away, but he was too fast.

"Rosa!" Jessie screamed as Vernon drove a fist into her face. The blow knocked her to the floor and Vernon kicked her in the side with his shoe. "Rosa!" She held her hands over her stomach to protect her child, curling into a fetal position. "No, no, not my baby."

He was about to drive a shoe into her face when Rosa came running. "Get away from her, you bastard!"

Vernon ran out the door and Rosa fell down beside her. "My *niña,* my *niña.* What happened?"

"Call Cadde," she gasped, her stomach cramping. "Call the police."

Felix came charging into the hallway with a gun, but it was too late.

CADDE WHISTLED AS HE DROVE down the highway. He hadn't done that in ages. This afternoon he was going to buy the biggest tree he could find. This was going to be a Christmas they'd never forget.

His cell rang and he clicked on.

"Mr. Cadde, come home fast. Miss Jessie's hurt bad."

"What!"

"Just come home. I have to take care of Miss Jessie."

What the hell? He weaved in and out of traffic, breaking the speed limit. An ambulance, siren blasting, passed him. He followed it all the way down the county road. As it turned into the Murdock house, Cadde's stomach roiled with a sick feeling. Something was terribly wrong. Was Jessie having a miscarriage? Was she okay? Rosa had said Jessie was hurt. How could that be? He'd just talked to her.

The ambulance roared up to the house and Cadde was out of his truck, running for the opened front door before the ambulance could even stop. His heart lurched into his throat as he saw Jessie lying in a pool of blood. No, no, no! The right side of her face was black and blue. Oh, my God! Rosa cooed to her in Spanish and Cadde's knees gave way and he fell down by her.

"Jessie."

"Cadde." Her right hand clutched for him and he grabbed it.

"The baby," she cried.

"What happened?" he asked in a voice he didn't recognize.

"She said the man who beat her was Vernon Lynch," Rosa replied. "If I hadn't stopped him he would probably have killed her."

What! They'd just talked about the man. Anger rose up in his chest.

The paramedics rushed in.

"She's three months pregnant," Cadde told them.

"Let's get her to a hospital." They put a C-collar on Jessie and loaded her onto a stretcher.

Jessie clutched his hand tighter. "Don't leave me."

"I won't," he told her. "I'm right here."

He crawled into the ambulance with her, never letting go of her hand. A paramedic checked her vitals and Cadde covered her with a blanket, still holding on to her hand.

The paramedic examined her. "She's going into premature labor. Hurry, Cal," he shouted to the driver.

"Take a deep breath, Mrs. Hardin. Try to calm down."

Cadde rested his face against hers. "Stay calm. I'm right here."

"The baby," she cried in a voice that squeezed his heart.

"Shh. We'll be at the hospital soon."

"I thought it was you. That's why I opened the door."

"Shh."

Cadde knew it only took minutes but it felt like hours. Once they reached the emergency room things happened fast. They whisked her away to labor and delivery. He held her hand the whole way, trying not to look at the blood on the blanket. *Please don't let her lose the baby,* he prayed as they rolled her into a room.

Dr. Barnes came in. "Cadde, would you like to step outside? We have to try and stop the labor and stabilize Jessie."

"No," Jessie yelled. "I want him here."

The doctor nodded and Cadde rested his face against hers again. "I'm here." The doctor and two nurses worked. Cadde averted his eyes, but not before he saw the bruises on her side. Oh, my God! The man must have kicked her. Son of a bitch! He gulped a breath and focused his concentration on Jessie. Their hands were locked on the bed and he saw how bloody they were. His chest contracted in pain.

He was aware of machines being pushed into the room. The nurse attached a monitor to Jessie's stomach and his eyes swung to the machine. A heartbeat was visible on it. He looked at Dr. Barnes. "Is that…"

The doctor pulled down his mask. "It's the baby's heartbeat. We've stopped the labor but the baby is still in distress. Now we wait and pray."

Cadde couldn't take his eyes off the monitor, the little beeps and the uneven line that signaled their baby was still alive. "Jessie, look." He pointed to the screen. "There's our baby's heartbeat."

"Oh, Cadde." Tears slipped from her eyes.

"Shh." He cradled her face.

Cadde knew they'd injected something into the IV to relax Jessie. She slowly closed her eyes. He reached for his phone to call Chance. For the first time in his life he truly needed a connection to family. He needed support. After he'd told Chance what had happened, he called Rosa and Felix to let them know how things were going. Then he laid his face against Jessie's and watched the monitor.

Jessie woke up. "Cadde."

"I'm here." He kissed her bruised face. "I'm watching the fetal monitor." They both stared at the machine and Jessie dozed on and off.

Cadde was beginning to hope the worst had passed when the monitor shrilled and nurses ran in. He gazed at the blips as they became slower and slower and then a solid line slashed across the screen. A nurse turned it off.

No!

"No!" Jessie screamed. "No, no!"

He caught her face and held it, his forehead against her.

"Cadde, make them turn it back on. Cadde," she begged, and his heart broke into jagged tiny pieces.

The doctor rushed in. "We have to get her to an operating room."

"No." Jessie began to fight and he had to hold her down.

"I'm sorry, Cadde," the doctor said as politely as he could. "The baby didn't make it."

"Cadde." His name echoed around the room with a chilling effect. The nurse injected something into the IV and Jessie went out. Then they quickly rolled the bed from the room. Cadde stood there as if someone had ripped out his heart. He couldn't breathe. He couldn't do anything but feel the pain.

Their baby was gone.

Jessie.

Chance walked in and pushed him into a chair. "Cadde."

"The baby died," he said in a voice that seemed to come from deep in his gut.

"Oh, God. I'm sorry." Chance looped an arm around his shoulder. "Where's Jessie?"

"In the operating room."

"I'm sorry, Cadde…"

"That lunatic killed our baby. There are bruises on her side and on her face. The bastard must have kicked her." He stood in an angry movement because he could no longer remain still.

Chance patted his shoulder. "The police are outside. Do you feel like you can talk to them?"

"Damn right." He hit the door and found two deputies in the hallway.

"Have you caught him?"

"We have an All Points Bulletin out on Vernon Lynch. We have someone at his house and at his workplace, but, no, we haven't located him yet."

Cadde pointed a finger in the deputy's face. "You find him or I will."

Chance laid a hand on his shoulder. "Cadde." He wanted to knock it away. He didn't need sympathy. He needed them to find Vernon Lynch.

The other deputy pulled a small notebook out of his pocket. "We spoke to Rosa Delgado and she said the man didn't break in. Mrs. Hardin must have let him in."

"She thought it was me," Cadde yelled. "I talked to her about five minutes before."

"Does she know Mr. Lynch?"

"Jessie counsels his wife, trying to get her out of that abusive relationship. I don't know why Lynch targeted my wife or felt a need to destroy her. Or how in the hell he got our address."

"I can answer that," a woman said.

Cadde turned to look at a woman he'd never seen before. "I'm Fran Turlock from Rachel's House. I'm so sorry, Mr. Hardin."

"Do you know anything?" was all he could say.

"After I heard what had happened to Jessie, I called Nina and she confirmed what I feared for a while now. She's obsessed with Jessie. She wants to look like her, wear nice clothes like her and have a loving husband like her."

"How does she know anything about Jessie? Isn't everything supposed to be private? First names only?"

"Yes, but with the media and the internet it's very hard to keep that privacy."

"What the hell are you talking about?"

"When Roscoe Murdock died, there was a photo of

him and Jessie in the paper. Nina recognized her and began searching on the internet for anything she could find about Jessie. She had a folder full of information on Jessie and Vernon must have found it after he was served divorce papers."

"Did Nina Lynch have a physical address for Mrs. Hardin?" a deputy asked.

"I asked her that. She said all she could find was a county road and that Roscoe Murdock had built a castle for his daughter."

"Son of a bitch!"

A nurse walked by and glared at him, but he didn't care. He wanted to physically hurt someone. How insane could this get?

Cadde got in the woman's face. "You knew the woman was obsessed with Jessie. Why in the hell didn't you do something?"

The woman paled and Chance pulled him away. "Let's go to the waiting room. Jessie will be out soon."

He let Chance lead him away because he knew at any minute he was going to lose it. Anger was bubbling in his system like a pot of water about to boil over.

Plopping into a chair in a waiting area, Cadde buried his face in his hands. "Jessie's probably not going to remember about the baby. I'll have to tell her all over again. How am I supposed to do that?"

Oh, God, how am I supposed to do that?

CHAPTER THIRTEEN

CADDE SAT WATCHING THE CLOCK and trying to keep his anger under control. He paced, ran his hands through his hair, jiggled the change in his pocket, but nothing eased the pain.

"Kid will be here any minute," Chance said.

Cadde didn't answer. The walls were closing in and he wanted to run until he had no breath—until there was no more agony.

Dr. Barnes came into the room in blue scrubs and Cadde rushed to him. "Everything went well and Jessie's resting comfortably. They'll take her to a room in a few minutes. She'll be out for a couple of hours." The doctor pulled off his surgical cap. "I don't know if you want to know, but the baby was a boy."

A choked sob clung in Cadde's throat and the pain seared all the restraints he had on his temper.

"Do you want the fetus or do you want the hospital to take care of it?"

What! For a moment he was paralyzed with what the man was saying. He cleared the sob in his throat. "We'll bury him. Jessie would want that." He wasn't letting his son be thrown away like garbage.

"I'll let the appropriate people know." The doctor fiddled with his cap. "I'm sorry, Cadde."

Cadde nodded, unable to speak.

"Are you okay?" Chance asked, placing a hand on his shoulder.

Again, he didn't respond.

Chance's cell rang and he turned away to talk to Shay.

Cadde hit the door leading to the stairwell, taking them two at a time.

"Cadde!" Chance shouted, but he kept running. Once he reached the ground floor, he called for a cab and went to Shilah. He took the private elevator up to his office. Losing no time he opened the safe on the wall and pulled out Roscoe's Glock with a clip. He jammed a clip in. Laying the gun on his desk, he sank into his chair.

Vernon Lynch was going to die tonight.

Chance and Kid burst through the door. They looked at him, the gun and then at each other.

"What are you doing?" Kid asked.

"I'm going to put a hole right through Vernon Lynch's dead heart."

Chance and Kid exchanged glances again.

"Cadde..." Chance moved toward him.

Kid grabbed the gun. "I'll do it. You have to get back to the hospital. Jessie's in her room and she needs you." Kid took a breath. "I'll kill the bastard for you and I can do the time."

Chance yanked the gun from Kid. "Nobody's killing anybody. The police haven't even caught him yet."

Abruptly, Cadde stood and his chair went flying backward. "Give me the gun. I have to do this for Jessie. When she wakes up, I have to tell her that bastard is dead."

"No," Chance replied. "You're not thinking straight."

Cadde leaped on his brother, determined to get the gun. Kid jumped on his back and they wrestled around the room, the gun slid beneath a table. Furniture crashed to the floor and two steel bands held him down. Then he did something uncharacteristic of a Hardin.

He cried.

Tears rolled from his eyes and his chest shook with sobs. The steel bands wrapped around him now in soothing comfort. Nothing was said for some time.

Cadde finally stood, wiping at his eyes, his momentary insanity gone. "I have to go to Jessie."

Chance drove him back to the hospital. Rosa, Felix and Myra were there. Jessie was still out.

"Where have you been?" Myra asked in a harsh whisper.

He didn't answer. Instead, he pulled a chair to Jessie's bedside and took her lifeless hand in his. He waited.

Everyone waited.

Suddenly, Jessie's dark eyelashes fluttered open. They were filled with undisguised pain. His stomach clenched.

"I…I'm…not pregnant anymore, am I?"

He swallowed. "No."

A guttural cry left her throat and she pulled her hand away.

"Jessie."

"Please leave."

"I'm not going anywhere," he said.

Myra walked up to the bed. "Hey, Kiddo…"

"Everybody get out of my room," she screeched, and a nurse came in.

"Mrs. Hardin, are you okay?"

"Make them leave."

The nurse looked at Cadde. "Maybe it's best if y'all give her some time."

Against every instinct in him, he did, but he didn't leave. He sat in a chair outside her door just in case she needed him. But she didn't. For three days, he sat and only left to shower and change his clothes. Jessie remained distant, not talking to anyone.

Fran from Rachel's House came by and told Jessie about Nina's obsession with her. She said she was sorry, but once again Jessie only stared ahead, not looking at the woman.

Outside in the hall, Fran spoke to him, "I'm sorry, Mr. Hardin. I feel so responsible."

"Yeah, me, too. I wish I had come home earlier. I wish Jessie had never gotten involved with Rachel's House, but she's so loving and giving…" He closed his eyes. "She's shutting me out. She's shutting everyone out."

"It's going to take time."

"Yeah." He drew a heavy breath, wanting to blame the woman, but he couldn't. Now his only concern was Jessie and her well-being.

"Ms. Delgado called me. I offered to testify against Vernon Lynch when they catch him and the trial is set."

"I've been so concerned about Jessie I wasn't aware

she was working on the case, but I hope they put that bastard away for life."

"I'll do everything I can to make sure he stays locked up."

"Thanks."

He sat in the chair, his elbows on his knees, his hands clasped between them. Chairs scraping against the tile drew his attention and he noticed Chance and Kid sitting beside him. They didn't speak. They didn't need to. They were his support system and he felt he was going to need them more than he ever had in his life.

CADDE HAD HAD THE BABY taken to a funeral home in Giddings. When the doctor released Jessie, he told her about the burial arrangements. All she said was, "Tell Rosa to bring my black suit."

He knew she was suffering and he didn't know how to reach her. Kid drove them to Shilah, where Chance waited with the helicopter. Myra was there, too, wanting to help Jessie. But Jessie wouldn't look at anyone nor did she speak. She sat in the chopper, drawn into herself, away from a world that had caused her so much pain. In her hand, she clutched the yellow booties Rosa had made.

Chance landed the chopper in High Cotton's country cemetery. Cadde planned to bury the baby next to his parents. His mother would have loved a grandson. A hearse was waiting and a small grave had been dug. He had asked Chance to tell the family to stay away. Jessie couldn't handle a crowd and he wasn't sure he could, either.

The cold north wind blew as he stepped off the chopper, scattering dried leaves against his feet. He tried to help Jessie off the aircraft, but she wouldn't let him touch her. Her reaction cut deep and he didn't understand it.

They gathered beneath two stately cedars that had stood the test of time. A man from the hearse carried a small coffin about the size of a shoe box and placed it in the ground. Cadde was numb as a preacher from a nearby church read a verse from the Bible. After he finished, Jessie knelt and dropped the booties on top of the box. He thought she'd cry, show some emotion, but she didn't. She stoically walked back to the chopper and boarded.

He'd given Chance instructions to drop them at the house. He hoped once she was home she'd cry and release her pent-up grief. But there was no emotion as she walked into the house and headed for the stairs.

"I don't know how to reach her," he said to Rosa.

"Mr. Cadde, she's grieving. She needs time to get over this tragedy."

"But why is she shutting me out?"

Rosa shrugged. "I don't know, Mr. Cadde. She's hurting."

Cadde walked toward the stairs to see if Jessie was okay. He opened the door and came to a dead stop. Jessie was throwing clothes into a suitcase.

"What are you doing?"

"I'm leaving."

"What?"

She turned to him, her eyes wild, her hair even wilder. "I'm the reason our baby is dead."

"What are you talking about?"

"Who do you think put the idea of marriage into Daddy's head?" She poked a finger into her chest, her voice rising with each word. "It was me."

"What?" He felt a sucker punch to his gut.

"When he knew he wasn't going to live much longer, he kept saying if I had any problems or fears I was to call Cadde. He'd take care of everything. Cadde's a good man." She zipped the suitcase and swung back. "I saw this as my opportunity to get what I wanted. I've been in love with you since the first time I met you, but you never noticed me. And I wanted you to notice me, so I said to Daddy that I might as well be married to you, and he was off to the races with the idea just like I wanted him to."

He frowned. "Did you suggest how to split the shares?"

"No, Daddy did that." She lifted the bag to the floor. "Even after the marriage you kept your distance, but since I'm like my manipulative father I offered you another deal—a baby for Shilah. How could you refuse? It was what you wanted, control of Shilah. But you can't make someone love you no matter how much you manipulate the situation, as my father found out. You've never loved me. When we were at High Five and I was playing with the kids, you walked over and kissed my cheek. All I wanted to hear was 'I love you.' But you didn't say the words. You never have."

"Jessie."

"Oh, please, do not say them now and insult my intelligence."

He just stared at her, trying to take in everything she was saying. But he just saw a woman overwrought with pain.

"So you see, Cadde, I brought all this misery on us because I tried to play God." She picked up the bag. "You'll receive divorce papers in the mail and the transfer of the share into your name." She pushed past him.

Divorce papers.

I've loved you from the first moment I met you.

You've never loved me.

You've never loved me.

It took a few minutes for him to come to his senses and then he tore from the room. In the kitchen, he asked Rosa, "Where's Jessie?"

Tears filled Rosa's eyes. "She's gone, Mr. Cadde. I don't think she's coming back. She told me to take care of Mirry."

Cadde ran into the garage, but Jessie's Suburban was gone. Jessie was gone. Where would she go?

He reached for his cell and called her number. It rang and rang and then went to voice mail. She wasn't taking his calls. Dammit!

He dashed back to the kitchen. "What's Myra's number?" Rosa gave it to him and he quickly dialed.

"Myra, Jessie's left and she might be coming to you. Call me when she gets there."

"She's in no condition to drive."

"I know. That's why I'm so worried. Just call me."

"Wait. They arrested Vernon Lynch. He was hiding out at his sister's."

Somehow that didn't make anything better. Jessie was gone. He had to find her. Running to his truck, which was still parked in the front yard, he prayed he could catch her. He watched the highway for the silver Suburban, but there wasn't a sign of it all the way into Houston.

Not knowing what else to do, he called his brothers and told them what had happened. They immediately started searching, too.

Frustrated, he called Myra again and again, but she still hadn't heard from Jessie. As the darkness ushered in colder temperatures, he drove home, hoping Jessie was there.

She wasn't.

Chance and Kid called. They hadn't found Jessie, either, and wanted to come out to be with him. He told them no. There was nothing they could do, and he had to be alone to face his own shortcomings.

Where would Jessie go? He racked his brain. *Gavin.* Grabbing his phone, he searched for the man's number. Jessie had spoken to Gavin from his phone so it had to be on his cell. He finally found it and called the number.

"Gavin, this is Cadde Hardin."

"Oh, I heard about the attack on the news. Is Jessie okay?"

"Jessie's very depressed and she left. I can't find her. Have you heard from her?"

"No. Not a word."

Cadde wasn't sure he was telling the truth. "Man, don't lie to me. If she's there, just say so. Jessie needs medical attention."

"I wouldn't lie about something like that."

By Gavin's concerned voice Cadde knew he wasn't lying. "If she calls or shows up, please let me know. We're all worried about her."

"I will."

Cadde walked into the living room in a daze. Where was Jessie? Falling onto the sofa, he stared at all the decorations Jessie had strewn about. This was his fault. How could he have never said the words? Didn't she feel them?

It didn't matter about the arranged marriage. He didn't care whose idea it was. Their relationship had gone way beyond that. They'd bonded in a way he had never thought possible. All he thought about was her. He couldn't even focus on the oil business. Didn't she see that?

Running his hands over his face, he knew the answer. Jessie was in so much agony she wasn't thinking. The pain was all she could feel. She blamed herself because of the arranged marriage and his failure to say the words she wanted to hear—the words that would have made their marriage valid were never said.

Oh, God.

He didn't know how long he sat there, but it had grown completely dark outside. He called Myra once again. Jessie wasn't there. In her state of mind, where would she go?

A whimpering caught his attention and he looked down to see Mirry at his feet. "Hey, Mirry."

The dog whimpered louder.

He knew that sound. "You have to pee. Okay." He picked her up, carrying her out the front door. Mirry played around in the grass and he noticed blood drops on the tiled porch. His stomach clamped tight. But, just then, his attention was riveted by headlights at the entry. *Jessie!* The car drove on and he sank down on the step. It wasn't Jessie.

Mirry whimpered again, not liking the colder temperature, and Cadde settled her in his lap.

Was Jessie ever coming back?

She had to. He couldn't survive without her.

JESSIE RAISED HER HEAD from the steering wheel and stared out at Blue Bell Creamery in Brenham. What was she doing here? It was late and the ice cream company was closed, but she could see lights inside.

Her father had brought her here many times as a child. She loved homemade vanilla and refused to try any other flavors. Her father had said she was stubborn. And she was—stubborn, manipulative, controlling. That's why she'd lost everything. She'd forced Cadde into marriage. She'd forced him into having a child. And now she suffered the ultimate punishment— the loss of her child. The loss of Cadde.

She couldn't think about it. She wouldn't allow herself to. It would kill her. And she had to be alive to feel the pain.

Starting the car, she drove toward Houston alone

in the darkest of nights. She wasn't afraid. There was nothing left to fear.

She checked into a hotel and people stared at her bruised face, but she ignored them. She slept for two days. When she woke up, she didn't know where she was and then it all came flooding back and she screamed into a pillow to stop the vivid nightmare.

After a moment she went through the motions of taking a shower and then ordered food even though she wasn't hungry. Forcing herself to eat, she wondered what she was going to do. She couldn't see Cadde. It would be too painful and they had to make a clean break. She had to let him go. The thought didn't even faze her. She was an awful person and he'd be better off without her.

With that concept firmly in her head, she called her lawyer, Hal, and had him file for a quick divorce. She also gave Cadde control of Shilah.

He'd earned it.

Pacing her room, she plotted what she needed to do next. She had to get away. But where? She could call Rosa or Myra, but they'd just try to change her mind. There had to be someone who would help—someone who would understand and not ask questions.

She picked up the house phone.

Within thirty minutes she opened the door to Hooter Caldwell.

"What is it? Oh, Jessie, your face."

"It'll heal." She didn't want to talk about her bruises or what had happened.

"Why are you in this hotel?"

"I need your help."

He removed his hat, chomping on his cigar. "Sure, anything. I heard—"

"Don't say it!" she shouted. She couldn't hear those words.

"Okay." He gave her a strange look.

"I need money."

"Jessie, honey, you have more money than I do."

"Cadde would know if I accessed my account. I've already used all my cash for the hotel and I want to be gone before Cadde finds out where I am."

"Jessie, go home. Talk to the man."

"Are you going to help me or not?"

He scratched his balding head. "I suppose. I'd do anything for you."

"Find out who my aunts in Italy are and their address."

One shaggy eyebrow rose. "How am I supposed to do that?"

"Chip at Shilah has all the information. You just have to get it."

"Cadde will be there and he's not stupid."

"But you're sneaky just like Daddy and I know you can find a way."

"Jessie, you're looking mighty pale. Why don't you take a nap and think about this first."

She clenched her hands at her side. "Get me the information."

"Okay, okay. Don't get upset."

"I'll also need a plane ticket to the town and some extra cash."

Hooter sighed. "You're asking a lot, Jessie. I wish you'd…"

"If you don't want to do it, I'll…"

"Now wait a minute." He plopped his hat on his head. "I'll see what I can do."

"Thank you."

"Hooter?"

He turned back. "If you tell Cadde, I'll never forgive you."

After Hooter left, she lay down and fell into a deep sleep. Four hours later she woke up, disoriented. It took a moment to get her bearings. She trembled, forcing memories away. A tap at the door had her scrambling to look through the peephole before opening it.

Hooter walked in and handed her a manila envelope. "There's the information you need including an open-ended return ticket—first-class."

"Thank you, Hooter, but I don't know if I'm coming back."

"What? Everything Roscoe built for you is here."

She placed the envelope on the bed. "My father built everything for himself—not me. He never thought about me or my feelings. It was all about him and having control. And, sadly, I'm just like him."

"I've never seen you like this, Jessie. Roscoe worshipped you."

"Like a statue in a closet."

Hooter removed his hat and scratched his head. "That's mighty bitter."

Jessie bit her lip to keep the trembling inside. "Thanks for everything you've done. I appreciate it."

"Call Cadde. He hasn't returned to work yet so getting the info from Chip was a snap."

"I'll repay you."

"Don't worry about it. Call your husband."

Jessie, feeling pressured, walked over and opened the door. "Thank you, Hooter."

The man left without another word.

She felt so tired, but she had to keep going and find a way out of Houston. But she would need her passport. It was in her father's study at the house. How did she get it without anyone seeing her?

Maybe she'd sleep and a plan would come to her. And that's what she did—until morning. After showering and dressing, she used her credit card to rent a car. She'd be long gone before Cadde could have it traced. An hour later she was headed for the house. It was Thursday and Felix always bought feed early on that day. She parked away from the entrance, but she could see Cadde's truck. How did she get past him for her passport?

She pulled her cell out of her purse and dialed the office. "Hi, Barbara, this is Jessie."

"Uh…Jessie…uh…"

She could hear the sympathy in the woman's voice and nausea rose in her throat. "Is Cadde there?"

"Uh…no…he's at home."

"Would you please let him know that I'm coming into the office?"

"Um…sure."

"Thank you."

Within minutes Cadde's truck tore out of the driveway and she drove slowly toward the house. Now she had to get past Rosa. She parked away from the kitchen so Rosa wouldn't see her. Since Cadde had just left she was betting the alarm system was off. Slowly, she inserted her key into the lock on the front door. It opened smoothly without a siren going off. Good!

For a moment she froze in the entry as that awful afternoon flashed through her mind. No, no! She forced it away and hurried into her dad's study. Kneeling, she opened the bottom drawer and pulled out her passport. Mirry appeared, wagging her nub of a tail.

"Oh, Mirry." She gathered the dog into her arms, kissing her face.

"Mirry, where are you?" Rosa called.

Jessie shrank beneath the desk, holding the little dog.

"Mirry?" She could hear Rosa going up the stairs.

"Bye." She kissed the dog's face and ran for the front door. It didn't click behind her, but there wasn't time to correct that. As she backed out, she saw Mirry on the porch. Tears stung the back of her eyes, but she didn't cry. She couldn't.

Driving away from everything she loved, she knew beyond a shadow of a doubt that she was the daughter of scheming, conniving Roscoe Murdock.

CHAPTER FOURTEEN

"ARE YOU SURE IT WAS JESSIE?" Cadde asked Barbara.

"Yes, Cadde, she said her name and I know her voice."

He glanced at his watch. "It's been over two hours and she's not here."

"I'm sorry. I don't know what else to tell you."

Cadde went back into his office, trying to figure out what had happened. Why wasn't Jessie here?

Chance and Kid walked in.

"Hey, any word on Jessie?" Kid asked.

He'd forgotten to call his brothers to let them know that Jessie had called. "She said she was coming in, but she hasn't arrived."

"That's odd," Kid replied.

"Yeah," Chance added. "Why would she come here instead of the house? She's hardly ever here unless it's to check her mail and lately you've been taking that home to her."

They were right. Jessie never came into the office anymore. If she was in town, she'd call and they'd meet in the apartment.

"Sounds like she wanted you out of the way," Kid remarked.

"That's it." Cadde snapped his fingers. "She wanted me out of the way." He grabbed his phone and called Rosa.

"Rosa, is Jessie there?"

"No, Mr. Cadde, but something strange happened."

"What?"

"I was looking for Mirry and I found her on the porch. The front door was opened and Mirry was gazing down the road, barking."

"I'll be right there." He jumped up and reached for his jacket.

"Don't you want the figures on the Louisiana well?" Kid asked, and he knew Kid was trying to distract him. But there was no distraction from this maelstrom of sadness.

"Leave it on my desk. I'll look at it later."

Since it was noon, the traffic was heavy. He weaved in and out of cars and trucks in a hurry to get home. He didn't know what for. Jessie wasn't going to be there. She'd made it very clear she didn't want to see him and had gone to extreme measures for him not to be there. That was just another hurt his loaded heart couldn't take.

But Jessie had come home for something. What?

On U.S. 290 he got behind an 18-wheeler and couldn't get around the big vehicle. He tapped his fingers on the steering wheel as cars zoomed past on his left—seemed like the whole world was headed into Houston to Christmas shop.

Finally, he turned down the county road and sped to the house. He hurried inside. "Rosa, I think Jessie came home. Is anything missing?"

"No, Mr. Cadde, and I looked. Everything's the same."

"Thanks."

He made his way into the living room and fell onto the sofa, rubbing the palms of his hands into his eyes. He needed to know she was okay—that she was safe. The enormity of the situation hit him like a sledgehammer to the head. He hadn't protected her. She'd been attacked by a Doberman and a lunatic, all on his watch. He'd let Roscoe down, but most of all he'd let Jessie down. How did he live with that?

A whimper sounded at his feet and he saw Mirry looking up at him. Lifting her, he cradled her in his lap. "Did you see Jessie today?"

Mirry wiggled her knob of a tail. "You did, didn't you?" Rubbing the dog's head, he got lost in his thoughts. Why hadn't Jessie taken Mirry? That surprised him. Maybe she was going somewhere the dog couldn't go. Where, though?

He went round and round the situation, but nothing made sense. How could they go from deliriously happy to this agonizing numbness?

"Cadde." Chance stood in the doorway. "Are you okay?"

"No. I'm never going to be the same again." He was honest. That was all he could be.

Chance took a seat in a wingback chair, placing his hat on the arm. Cadde had no idea where his own hat was. Jessie used to tease him about that. He'd never had a problem with his Stetson until he moved into the house for good. Jessie had his emotions turned upside down and he didn't care about his hat—only her.

"Kid and I did something I need to tell you," Chance said.

For a moment he was shocked someone else was in the room and then he saw Chance's worried face.

"What?"

"We had a marker made for thc baby's grave."

"Oh."

"They'll set it tomorrow if it's okay with you. It's small, just something to mark the site. We put Baby Cadde Hardin and the date on it."

Cadde held a hand over his eyes and felt a gut-wrenching pain. He waited for it to subside. "Thanks. I appreciate that. Jessie will, too, if she ever comes home."

"She will. She's just hurting right now."

He clenched his hands between his knees. "Did you tell Shay you loved her when you were dating?"

"Uh…yes, and she told me she didn't love me."

"I remember. You were devastated."

"Yeah. That's not something a man wants to hear." He took a breath. "I never told Jessie I loved her."

"Why?"

"I don't know. I was stupid." He jerked his hands through his hair.

He took a moment to try and understand his own behavior. "Everything was going so great. We were happy, yet…"

"Remember how Mom used to make you say it?" Chance asked. "When she'd drive us to school, Kid and I would jump out yelling, 'Love you, Mom.' She'd have to call you back and make you say it."

"Yeah, and if Dad was there he'd say, 'Leave the boy alone. He doesn't have to say anything he doesn't want to. You're making a sissy, a momma's boy out of him.'"

And there it was—the big ugly monster in the room—his father's opinion mattered. He'd grown up trying to be like him—tough, strong, with his feelings bottled up inside. He was a man and didn't have to bow to a woman's will. But in the end his father had bent over backward to please his mistress.

Cadde buried his face in his hands. "Oh, God. I'm just like him—emotionally unavailable."

"No, you're not."

He raised his head. "Do you ever remember Dad saying 'I love you' to any of us?"

Chance studied the Oriental rug on the floor. "No."

"There was always 'That's my boy,' 'I'm proud of you,' 'You did good,' but not ever 'I love you.' How could I emulate a man like that?"

"Cadde…"

"Jessie needed to hear those words. I felt them, but that's not enough. A woman wants to hear them. That's why Mom pushed us to say the words she never heard from him. Son of a bitch!"

Silence followed—a heartrending quiet.

"I've lost her, Chance," he said in a low voice.

"No, you haven't. You hit a big bump in the road, but you'll both get through this—together."

"Jessie blames herself for the baby's death."

"Why would she do that?"

"She's the one who put the idea of marriage into Roscoe's head. She said…she's been in love with me ever since we met. But I couldn't see *her* for Shilah. And now…"

"Oh, man."

"The boardroom antics were to get my attention. I never saw the signs, so she thought of the baby deal. She's blaming herself for manipulating the circumstances and she feels the loss of our son is her punishment."

"You don't blame her, do you?"

"Hell, no, but she wouldn't listen to me. She's out there—" he waved a hand toward the window "—all alone in a world that's not safe."

"Just give her time," Chance suggested, standing. He looked down at all the Christmas decorations. "You might want to get rid of this stuff."

Cadde got to his feet. "I have a baby's room to undo, too. I don't want Jessie to see it when she comes home."

Chance gave him a hug. "Hang in there, brother."

"Thanks for the marker."

"Anytime." Chance headed for the door and stopped. "The Louisiana well is right on track. No problems yet and the office is running smoothly, just in case you wanted to know."

"Thanks."

Cadde sat in the living room until midnight, dozing on and off, waiting for Jessie to come home. He trudged up to bed. He slept in his old room, not able to sleep in the master bedroom without Jessie.

Almost asleep, he heard Mirry whimpering. He

picked her up and placed her on the blanket. She was missing Jessie, too.

Jessie, please, come home.

THE NEXT MORNING JESSIE WAITED for the divorce papers so she could sign them. When they arrived, she scribbled her name without allowing herself to think. She had the hotel courier them to Hal's office and then he'd send them to Cadde for his signature.

Their marriage was over.

At ten she was on a plane for New York. She had to wait several hours, curled up in a chair, for her flight to Rome. Her aunts, Teresa and Margaret Martinez, worked in an orphanage on the outskirts of the city. She had no idea what she was going to find across the ocean. Her aunts didn't even know she was coming. All Jessie knew was that she had to get away and make some sense of her shattered, broken life.

Before she boarded the plane, she called Myra and left a message. It was simple: *I'm fine. Please don't search for me.* She didn't want the people who cared about her to worry.

A man who sat beside her in first class wore a Stetson and cowboy boots. She avoided looking at him. He was too vivid a reminder. She'd left her hair down to cover her bruised face. Suddenly, she felt hot and weak and had to take a couple of deep breaths. She should have eaten something.

"Ma'am, are you okay?" the man asked.

"Yes. I'm just a little nervous about flying. Thank you." She curled up and turned away from him, hoping the weakness would leave. Her hair fell forward, covering her face. Exhaustion consumed her and she fell asleep. When she awoke, she saw that a blanket was around her.

The man's long legs were stretched out with his boots crossed one over the other. They were sitting in the first seats. She guessed that's why he was here, 'cause he needed leg room. He was tall like… No, no, no! She couldn't think his name. She'd fall apart.

She went back to sleep. The stewardess woke her when she served food. Jessie tried to eat, but nothing tasted good to her. She could feel the man's eyes on her, so she shifted away to her own thoughts and her own private hell. But sleep eventually overtook her.

A long time later the stewardess gently shook her. "We're fixing to land. Buckle up." Jessie had lost track of time. She didn't even know what day it was. Nor did she care. When the plane landed, the man quickly grabbed his bag and joined the exit line.

Jessie watched as if from a distance. Slowly, she got to her feet, the weakness returning. Somehow she made it through customs, even managed to change her money into euros. There was so much confusion, people speaking Italian and wanting answers. She just wanted to lie down and close her eyes. Someone directed her to a cab and she crawled inside.

"Dove vuoi andare?" the man asked.

She had no idea what he'd said, but she dug in her purse for the address and showed it to him.

"Sì. Benvenuti a Roma."

The white cab took off at a dangerous speed. Jessie held on to the door. A busy ancient city flashed by so different from the world she'd left. Soon there were stone houses with English ivy growing up the sides, clothes hanging outside on a line, people on bicycles and everyone seemed to be shouting or gesturing.

The scenes faded in and out as dizziness assailed her. She tried to focus on the hilly Italian countryside of pines, orange and palm trees but couldn't. The man braked to a sudden stop and she saw the big stone structure attached to a church with a bell tower. Children played in a courtyard.

The man flung out an arm. "The good sisters. You nun?" He said the words in English.

She shook her head, not wanting to talk to him. Not having a clue what to pay, she handed him some euros, hoping it was enough.

"Grazie. Grazie." He happily nodded his head and she got out, clutching her bag. The temperature was chilly and felt good. The cab zoomed away and she stared at the cold, foreign building that had to be hundreds of years old.

What was she doing here?

Her eyes went to the bright blue sky and her head spun. Dizziness gripped her and suddenly she was falling, falling onto the cobblestones. And everything went black.

"CADDE, I'VE HEARD FROM Jessie!" Myra shouted, charging into the living room.

He was immediately on his feet. "When? What did she say?"

"I was in court so she left a message saying she's fine and not to search for her."

"But she's not fine."

"I know that and you know that, but it seems Jessie has to grieve alone. I say let's give her some time."

He gritted his teeth and against every instinct in him he said, "Okay."

"I had the police on the lookout for her vehicle."

"And?"

"They got a call from the Marriott Hotel that a silver Suburban had been parked in their garage for several days. It's Jessie's."

"There's no charge on her credit card for that. She must have used cash."

"Yes. She checked out two days ago."

Cadde eased onto the sofa. "Since she left the vehicle behind, I'm guessing she took a flight somewhere."

"That's my guess, too. I could continue checking, but I'm going to leave that up to you. Personally, I think we have to give her time and I believe she'll come home."

"I...uh..." Cadde wanted to find her as soon as possible, but Jessie didn't want to see him. She'd made that very clear. Giving her space and time was the hardest thing he'd ever had to do, except for losing his child. He drew a deep breath. "Okay. Tell the hotel I'll pick up the car."

Before Myra could leave, his cell buzzed and he reached for it. "Damn, thanks, Arnie."

Slipping the phone in its case, he said to Myra, "I had Arnie, one of the accountants, checking credit card purchases. A charge for a rental car came through on

Jessie's. That's how she came to the house undetected."
He sighed.

"Cadde, I'm sorry."

"I know. I have to believe she'll come home."

That afternoon he called Kid. They brought the vehicle back to the house and parked it in the garage, in
her spot, waiting for her return.

THE DAYS PASSED SLOWLY for Cadde. He didn't have the
mind-set to go back to work. Chance and Kid were
doing fine without him. He went into town and bought
the biggest Christmas tree he could find and placed it
in the window where Jessie had wanted it. As he stared
at the baby ornament in his hand, his throat closed up
and he had to force himself to hang it high on the tree.

Jessie would be home by Christmas and then they'd
decorate the tree like they'd planned. He sat in a stupor,
waiting, Mirry at his feet. She followed him everywhere
these days. He fed her, took care of her just like Jessie
would want. He also tended to her other animals. He
thought of letting the fawn go, but Jessie might want to
see her one more time.

Rosa and Felix watched him from a distance and he
knew they thought he was losing his mind. Maybe he
was.

The day he received the divorce papers he lost it.
Kid brought them out and Cadde tore the document
along with the transfer of one share into shreds and
burned the pieces in the fireplace. He kicked the furniture and threw a vase. Kid tackled him as if they were

playing football and Felix rushed in. They tried to hold him down.

"Mr. Cadde, please," Felix begged.

Cadde relaxed, took a deep breath and sat up. "Sorry," he muttered, and staggered to his feet.

Kid looped an arm across his shoulder. "Let's go paint the baby's room and put all the stuff up so Jessie doesn't have to see it."

"I don't have any paint."

"I brought it."

"What?"

"Yeah. The lady at the store said it was a popular color and whatever the hell it is, we're putting it on the wall."

"Kid…"

Before Cadde knew it, he was painting. The sweeping strokes of the roller eased some of the tension in him. The pale gold color was nice. They put the crib and the baby things in the attic and moved the bedroom set back in. The room didn't even look like it had been planned for a baby.

Kid left and Cadde returned to the living room, staring at the tree. He couldn't think about the divorce papers. All he knew was that he wasn't signing anything. Jessie would be home by Christmas.

He clung to that one thought.

JESSIE WOKE UP IN A STERILE-looking room. She lay on a metal-framed single bed. A stiff white sheet and a brown blanket covered her. There was a small dresser and a nightstand with a pitcher of water and a glass.

The walls were a gray stone, as was the floor. Sunshine poured in from a slim window.

Where was she?

A woman poked her head around the door. "Ah, you're awake."

"Where am I?"

"In an orphanage outside Rome."

"Oh." It all came flooding back and she gasped for breath as the pain hit her.

"Rest. Rest." The woman pulled the blanket up to Jessie's chin. "You've been very ill."

"Have I?"

"High temperature, so we called the doctor and he examined you." The woman stroked Jessie's hair. "You're Angela's daughter, *sì?* You look like her."

Jessie stared at the dark hair and the dark eyes of the woman. "Are you my aunt?"

"I'm Teresa, *sì.*" She nodded vigorously and rubbed her stomach. "You lose bambino, *sì?*"

No, no, no! Don't say that. She wanted to cry. She wanted to scream. She did neither.

"You rest. Doctor leave pills for you and you have to eat. Margaret and I will take care of you. Rest."

Teresa disappeared out the door. Jessie threw back the covers and tried to stand. The room spun. Weakly, she sank on the bed, noticing she was wearing a tan nightshirt. It was very plain, with no frill or lace.

Another woman dressed in a long black skirt and long-sleeved white blouse walked in and immediately ran to Jessie's side. "Child, what are you doing? Get back in bed." She covered Jessie, clicking her tongue.

"Teresa's bringing you some food. You have to eat. You have to heal."

"Are you Margaret Martinez?"

"*Sí.* I'm Sister Margaret."

She placed her hand on Jessie's forehead. "What are you doing here, child?"

"I don't know. I don't know."

CADDE SAT IN THE LIVING ROOM, Mirry in his arms, staring at the Christmas tree. He couldn't seem to force himself to do anything else. He just needed to know that Jessie was okay, but as each day passed he knew that she wasn't. And there wasn't a damn thing he could do about it.

Dr. Barnes's secretary called. Jessie had missed her appointment. There was nothing he could do about that, either. Except worry.

Suddenly, Myra came in and threw her purse into a chair. "Why in the hell don't you answer your cell?"

He lifted the phone from its case on his belt. "I forgot to charge it."

"What if Jessie calls you?"

Oh, God. How could he forget that? He placed Mirry on the floor and stood.

"Just wait a minute, big guy. I have some news."

"Jessie called you again?" He grew hopeful.

"No." Myra took a seat. "It's about Vernon Lynch."

Cadde stiffened.

"The D.A. won't let me work on the case because I'm too closely involved, but I'm pulling all the strings

I can backstage. I've talked them into going for murder one and the death penalty."

"Oh."

"Lynch came into this house knowingly and willingly to kill Jessie and the baby. I wanted to fry that bastard."

"Can you prove that?"

"Believe me, I was going to give it a damn good shot."

"Was?"

"Vernon Lynch hung himself in his jail cell about an hour and a half ago. I got here as fast as I could. I didn't want you to hear it on the news."

Cadde plopped onto the sofa. "Damn!"

"Even he couldn't live with what he'd done."

Cadde rubbed his hands together. Somehow the news didn't make him feel better. It didn't bring the baby back. And it didn't bring Jessie home.

All the pain was still there.

CHAPTER FIFTEEN

"I RECEIVED DIVORCE PAPERS," Cadde told Myra.

"What?" Her eyebrows knitted together in confusion. "Jessie took the time to do that?"

He shared what Jessie had told him before she'd left about being responsible for the baby's death.

"Oh, crap, this just gets worse." She looked at him. "Did you sign them?"

"Hell, no, and I don't plan to. I burned them."

"I used to not like you, but you're turning into a pretty decent guy. I thought you were after the money."

"Ever since I was a kid I dreamed of being in the oil business, not as a roughneck like my father, but someone in control, running the company. I guess money was part of it. Roscoe brought me into the office and for ten years I spent almost every day with him, learning everything I could. I had offers from other companies, but I turned them down. I liked working with Roscoe. He was different, hard to please, but he knew the oil business. I had no idea Roscoe was going to give me twenty-five percent."

"And a wife."

"Yeah." He ran his hands over his face. "That hit me like a blow."

"Why? Couldn't you see how Jessie felt about you?"

"Honestly, no. From day one Roscoe made it very clear I wasn't to mess with his daughter. I pretty much had that tattooed on my brain."

Myra's cell rang and she reached for it in her purse, turning it off. "I thought she was just infatuated with you. After Roscoe died, I took her to a few parties to..."

"You took my wife to parties?" He couldn't keep the anger out of his voice.

"Now don't get your nose out of joint, big guy. Jessie's never been around men her age and she needed to realize she was a desirable, beautiful woman. Guys were buzzing around her like deranged bees, but she didn't see any of them. It was always you."

He drew a deep breath. "When I was with her, she never showed any signs. We talked about Shilah and its future, but we never got into anything personal."

"Because she was scared. That's why she came up with that insane baby deal."

"We tore it up and got beyond that."

"I know. I wish I had some answers for you, but I don't. I'm just worried."

"Me, too." He jammed his hands through his hair. "I told you not to investigate further to give Jessie some space and time, but now I'm changing my mind. I have to know she's okay. I won't try to see her. I need to know."

"Okay." Myra got to her feet. "I was only waiting for the go-ahead." She swung toward the door. "I'll be in touch."

Maybe if he knew he could find some peace in his private hell.

JESSIE DIDN'T KNOW HOW many days had passed when she woke up again, but she was better. She wasn't hot or tired and her mind was functioning. Slipping out of bed, she found her clothes in the dresser and changed into jeans and a knit top.

She vaguely remembered a portly man with a black moustache examining her, Teresa bringing her food, brushing her hair, helping her down the hall to the bathroom and giving her a sponge bath.

The room did a crazy spin and she sank onto the bed, feeling weak. She glanced at the stone walls. What was she doing here? So far from home. If she was planning to outrun the pain, it hadn't worked. It was just as vivid as ever.

Teresa poked her head around the door. "Ah, you're awake."

"Yes, and I feel better."

"Good, you can come for breakfast in the dining room with the children."

"Oh, no, Teresa, please. I don't want to be around anyone."

"They're just kids and well disciplined."

"No, no, please." She wasn't ready to face the world, especially children.

"Okay. You have to leave this room soon, though. Sister Margaret will insist on it." Teresa walked closer. "I don't want to upset you, but since you had bruises we need to know if you were beaten by someone. We have to inform the authorities."

"No, no." She shook her head. "It was taken care of in the States."

Teresa eyed her. "You sure you don't want Mother Superior to call someone?"

"No, please. I'm hoping you'll let me stay here—to heal."

"You can tell me anything, Jessie."

"I know, and thanks. I just need some time."

"Sí."

Teresa left and Jessie scooted back on the small bed. She heard children's voices and stood to look out the window. Suddenly, a loud bell rang and children, single file, marched into the church. The boys wore black slacks and white shirts; the girls were dressed in black skirts and white blouses. They were all ages from six to sixteen.

Teresa rushed back in with Jessie's breakfast.

"Where are the children going?" she asked.

"To mass. We have mass every morning and I have to run."

"Teresa," she called. "What's the date?"

"December 23 and we're getting ready to celebrate the birth of Christ. The children are so excited."

Christmas. She pushed the thought from her mind.

"I don't know much about religion."

"It's not difficult." Teresa placed her hand over her chest. "You feel it in your heart, you know it in your mind—" she touched her forehead "—and you treasure it in your soul. We'll talk later."

Jessie kept watching out the window and saw Teresa flying across the courtyard. What were they doing in there? What was mass like? She gave up trying to figure it out and ate her breakfast. The homemade thick bread slathered in butter was decadent. Rosa had never made anything like this. *Rosa...home.* The memories seemed to trap her in a purgatory she couldn't escape.

The children's voices tempted her again and she returned to the window. The kids were laughing, running, playing. They were happy. How could that be in an orphanage? Maybe it had something to do with their religion.

Teresa rushed back in for the breakfast tray. "Try to walk some today."

"Could you spare a few minutes?"

"Yes, but not long. The children are out of school for the holiday and someone has to be with them."

"Where do they go to school?" Jessie was curious.

Teresa looked out the window and pointed. "There is the church, the classrooms, the dormitory, the office and we're in the sisters' quarters. The children live here until they're eighteen and then Mother Superior finds them a job so they can support themselves and live on their own. Some are adopted, some are not."

"Are...are there babies here?" Why did she ask that? It only made her think and she immediately closed her mind. It was still too painful.

"Ah, babies go quickly. Every couple who comes here wants a *bambino.*"

Jessie sat on the bed and wrapped her arms around her waist. Babies were something she couldn't discuss. "Please tell me about my mother."

Teresa lifted a dark eyebrow. "Is that why you came here?"

"I'm not sure. I'm just curious about her."

Teresa pulled up a metal chair. "She was *bellissima,* like you."

"I know. My dad had pictures of her."

"Did he? That surprises me."

"I didn't see the photos until after his death."

Teresa nodded. "That I understand."

"What was she like?"

"Angela was the oldest, fun-loving and impulsive. She feared nothing but poverty. When our father died unexpectedly, she went to work to help support the family."

"Stripping?"

Teresa's eyes opened wide. "You know that?"

"Yes, but little else."

Teresa seemed uncomfortable and shifted in the chair.

"It's okay if…"

"No, no." Teresa waved a hand. "Angela grew up fast in the strip clubs and I wanted to be like her, beautiful, seductive."

"But it didn't work out?"

"No, I got in with a bad crowd and did bad things… that's why I'm here to find some peace so I can live with myself."

"Did Angela find any peace?"

"Sadly, no. Mr. Murdock was older and she thought she could bend him to her will."

"What do you mean?"

Teresa shrugged. "She thought she could get the money and the baby."

"Oh." That shocked Jessie. "So she never planned to give me up?"

"No. Angela used Mr. Murdock because he had money, but she learned the hard way that nobody uses Mr. Murdock." Teresa took a heavy breath. "I'm not sure what kind of childhood you would have had with Angela. I loved her but she lived a rough life with many, many…you know. Our neighborhood was rough, too, and my brothers got into gangs. You were better off in Texas."

"My father…was very controlling, but loved me more than anything on this earth. Maybe a little too much." Jessie said that from the bottom of her heart, and she meant it. For a moment she hesitated in telling Teresa about her life, but the nuns had been so good to her that she had to speak the truth.

After she told Teresa the story of the guards and the protection, Teresa clicked her tongue. "How sad for you."

"I never wanted for anything but my freedom."

Teresa flung out her arms. "You're free now. You come all the way to Rome."

Jessie managed a half smile. "I think I was delirious with fever."

Teresa touched Jessie's hands. "Are you well enough to talk about why you came?"

Jessie shook her head. "Not yet." She wasn't strong enough to open up those feelings. She wasn't strong enough to face what she'd done.

"I have to go help prepare the meal." Teresa shoved the chair back against the wall and looked at Jessie.

"Angela loved you and she never gave up hope that one day her little girl would be with her."

"Thank you."

After Teresa left, Jessie watched the children and marveled how they found pleasure in a simple thing like kicking a ball. She wondered if she'd ever feel pleasure again or would there always be this emptiness inside her?

In the afternoon she grew restless and ventured out into the long hallway. She came into a large room with sofas and chairs, a TV was in one corner and in the other was a large Christmas tree. She gasped. Oh, no! She ran from the room and opened a door. Suddenly, she was in the courtyard with the children. They stared at her with soulful dark eyes but they made no attempt to approach her.

She eased onto a stone bench and enjoyed the sun on her face. The temperature was chilly, though. She wrapped her arms around her waist. One of the nuns clapped her hands and the children immediately formed a line and marched inside.

Religious statues were here and there. Jesus on a cross was at the front of the courtyard and another was of a woman in a white flowing robe with her hands out-stretched to three children at her feet. She'd read enough to know this was Mary, the mother of Jesus. The place had a somber but peaceful feel about it and she sat long into the evening.

The next day everyone seemed to be busy so Jessie explored on her own. There was a girls' dormitory and a boys', plus a babies' room. She didn't freak out. She just didn't go in. Mother Superior was in the office, but since Jessie couldn't speak Italian they couldn't converse, or so she'd thought. The elderly nun spoke broken English and Jessie found out Teresa had given up her room for Jessie and was now sharing with Margaret. She tried to talk to Teresa, but she was busy getting ready for Christmas Eve mass. The children had a special program and Teresa was in charge.

As Jessie prepared for bed, she saw the children file into the church again. They were dressed differently. The girls wore long gray jumpers with white blouses while the boys still had the black pants and white shirts, but they had donned black bow ties. They looked so cute.

She tossed and turned, unable to sleep. Slipping from the bed, she grabbed her clothes and put them on. She had no idea what she was doing or why she felt a need to go to the church, but that's where her feet took her. Her hand shook as she reached for the large wood-carved door lever.

The church was in darkness except for the flickering candles that seemed to be everywhere. She made her way down the side aisle to the back row. Some of the children were to the right of the altar, holding hymnals. Teresa stood beside them in a long gray dress.

A bell rang loudly and everyone got to their feet. The children began to sing. She glanced to the aisle and saw four of the older children in white robes. One held a huge cross. A priest dressed in gold robes stood behind them with baby Jesus cradled in his arms. They all marched in. When they reached the altar, the priest knelt and placed the statue in the nativity display on the left. Everyone joined in prayer.

Then the priest stood, made the sign of the cross and everyone took their seats as the mass began. Jessie sat, mesmerized, the whiff of incense comforting her senses. Everything was in Italian and she didn't understand the words but she felt them. The children sometimes sang responses and it was lovely. The people got to their feet to form a line to the front to receive communion. Jessie sat alone, unmoving, but she didn't feel as lonely.

When the mass ended, the priest took his seat and the children moved in front of the altar with Teresa instructing them. She noticed that black lace covered Teresa's head, and the girls' were also covered. She hadn't seen that earlier. All the women in the church had something on their heads and the nuns wore black veils.

An organ played and the children began to sing. Once again Jessie was mesmerized as the young innocent voices rang out with a message of faith, hope and love. She didn't need to understand the words; the sound was universal and it moved her in a way she hadn't expected. As the lovely notes filled her, her broken heart began to beat again and her closed mind opened. In the old, old church she admitted something to herself that she thought she never would.

I lost my child.

I lost Cadde's child.

Cadde.

Tears clogged her throat and she wanted to cry. She needed to cry. But she couldn't.

CADDE SAT ON THE FRONT PORCH, with Mirry in his arms, waiting for Jessie. It was Christmas Eve. She'd come home tonight because they had to decorate the tree. A cool breeze reminded him that the weather was getting colder. At 2:00 a.m. he went inside.

In his mind he knew Jessie wasn't coming home, but in his heart, he would never *ever* give up hope.

On Christmas Day he sat in the living room, staring at the tree. He talked to Aunt Etta, Chance and Kid and they begged him to come to High Five, but he wasn't in the mood to celebrate anything.

Myra came for lunch with her parents and she gnawed on him, too.

"Cadde, the tree is dying. I'll get Papa to take it out."

"Don't you dare." His stern voice stopped her in the doorway.

"You have to snap out of it." She walked back into the room. "Go upstairs, shower and shave."

He looked at her. "How come you haven't found Jessie?"

"The investigator is working on it, but it's a big holiday and a lot of people are off, including the investigator."

"Can't you twist his arm? Aren't you the fire and brimstone lawyer?"

She heaved a breath and he could see she wanted to say more than she did. "I got a court order to search airline records. We'll probably know something tomorrow."

"Fine."

Cadde leaned his head back on the sofa. This Christmas was going to be different—special. It certainly was different, all because of him and the traits he'd inherited from his father. If he'd just told Jessie how he felt, they would be together. They'd be sad because of the baby, but they would have dealt with it as husband and wife. Now Jessie was gone and he felt responsible, inadequate and angry.

Kid arrived in the late afternoon with a piece of coconut pie in his hand.

"What are you doing here?"

"Aunt Etta sent your favorite pie."

"Thanks, but I'm not hungry."

Kid placed the pie on the coffee table, sat on the sofa beside Cadde and propped his boots on the table.

Nothing was said for a few minutes.

"You do know that tree is almost dead?" Kid remarked. "You haven't watered it." Kid swung his feet to the floor. "I'll throw it into the back of my truck and get rid of it."

"Don't touch it."

"Come on, Cadde, you're killing me here." Kid flung out his arms. "Do something. Don't just sit there and stare at that tree."

"Go away, Kid."

Kid got to his feet. "I'm not going anywhere until you shave that stubble off your face."

"Go away, Kid."

"With you it's always the easy way or the hard way," Kid told him. "You can either go upstairs on your own or we can fight all the way. Your choice."

"Okay. Okay. Anything to get you out of my hair."

He lifted Mirry and went upstairs. Ten minutes later he came down in jeans and a T-shirt, cleanly shaven. Kid had his feet propped on the coffee table, eating Cadde's pie.

For a brief moment, a note of laughter pierced his numb heart. Kid was Kid, and his brother always had a way of making him laugh. The moment didn't last long.

"Thanks for the pie."

"Uh…" Kid swallowed a mouthful. "You said you didn't want it."

"I don't." Cadde resumed his seat. "Didn't you eat at High Five?"

"Yeah, but I'm not letting Aunt Etta's pie go to waste."

Cadde just shook his head.

"Let's watch a movie," Kid suggested. "You got any movies around here?"

"Yes, but I'm not in the mood, and don't try the easy or hard way again. It won't work."

Kid swung to his feet. "You're as stubborn as…"

"Dad," Cadde finished for him.

"You're nothing like Dad."

"Oh, but I am. I'm just like him."

"You resemble him, but you're bigger, taller and have morals. Not once did you cheat on Jessie during that sham of a marriage. Believe me, I know, because I had to put up with your grouchiness. Dad probably cheated on Mom from the get-go. So you're not good with the flowery words, but you show your emotions through actions. Jessie's going to realize that sooner or later.

Right now she can't see beyond the pain of losing the baby."

Cadde rubbed his hands together. "I lost a baby and…a wife."

There was nothing but silence.

"Okay, wallow in whatever misery you have to," Kid finally said. "Just call if you need anything."

"Thanks."

Kid stopped at the door. "Chance and I are flying to Louisiana in the morning. We're drilling deep like you wanted, but there are times I think we're going to hit China before the desired depth. Why don't you come with us and see the action?"

"I have to stay here," he murmured. "You and Chance can handle things."

After Kid left, he went outside to feed Jessie's animals. That was the only thing that brought him comfort. Winky was becoming a pest, braying and nudging him for more food. He couldn't seem to fill the donkey up, but he wanted them healthy for when Jessie returned.

And she would.

Eventually.

THE NEXT MORNING JESSIE went to mass again with the children and loved listening to them sing. Afterward they all gathered in the big room around the tree. She could now look at it without feeling that crippling pain. It was there, though, and she fought that sickening sensation.

The nuns passed out paper bags filled with candy and an apple and an orange. *"I dolci,"* the children shouted, excited as if they'd received a bicycle or some-thing equally expensive. Everything here was simple and down-to-earth and revolved around faith.

Later they gathered in the dining room for the noon meal. There was ham, ravioli, pasta, sauces, vegetables and panettone bread that was heavenly, plus milk or water to drink.

She finally had a chance to talk to Teresa about the room and Teresa said the nuns doubled up when they had guests. But Jessie decided she shouldn't be a guest and she shouldn't be a burden on the nuns. So she vol-unteered for work.

She swept and scrubbed the floors, helped in the kitchen and with the laundry. It was a bit of a shock to find there were no washing machines or dryers. The clothes were washed by hand on a board, hung out to dry and then ironed. Jessie had never ironed anything in her life but she learned. Sister Alice and two of the older girls did the laundry and they were glad of an extra pair of hands. They laughed at her a lot. Laugh-ter was universal, just like music.

At night she was exhausted and fell into a deep sleep, but before she slipped into oblivion, she'd see Cadde's face. She held it in her heart and in her mind, even though she knew she shouldn't.

CHAPTER SIXTEEN

Rosa was fussing at Cadde for not eating when the doorbell rang. He leaped off the sofa and yanked opened the door, hoping with everything in him that it was Jessie. Hooter Caldwell stood outside. Cadde's heart sank.

"Mornin', Cadde." Hoot had his hat in his hand, chomping on a cigar, which reminded him so much of Roscoe.

"Hooter." What was he doing here?

"Could I talk to you a minute?"

It had to be about Shilah and Cadde's absence from the office. He wanted to slam the door in his face, but as a business courtesy he thought he'd hear the man out and then slam the door in his face.

"Sure." Cadde led the way into the living room.

Hooter stared at the tree and the decorations on the floor. "Man, Christmas is over with."

Cadde sat on the sofa. "What do you want?"

Hoot's eyes were on Mirry lying beside Cadde. "What the hell happened to that dog?"

"What do you want, Hooter?" He felt he didn't need to explain anything.

"Is Jessie here?"

Cadde looked at the man. "No. Why?"

"From the tree and decorations I'd say she hasn't been here in a while."

"No. What about it?"

"Well, now—" Hoot eased into a chair and placed his hat in his lap with extra care "—I did something and it's been on my conscience."

"You don't have a conscience."

"When it comes to Jessie, I do."

Jessie. What did he know about his wife? The man was fixated on her. He knew that from the board meetings.

"What did you do?" Cadde thought he'd better get to the heart of Hooter's visit.

"Stay calm, okay?"

"What did you do?" Cadde asked with as much calm as he could muster.

"Jessie called me about four days after that man attacked her and she lost the baby."

Cadde curled his hands into fists. "What did she want?"

"Money and information."

"What?"

"You said you'd stay calm."

"Tell me what the hell you did."

"She wanted information on Angela's sisters and I paid the computer kid at Shilah for everything he had on Jessie's mother and her family. Jessie then wanted a plane ticket to the village outside Rome where they lived."

Cadde was on his feet, his calm forgotten. "You let her go to Rome all by herself? In her state of mind?"

"Jessie's pretty stubborn and I could see she was all messed up in her head. I begged her to call you, but she wouldn't."

"So you just let her go to Rome." Anger coiled through him, but something registered in his mind—something about the way Hooter had said Angela.

"Did you know Angela?"

"Hell, yeah. I was with Roscoe when he met her. I told him she was too young and that she'd take him for every dime he had, but he wouldn't listen. He was besotted." Hoot fingered his hat. "I thought Shilah would go under for sure, but I underestimated ol' Roscoe. He kept his money and the baby."

"Did either of you ever think about Jessie or her life?"

"That was Roscoe's business, not mine."

Cadde ran his hands through his hair. "Just get out."

Hooter stood with his hat in one hand. With the other he pulled a slip of paper from his left pocket. "Here's the address. Knocked me for a loop to find out Angela's sister is a nun and her other sister is at this orphanage, too."

He didn't take the paper. "I know where her aunts live. I just never imagined Jessie would go there, but you made it easy for a severely depressed woman to do that." He took a deep breath. "Get out, Hooter, before I hit you."

"Now, Cadde, I risked a lot coming here. You can remove me from the board and my investment in Shilah will be…"

"Get out," he shouted. "I don't give a damn about you and I don't give a damn about Shilah."

"I don't like the sound of that. Someone has to be at the helm to protect all our investments. I could take over..."

"Get out!"

Cadde paced in the living room, trying to control his anger. How could that old fool think he was helping Jessie? How could...

His cell rang and he answered.

"I know where Jessie is," Myra said.

"So do I. She's at an orphanage outside Rome."

"How do you know that?"

"An old friend of Roscoe's just dropped by. He helped her get there."

"And he's just now telling you this?"

"Yeah. Kind of blew my mind, too."

"Forget about him. I called the orphanage and Jessie is there. The woman who answered the phone spoke broken English, but when I asked about Jessie she said, '*Sì*,' and something about a laundry room. I gave her my number and asked for Jessie to call me—whether she understood me or not I don't know."

"Let me have the number."

"Cadde." There was a long pause. "Jessie went there for some sort of peace or maybe to feel a connection to her mother. Whatever it is she needs to do it on her own. She's feeling a lot of guilt over the forced marriage and the baby deal."

Cadde gripped his cell. "She didn't force me into anything. Please stop saying that."

"But Jessie feels it. Give her time."

"Myra..."

"I know it's hard, but she's okay and if she calls, I'll phone right away."

"Thanks. Oh, Myra, I just thought of something. Jessie came home for her passport. That's why Rosa found the front door opened that day with Mirry on the front porch."

"Makes sense now, but I would never have suspected Jessie of doing something like that."

"Me, neither. That just shows how depressed she really was." He gripped the phone. "Are you sure she's okay?"

"She's with her aunts and they'll take care of her."

"Yeah."

Cadde ended the call and hurried into Roscoe's study. Opening the bottom drawer, he pulled out the security box that held some important papers and Roscoe's and Jessie's passports. Roscoe's was there, but Jessie's was not.

His heart took another hit. He'd thought their marriage was based on trust and honesty. In her grief Jessie must have forgotten that. Why couldn't she have trusted him to understand about her part in the marriage arrangement? Why couldn't she trust him?

It took everything in him not to find the number of the orphanage and call. Since Jessie didn't want to talk to him or see him, he'd respect her wishes. But he had to show her how much he loved her and there was only one way.

He reached for paper and a pen. Placing it in front of him, he began to write.

THE DAYS PASSED QUICKLY for Jessie. She had ironing down to a fine art. The children's clothes were cotton and she went after wrinkles with a vengeance. Her time was getting better than the older girls. While she worked she didn't have an opportunity to brood. She was busy.

Her favorite thing was taking long walks. There were no towering trees like in Texas but the maritime pines and cypresses were lovely. All the people she met on her strolls were friendly yelling, *"Ciao,"* or *"Buonasera."* She'd nod and keep walking. In the distance she could see rows and rows of vineyards. The area was very hilly and rocky. Sitting on a rock, she gazed at the blue water of the Tiber River and soaked up the ambience of this ancient place.

As always, her thoughts turned to Cadde and she wondered if they were still married. Had he signed the divorce papers? She stared at her platinum wedding band and couldn't bring herself to remove it. She'd tried to force him to love her but she'd found that love couldn't be forced. It had to be there from the start. And Cadde had never loved her. He loved Shilah—not her. The loss of their child had made her realize the truth.

Maybe she had to come to this place for her penance, like Margaret and Teresa. She'd learned that Margaret had been raped by a gang member and he'd attempted to stab her to death. Bleeding severely she'd made it to a church and a priest had taken her to a hospital. From there the priest had found her a place to live, with an elderly Catholic couple. Margaret had attended church every day and when she graduated high school, she'd joined a convent.

Teresa's life had been riddled with turmoil, too. She

had been a stripper like Angela, got into prostitution and drugs. While she was on drugs she had an abortion. When she'd sobered up in a jail cell and realized the horror of what she'd done, she'd called Margaret for help. Now her life was devoted to the children no one wanted.

Everyone made mistakes and her parents had made huge ones. Jessie found the strength to forgive because she was no better. Manipulation was not a part of love.

IN MID-JANUARY, KID WALKED into the living room and threw his hat across the room. "Hot damn, Cadde, I have great news. The well came in big, better than we ever dreamed, oil and gas. You were right. Roscoe held on to those leases for a reason. Cadde, do you hear me?"

Cadde rubbed his hands together. "That's good."

"What? Why aren't you jumping up and down? Oh, crap, you still have that damn tree up. Cadde, come on, snap out of it."

"I have something to tell you."

"Cadde, are you listening to me? The Louisiana well came in big."

"I heard you the first time. Now listen to me.

"What?"

"I resigned as CEO of Shilah."

"What the hell?"

"I've appointed you and Chance as interim CEOs until the board meets the first week in February."

"I'm not working for anybody else, Cadde. I'll tell you that right now."

"You'd be the boss."

"I'm not working for myself, either. There's only one person to lead Shilah and that's you."

Cadde stood. "Please try to understand I have to do this. I have to prove to Jessie she means more to me than that oil company."

"Dammit, Cadde."

"I know you and Chance can run the company. You've been doing it for weeks. Don't let Hooter and the board hire some yahoo who'll run Shilah into the ground. Fight to remain CEOs, but it's up to you."

"Have you told Chance?"

"I'll call him as soon as you leave."

Kid picked up his hat from the floor. "I don't understand this. The oil business has always been your dream."

"Not anymore."

Kid placed his hat on his head. "Okay, you want us to fight. We'll fight. Hell, the Hardin boys do that better than anyone."

"Barbara will hand in my resignation at the board meeting. It will be the first order of business. If you want control, be there. If not…it's up to you and Chance."

"We'll take care of it." Kid glanced at the tree and decorations. "Throw the tree out and put away the decorations. For heaven's sake, get a grip on reality."

"I don't even know what that is anymore."

"Cadde."

He held up his hand. "Yes, I'm losing it if that's what you're thinking."

"What can I do to help?"

"Just leave me alone. And protect your investment in Shilah."

Kid turned to leave.

"One more thing. Fire Chip the computer guy."

Kid swung back. "Why?"

"He can be bought and someone like that shouldn't be working for Shilah." Cadde told his brother about Hooter and how he made it possible for Jessie to fly to Rome.

"That son of a bitch! I'll take care of it, Cadde. You don't have to worry."

Kid walked out with murder in his eyes. Cadde ran his hands over his face. He didn't want his brothers to lose what they'd invested in Shilah. Personally, he wasn't worried about losing what he'd worked his whole life for. He only worried about Jessie.

JESSIE WOKE UP TO SOMEONE screaming. It was faint but she could hear it. She padded to the door and opened it. Teresa ran by.

"Teresa," she called. "What's happening?"

"Go back to bed, Jessie. A pregnant teenage girl came in and she's giving birth. Sister Alice and Margaret are with her. I have to go."

Jessie went back into her room but she didn't sleep. She listened to the screams until they stopped and then she opened her door again, waiting for Teresa.

"Jessie, what are you doing still up?" Teresa asked when she saw her.

"Is everything okay?"

"*Sí*, mother and baby are fine. Sister Frances called

the adoptive parents and they will be here in the morning for the baby girl."

"The mother's giving the baby up?"

"*Sí*. That's why she came here. We don't ask any questions. We protect the child. It gives young girls another choice instead of abortion. The church is against abortion."

Teresa's face changed and Jessie knew Teresa was thinking about her own mistakes. Jessie hugged her.

The next morning she saw a couple leave with the baby. Just like that, four lives were changed and it stayed with her for a long time. It was sad, but uplifting, too.

Couples came quite often to the orphanage looking for a child. It was a long interview process, Teresa had told her, which ensured the child and family were suited to each other. When Jessie noticed a child missing from the playground, she knew the child had finally found a real home. Again, it was sad, yet uplifting.

That evening as Jessie hurried from the laundry room to help with the meal, Margaret stopped her.

"Could we talk, Jessie?"

She followed her into the courtyard. Everything was quiet because the kids were inside. They sat side by side on the stone bench.

"You've been here for a while, child, and your bruises have healed."

"Yes." Jessie touched her face. "I'm better."

"Are you strong enough to talk about what happened to you?"

"Uh…"

"The outward bruises have healed. Now you have to deal with the inner ones."

"Uh…" Jessie stared at the clenched hands in her lap, and before she knew it the words came tumbling out. She told Margaret about her life, her animals, her counseling, Nina, Vernon and Cadde. "You see, I tricked him, I knew his weak spot and I played on that. I'm an awful person."

Margaret patted her hands. "You're a very caring person."

"A caring person wouldn't trick a man into marrying someone he doesn't love."

"Did he say this?"

"No, I didn't give him time and I couldn't stand to hear the truth after…"

"Say it," Margaret urged.

"After losing the baby." Her stomach cramped and she fought to breathe.

Margaret gave her a moment. "Tell me about your husband."

"Oh, Cadde…he's thoughtful and kind, very serious, businesslike but once you reach his soft side he's like a big cuddle bear. He took excellent care of me after the Doberman attack. He started coming home earlier and earlier. He bought a special baby ornament and we were planning on putting up a tree when Vernon Lynch decided to take his frustrations out on me."

"This doesn't sound like a man who doesn't love you. He would be distant and spending more and more time away from you, *si?*"

"I suppose." Jessie recalled how Cadde had torn up

the baby agreement because he'd thought he'd hurt her. He'd told her he wasn't good at expressing his feelings. Oh, no! In her grief, could she have forgotten his words and his concerns? His touch? His strong yet gentle embrace?

But then, he didn't know what she'd done.

"I'm sure he hates me now that he knows the truth." She looked down at the burns on her hands from the iron. "Do you think Mother Superior would mind if I stayed here for a while longer?"

"You do not belong here, Jessie." Margaret patted her hands again. "It is time for you to go home and tell your husband how you feel. You're strong enough to do that now."

"Yes." She was. She missed Myra, Rosa, Felix, Mirry…and Cadde. But she hesitated, unsure of what waited for her so many miles away.

"Why did you come here, child?"

"You've asked me that before and I couldn't answer. I still can't. I don't have any other living relatives and in my agony, I guess I was coming to find comfort and strength from my aunts."

"We enjoyed meeting you and we don't have to wonder about you anymore. You're a beautiful young woman with incredible strength and I know, unlike your father and mother, you will find the happiness you crave."

She hugged Margaret, hoping what she said was true.

THE NEXT MORNING JESSIE was packed and ready to go. She said a sad goodbye to everyone, clinging to her aunts a little longer than she should have. The white cab roared to a stop and Jessie climbed in.

The children shouted, *"Arrivederci."* Jessie waved until she couldn't see them anymore and she realized she'd left a part of her broken heart in a place that seemed untouched by time.

Her flight arrived late in New York. The closer she got to home, the more she worried. While she waited she wondered if she and Cadde were still married. Had he signed the papers?

It was 5:00 a.m. when she arrived in Houston. She wanted to go home, but for her own peace of mind she had to do something else.

She had to face Nina.

CHAPTER SEVENTEEN

BY EIGHT THAT MORNING Jessie was in Amarillo. She'd slept on the flights so she wasn't tired. As she rode in the cab she had no idea what she was going to say to Nina, but she had to face her to deal with what had happened for her own sanity.

She'd charged her phone at the orphanage and saw she had lots of calls from Cadde, Myra and Rosa. She didn't listen to any of the messages—not yet.

Using her phone she tracked down Nina's aunt. She knew the name and the street and it was no problem to find the number. Information was easily available and Jessie realized how dangerous that was for demented people. There was no privacy anymore as she acknowledged to her detriment. All the security in the world didn't work if a person was determined to get in. Ironically, she'd opened the door for Vernon.

She should be afraid, but she wasn't. The fear that always had been there had been obliterated by grief. She was stronger now than she'd ever been and no one was going to take advantage of her good nature again.

The cab stopped at an older clapboard house with black shutters. The long front porch was enclosed with railing. Nina sat in a chair, smoking a cigarette. Jessie asked the driver to wait and she made her way to the steps. Climbing them, she thought of what she wanted to say, but nothing came to mind.

Nina was immediately on her feet. "I'm sorry, Jessie."

Suddenly, everything clicked. She wanted to hit the woman, scratch her eyes out, but she did neither. She wasn't a violent person. "Every time I tried to help you, you always said I didn't know what your life was like." She stepped closer. "Thanks to you, Nina, I know exactly what your life is like, blow by blow."

"I didn't know Vern was going to do that."

"You broke the honor code of Rachel's House and you put everyone's safety in jeopardy, mainly mine."

"I'm sorry."

"Don't say you're sorry. Get off your ass and do something about your life. Stop depending on everyone else."

The door opened and a middle-aged woman with short brown hair stood there. "Watch TV," she said to the kids behind her, and stepped out onto the porch.

"Hi, I'm Lois Winslow," she introduced herself.

"I'm Jessie Hardin."

"Oh, Mrs. Hardin, I'm so sorry."

"Yes. That seems to be the phrase of choice." She looked at Nina, but spoke to Lois. "Don't let her take advantage of you. She's good at working people, the system."

"I told her she has to find a job or get out. With Vernon dead, she has no reason to go back to Houston."

"Dead?" She was confused for a moment.

"He was arrested and he hung himself in his cell," Lois told her.

"Oh." Jessie was taken aback for a moment. "I didn't know, but it doesn't bring my baby back." Once again she glanced at Nina. "You took everything from me— my child, my husband, my life."

"I didn't. Vern did." Nina readily placed the blame elsewhere.

"You did." Jessie pointed a finger at her. "You talked about me, held me up as an example to your husband when you knew it was against the rules of Rachel's House."

"I…I wish…"

"Don't wish. Do something about your life. If you screw up just once more I'll make sure you never see your kids again." Jessie took the steps quickly, completely spent.

Vernon Lynch was dead. It froze her for a moment in vivid gut-wrenching pain and she took a deep breath and let it go. There wasn't anything else she could do about it. Her focus was now on Cadde…and home.

Her cell buzzed and she looked at the caller ID. It was Myra and she did something she hadn't been able to do in weeks. She clicked on as she slid into the cab.

"Jessie, Jessie? Is that you?"

"Yes, Myra, it's me." She put her hand over the phone. "Rick Husband Airport," she said to the driver.

"Oh, my God! Are you okay?"

"Yes."

"You have to come home. Things have gotten really bad."

"What do you mean?"

"Cadde resigned as CEO of Shilah."

"What?" Her heart missed a beat. "Why would he do that?"

"He hasn't been the same since you left. He just sits in the living room staring at that damn dead tree."

"What tree?"

"He put up a Christmas tree and has the baby ornament on it. Mama said he's losing his mind and I believe she's right."

"Oh, no." She closed her eyes for a moment. What had she done?

"Are you still in Italy?"

"I'm in Amarillo." She watched the dry, flat landscape slip by.

"What are you doing there?"

"I had to see Nina."

There was a long sigh on the other end. "Why do you make this so hard on yourself?"

"It's something I had to do. My flight is at ten-thirty and I'll be in Houston soon."

"There's a board meeting at one, and Chance and Kid are going to try and stop them from appointing anyone else. But you're the only one who can stop this."

"Are you a fan of Cadde's now?"

"He's a good guy. I just didn't see that before because I was trying to protect you."

"I can take care of myself."

"Kiddo, I believe you can."

"May I ask you a question?"

"Anything."

"Did Cadde sign the divorce papers?" She bit her lip as she waited for the answer.

"Kiddo, you were married to the man for months, what do you think?"

"I…I…" She closed her eyes and saw Cadde's face. "I think he tore them up."

"Yes, and then he burned them."

The ache in her heart eased. "Thank you. I'm at the airport. I'm on my way."

Jessie counted off the minutes, but everything took so much time. Hooter was not appointing another CEO. The man had wanted control of the company ever since her father had died. He'd even approached her father on his deathbed about taking over. The answer had been a resounding no.

She tried Hooter's cell. No answer. He was probably in a bar celebrating his victory over Cadde. She arrived in Houston at twelve and rushed to rent a car. She wanted to go home, but instead she had to deal with this insanity.

It was 1:05 p.m. when she took the elevator up to the boardroom. The door was slightly ajar and she listened to what was being said.

Kid was speaking. "I think we need to do as Cadde suggested. Chance and I will run Shilah until Cadde returns."

"Read the letter, Kid," Hooter said. "Cadde resigned. Kaput. He's out of here."

Jessie clenched her hands at her side.

"Hoot's right," Owen chimed in. "It's a resignation letter. It doesn't say anything about Cadde coming back."

"But in it Cadde is asking the board to consider

Chance and me to run the company as we have been since the tragedy."

"You boys have no business sense."

Something hit the table. "Read the numbers, Hooter, and tell me we don't have any business sense. The Louisiana well is going to put a lot of money in your pocket."

"You boys are good oil well drillers but when it comes to crunching the numbers you have no experience."

"Don't make me jump across this table and stuff that cigar down your throat."

"Calm down." That was Owen again.

"Everyone calm down." Chance joined the conversation. "Looks like you guys are holding all the aces here, but out of respect for Jessie and Cadde and everything they've been through I thought you'd be more understanding."

"We're not heartless." George Pettibone put in his two cents. "We're thinking about the company."

"Cadde's done a great job since Roscoe left us." J. T. Hardeson spoke up for the first time.

"I've never had a problem with Cadde," Hank Parker added.

"Me neither," Hub Gillespie said.

"You're losing the gist of the conversation. Cadde's not here anymore." Hooter was nudging Hub like he always did.

"Yeah, that's right," Hub veered in Hooter's favor as Hooter knew he would.

"Okay. It comes down to a vote." Chance continued in his easy, smooth-talking way.

"Wait a minute," Kid interrupted. "You're all fond of Jessie. Just remember you're going to eventually have to look her in the eye and explain your vote."

Someone coughed and a chair scraped the floor.

"I make a motion that we ignore the resignation letter and leave Shilah as is." Chance brought everything to a head.

"I second that." Kid followed suit.

Jessie had had enough. She walked in and "Jessie" echoed around the room as the men got to their feet.

"Jessie, honey, how are you?" Hooter asked.

"I'm fine. At least I was until I heard the conversation outside the boardroom door. You will not take control of my father's company."

"Now, Jessie, you know you mean the world to me."

"Yes, that's why I called you when I was so depressed."

"I was happy to help."

"I should have listened to you, but I was out of my mind with grief."

"Don't worry about it, honey."

"I'm not." She reached across the table, picked up the letter and tore it in half. Throwing the pieces in front of Hooter, she said, "Cadde Hardin remains as CEO of Shilah and he will come back as soon as he chooses. In the meantime, Chance and Kid will run the company. Is that understood?"

She looked straight at the man. She'd manipulated Hooter, just as her father had manipulated people. So she didn't blame Hooter for her actions. But if he thought she owed him any favors, he was sadly mistaken.

"Yes. I understand," Hooter replied, working the cigar in his mouth.

"Any objection?" She looked around the table and everyone shook their heads. "Do not call Cadde," Jessie whispered to Chance. She and Cadde had to talk without interference.

Walking out, she heard Kid say, "I think that's what you call a slam dunk, boys. Kaput. It's over."

Jessie took the stairwell, not wanting to speak to Chance or Kid or anyone on the board. Cadde was the only person she wanted to talk to.

She headed out of Houston toward home. She had no idea where her suitcase was. It was probably somewhere between New York and Houston. She'd check on it later. Her focus was now on Cadde and his welfare. She wasn't quite sure why she'd asked Chance not to call Cadde but they had to meet again with unguarded hearts and deal with all the pain inside without any warning, without time to think. Their emotions had to come from within.

Driving the small Chevy into the garage, she noticed her Suburban. How did it get here? She remembered leaving in it. Her fever had been so high she didn't remember much after that. Evidently, Cadde had been looking for her. How she wished he'd found her, but, like Margaret and Teresa, she had to find her own peace and forgiveness first.

When she walked into the kitchen, Rosa dropped a plate and it shattered on the tile floor. "Miss Jessie.

Oh." Rosa stepped on the broken pieces and grabbed her in a bearlike hug. "My *niña*," she cooed.

Jessie hugged her back. "I'm fine, Rosa."

Rosa leaned away and searched Jessie's face. "I'm sorry."

"I know." She kissed Rosa's cheek. "Where's Cadde?"

"In the living room." Rosa clicked her tongue. "So sad. So sad."

Jessie avoided the broken pieces and made her way through the dining area to the living room. She paused in the doorway. Cadde sat on the sofa, his elbows on his knees, his hands clasped tightly between them. A dead Christmas tree stood in the window where they'd planned to put it and the baby ornament hung high on the top. Her throat closed up and she struggled for breath.

Her eyes centered on Cadde. He looked tired and haggard. What had she done to him? What had they done to each other?

"Cadde," she murmured, stepping farther into the room.

He jumped from the sofa, his eyes wide. "Jessie."

The moment he said her name, tears rolled from her eyes and sobs racked her body. He gathered her into his arms, stroking her hair. "Shh, shh."

"I lost our baby," she sobbed into his chest.

"Jessie, don't, please." His voice wavered.

"I lost our baby," she wailed, unable to stop the flow of tears. This is what she needed—to share her grief with Cadde. That's why she hadn't been able to cry before. And now the floodgates were wide-open.

Her knees gave way and they sank to the floor, both crying, both holding on for dear life. "I'm sorry," she blubbered.

He cradled her in his arms, bracing his back against a chair. Rosa came into the room and Cadde waved her away. She looked up and wiped the tears from his face. "I'm sorry for everything."

"There's nothing to be sorry for." He kissed her lips gently, softly. He tasted of salt. He tasted of love.

"I manipulated you."

"You didn't force anything on me that I wasn't willing to do." He flung a tear away. "I know I've never said it, but I felt it from the moment I made love to you, probably way before that." Both his hands cupped her face. "I love you. I can't live without you."

She rested her face in the warmth of his neck, feeling his love deep in her heart. "I've loved you forever and when we lost the baby, I blamed myself. The pain was too strong. I couldn't even cry…until today." She kissed his neck. "You're the only person I can share that grief with."

"Because we love each other and we share the pain."

"Mmm."

Mirry sneaked into her lap. She stroked the little dog. "Oh, Mirry. Mirry."

"She's missed you," he said, stroking Mirry, too.

"I've missed her." She picked up the dog. "What have you been feeding her? She's fat."

"Anything she wants."

"Cadde."

"Wait until you see Winky."

"Oh, Cadde, you can never fill that donkey up."

"Yes. I found that out."

They laughed for the first time in weeks and Jessie settled into his arms. They talked well into the evening. He told her about his father. She told him about the fever, her trip to Rome, her aunts, Nina and the board meeting.

His hands ran over her body. "Are you okay?"

She moved against him. "I am now."

"I cringe when I think of you seeing Nina alone."

"I had to."

He rubbed her arm. "I was so worried."

"The fever had my mind messed up and all I wanted to do was get away from everything here and to find some sort of peace and forgiveness."

"Did you find that?"

"Yes." She kissed his lips. "I was able to forgive my father and Angela. They were both very manipulative people and they both loved me in their own destructive way. They weren't perfect, but neither am I."

He cupped her face. "To me you are." He kissed her long and deep and she melted into everything that was right in her world. "Please don't ever leave me again."

"I won't," she promised, and poked a finger into his chest. "You're going back to work."

"I don't know. I don't have the drive anymore."

"Excuse me." She drew back. "Where's my Cadde?

The man who eats, breathes and is consumed with the oil business?"

He tucked her hair behind her ear. "He found something more important…love."

"Oh, Cadde." She wrapped her arms around him. "But you're still going back to Shilah. No way is Hooter taking control. We'll consolidate our shares and the Hardins will own fifty-one percent." When he tried to speak, she placed her forefinger over his lips. "I'm Roscoe Murdock's daughter and I always get my way."

He smiled. She smiled.

"Maybe in a few days, then," he conceded.

"And now we have to take down this tree, put the decorations and ornament away. At Christmas we'll look at it and remember the child that brought us together."

"I just wasn't taking it down until you came home."

She caressed his face and marveled at the strong love they shared. Against the odds their bond had survived. "What's that?" She pointed to the small silver-wrapped box beneath the tree.

"I bought that for you for Christmas."

She crawled on her hands and knees to get it. Ripping off the paper, she threw it to the side. Mirry sniffed the ribbon just in case it was something to eat. Opening the box, she gasped.

"It's an…"

"Engagement ring," he finished for her. "I was going to ask you to marry me for real this time and I thought we'd get remarried in a church."

Tears rolled from her eyes and once again she couldn't stop them.

He crawled to her side and took her hand. "Have you ever looked at the inside of your wedding band?"

"No. Why?" She smiled at him through happy tears.

"*Forever* is inscribed inside, as is mine."

She removed her ring to see and there it was in very tiny letters. Her heart wobbled. "I've never taken it off and I never thought to look. Did you have it inscribed?"

"No. Roscoe said, 'Boy, my girl needs a ring,' so I went to a jewelry store. They just happened to have these rings. The jeweler said that sometimes a couple likes a message inside so I bought them. It was easy and quick, but deep down in my heart I must have known we'd make this marriage work. Now I'm glad I bought them 'cause the message fits. And…and I'm a one marriage type of guy."

A shadow marred his handsome face and she knew what he was thinking. She kissed his cheek. "You're nothing like your father."

He lifted her hand. "Jessie Murdock Hardin, will you marry me?"

"Yes, yes, yes!" She flew into his arms and knocked him backward, rings and all. Cadde reached for the engagement ring and managed to slip them onto her finger.

"I love you," he murmured, holding her face. "No force, no manipulation, just an everlasting love."

"I love you, too—forever," she replied, meeting his lips.

Jessie thought she would never feel joy or happiness again, but she did and could. That was a miracle in itself.

They were going to make it.

With this much love, how could they not?

EPILOGUE

One year later

CADDE GLANCED AT HIS WATCH. Jessie had a doctor's appointment this morning and she should have called by now. Pushing the worry away, he went back to his laptop and the numbers. They had drilled the second Louisiana well and it came in as big as the first one. Shilah was in the black—big-time. He was proud of that, but the company was never more important than Jessie.

Leaning back, he placed his hands behind his head. A lot had happened in the past year. They'd gotten remarried in the little country church in High Cotton, Texas, with family and friends around them. Jessie had worn white and she'd never looked more beautiful. As he'd stared into her eyes that day he knew he had to keep her safe and the only way to do that was to move away from the horrible memories of the Murdock house.

Later, they talked about it and decided to build a house in High Cotton like Chance. They'd be surrounded by family, friends and neighbors in a community that had to be as safe as it could get. It had worked out fine and Jessie wasn't paranoid or fearful. Sometimes she was a little too independent for his peace of mind.

He glanced at his watch again. Jessie was meeting

Myra for lunch and it was already eleven-thirty. Why hadn't she called?

Again, he put his fears aside and went back to the numbers. His fingers paused over the keyboard as he remembered the busy year. They had to do something for Rosa and Felix. They'd given many years of their lives to Jessie so Cadde gave them a choice. He would buy them a house anywhere in Houston or build one next to them in High Cotton. He and Jessie had decided they wanted their home to themselves. Rosa and Felix had opted for the home in High Cotton. Jessie was like a daughter to them.

The plan worked well. Rosa and Felix now had a life and so did Jessie.

It seemed the Hardin boys were returning to the place of their birth, except Kid. He owned the property between Chance and Cadde where their parents' house sat, crumbling. It was an eyesore and soon they'd have to do something about that.

Cadde was happier than he'd ever been. They'd managed to survive the tragedy and they talked about the baby from time to time without the numbing pain. Happiness and time had worked miracles. Now, if Jessie would just call.

The door opened. Jessie slipped in and was in his lap before he knew it. She cupped his face. "Feel my hands. They're like ice. It's so cold."

Every worry in him relaxed and he kissed her deeply, his arms holding her tight. "Where's your coat?" he asked against her lips.

"I left it in Barbara's office. I don't need it in here. I have two strong arms to warm me."

He stroked her dark hair. She'd cut it a little shorter but it still tumbled down her back, the way he liked. "Aren't you supposed to meet Myra for lunch?"

She kissed his nose. "I canceled."

"Why?"

"I wanted to talk to you."

There was that voice. That I'm-gonna-knock-you-for-a-loop voice. "Something's wrong. What is it?" He looked at her and then at the door. "Didn't you forget something?"

She poked him in the ribs. "No, silly. He's with Barbara because I need to…"

He stood, holding her by the arms. "I'll get him. I haven't seen him since this morning."

Their three-month-old son had been born in November and they had been overwhelmed with joy. They were still adjusting to parenthood. He was over-the-top nervous. She was relaxed.

He pushed the stroller into the room and knelt down to look at his son, Jacob Hardin. His head tilted to the side. His cheeks were kissable fat, as Jessie called them. When he opened his eyes, they were black like his mother's. His boy had inherited the cap of brown hair from him, along with the shape of his face. Everytime he stared at his son, he felt an incredible weakness of pure joy at the miracle they'd been given. His love soared to the rooftops.

"Cadde, honey, please don't wake him. He'll want to nurse and we have to talk."

He kissed the top of his son's head and stood, bracing himself. "What is it? What's wrong?" He knew something was by the note in her voice and he was avoiding it every way he could. They were happy. If anything was wrong with Jessie, it would be another blow that would bring him to his knees.

She reached for his hand and led him to his chair. "Just stay calm. It's not bad."

"What is it?"

"Are you calm?"

"Yes."

"I'm pregnant."

"What!" He took a step backward and fell into his chair. "No. We have a baby. See." He pointed to Jacob. "There he is. And Rosa said you couldn't get pregnant while nursing."

Jessie sat in his lap and wrapped her arms around his neck. "Well, we've proved that old wives' tale wrong." She rested her face in his neck and he melted like chocolate on a warm day. "Please don't be upset. I'm looking at it as a blessing for everything we've been through."

He kissed her cheek. "I'm just worried about your health. That's three pregnancies too close together."

"The doctor says I'm fine. The baby is fine and Jacob is growing by leaps and bounds."

"Oh, Jessie." He smoothed back her hair and looked into her gorgeous eyes. "You have to stop hitting me with things out of left field. It's making me crazy."

"It keeps us on our toes." She snuggled into him.

"Oh, no."

"What?"

"We'll have to get a bigger stroller, another car seat and a larger car. And we were going to visit your aunts this summer. Now we'll have to postpone."

She drew back. "Cadde, pregnant women can fly."

"But…"

"No buts. We're going. I want them to meet you so they can see I have a wonderful husband and that we got through all the bad stuff."

"We could go earlier," he suggested.

"I don't think so. It's February and Shay's baby shower is in late March at our house and the baby is due in early June. We can't miss that."

"No, we can't." Chance and Shay were expecting their first child and they'd planned its arrival for when Shay wasn't teaching. It must be nice to plan those important events. He and Jessie seemed to roll the dice on birth control, but he was happy. Like Jessie had said, it was another blessing.

She lifted an eyebrow. "You okay now?"

"As long as you're in my arms. That's…"

A loud wail interrupted them and Jessie immediately went to their son. "The doctor said I have to put him on a bottle real soon."

"He's not going to like that."

Before she could reach Jacob, the door swung open and Kid stood there.

"Did I hear a baby cry?"

"He's hungry." Cadde explained the baby's wails. "Jessie's going to nurse him."

As usual, Kid paid him no attention and unstrapped

Jacob, lifting him out. The baby stopped crying, happily flailing his fists at Kid.

Jiggling him in the air, Kid cooed, "Hey, partner, you like breasts?" Slobber fell on Kid's shirt, but he didn't seem to notice.

"Put him down," Cadde said.

"Uncle Kid has a calendar in his office that has nice breasts. I'll show you."

"Do not show Jacob naked women. Hand him over to Jessie."

Kid walked out the door with the baby in his arms.

Cadde sighed. "That's the man who didn't like kids. Go figure."

Jessie slid onto his lap again. "Go figure." She ran her finger down his nose. "People change."

"Mmm."

"There are baby wipes in your truck and milk stains on the carpet. Not to mention mustard on the steering wheel. Go figure."

He smiled. "I love you."

"I'll love you forever," she whispered, and that sounded about right to him.

* * * * *

Harlequin *Super Romance*

COMING NEXT MONTH

Available November 8, 2011

*Harlequin® Special Edition® is thrilled to present a new
installment in* USA TODAY *bestselling author
RaeAnne Thayne's reader-favorite miniseries,*
THE COWBOYS OF COLD CREEK.

*Join the excitement as we meet the Bowmans—four
siblings who lost their parents but keep family ties alive
in Pine Gulch. First up is Trace. Only two things get under
this rugged lawman's skin: beautiful women and secrets.
And in Rebecca Parsons, he finds both!*

Read on for a sneak peek of
CHRISTMAS IN COLD CREEK.
Available November 2011 from Harlequin® Special Edition®.

On impulse, he unfolded himself from the bar stool. "Need
a hand?"

"Thank you! I…" She lifted her gaze from the floor to
his jeans and then raised her eyes. When she identified him
her hazel eyes turned from grateful to unfriendly and cold,
as if he'd somehow thrown the broken glasses at her head.

He also thought he saw a glimmer of panic in those
interesting depths, which instantly stirred his curiosity like
cream swirling through coffee.

"I've got it, Officer. Thank you." Her voice was several
degrees colder than the whirl of sleet outside the windows.

Despite her protests, he knelt down beside her and began
to pick up shards of broken glass. "No problem. Those trays
can be slippery."

This close, he picked up the scent of her, something fresh
and flowery that made him think of a mountain meadow on
a July afternoon. She had a soft, lush mouth and for one
brief, insane moment, he wanted to push aside that stray lock

of hair slipping from her ponytail and taste her. Apparently he needed to spend a lot less time working and a great deal *more* time recreating with the opposite sex if he could have sudden random fantasies about a woman he wasn't even inclined to like, pretty or not.

"I'm Trace Bowman. You must be new in town."

She didn't answer immediately and he could almost see the wheels turning in her head. Why the hesitancy? And why that little hint of unease he could see clouding the edge of her gaze? His presence was obviously making her uncomfortable and Trace couldn't help wondering why.

"Yes. We've been here a few weeks."

"Well, I'm just up the road about four lots, in the white house with the cedar shake roof, if you or your daughter need anything." He smiled at her as he picked up the last shard of glass and set it on her tray.

Definitely a story there, he thought as she hurried away. He just might need to dig a little into her background to find out why someone with fine clothes and nice jewelry, and who so obviously didn't have experience as a waitress, would be here slinging hash at The Gulch. Was she running away from someone? A bad marriage?

So…Rebecca Parsons. Not Becky. An intriguing woman. It had been a long time since one of those had crossed his path here in Pine Gulch.

Trace won't rest until he finds out Rebecca's secret, but will he still have that same attraction to her once he does? Find out in CHRISTMAS IN COLD CREEK. Available November 2011 from Harlequin® Special Edition®.

Harlequin
Super Romance

*Discover a fresh, heartfelt new romance
from acclaimed author*

Sarah Mayberry

Businessman Flynn Randall's life is
complicated. So he doesn't need the
distraction of fun, spontaneous Mel Porter.
But he can't stop thinking about her. Maybe
he can handle one more complication....

All They Need

*Available November 8, 2011,
wherever books are sold!*